**He lost his temper at his own helplessness, and now he could lose the one thing that mattered most...**

The door creaked as it opened, clicking when it shut. Emmett shrugged his way out of his shirt, felt its stiffness from dried blood, and had to choke back nausea. His hand reached past the shower curtain, and the hot gush on his cold skin had him quivering, hard, fit to have him falling apart at the seams. He fumbled for the wall, found the hand towel, and buried his face in the thick terry cloth as the sobs rose up. A howl wasn't too far off.

The door swung open again, and she was back, the curtain of her hair swinging against his cheek and neck as her sturdy arm wrapped around his waist. "Emmett, let me help you. You've been through a lot, more than you realize, and it's socking it to you. Don't be so tough. Let me get you undressed and in that shower. You'll feel better. Promise."

*Miss Sunshine again, probably has birds flitting around her head.* Something inside of him snapped, made him nasty. "I don't need any help! I'm sick and tired of everyone coddling me, treating me like I'll break. I'm blind, damn it, and today's little joy ride has taught me I have to accept my limitations. It's pure luck that man is all right, and I need a little time to process that, so how about you get out of here and leave me alone?"

Emmett could feel her withdrawal even before Casey stepped outside the door, as if he'd slapped her—hard. The pain welled up, forcing him to chew on it, swallow it, and choke it down, forming a cold, hard lump in his stomach. He wouldn't blame her if she kicked him out. Emmett couldn't even stand himself. Why would anyone else? *What are you doing, biting the hand that feeds you? Big mistake.*

**You met Casey and Emmett Henry in *A Man of Few Words*—now see where it all began…**

On a cold winter night, Casey Mitchell leaves her stalled car in the middle of a blizzard and heads for the only light she can see—a distant farmhouse. There she meets Emmett Henry, who has been blind for nearly a year after an injury in a bar fight. Casey is the new doctor at the clinic in town, so when Emmett's brother Wyatt calls in a panic because his wife has gone into labor, Casey and Emmett brave the elements on foot to Wyatt's house to deliver a baby, starting a journey that will take the two of them on the road to a future neither could have ever imagined…

KUDOS for *Hindsight's 20/20*

In *Hindsight's 20/20* by Heidi Sprouse, we are reunited with Emmett Henry and Casey Mitchell Henry back where it all began. Casey Mitchell is new in town, replacing a doctor who has just retired at the local clinic. On a cold winter night, her car stalls in the middle of a blizzard, and Casey makes her way to a farmhouse in the distance—Emmett's. He has been blind for about a year, due to a brain injury he received when rescuing a girl in a bar. Being a Henry, he is stubborn and obstinate and won't let anyone help him. But shortly after Casey arrives at his house that night, he gets a call from his brother whose wife is in labor, and Casey and Emmett head through the woods to Wyatt's house so Casey can deliver the baby. Their relationship gets off to a rocky start since Emmett feels that his disability makes him unlovable and Casey could do much better. But she is as stubborn as he is, and she is determined to help the man she has grown to love whether he likes it or not—even if it means losing his love. Written in Sprouse's refreshing voice, filled with lots of sex, drama, and tension, it will break your heart and warm it at the same time. Have a box of tissues handy and enjoy a very good read. ~ *Taylor Jones, The Review Team of Taylor Jones & Regan Murphy*

*Hindsight's 20/20* by Heidi Sprouse is the story of a proud young man brought down by a blow to head that leaves him blind. A horse farmer and active outdoors man, Emmett Henry doesn't know how to go on living without the ability to see, which means that he can no longer do what he has done all his life and is now dependent on others to do for him what he cannot do for himself. He has been blind for approximately a year the night that Casey Mitchell gets stranded in a blizzard and shows up at his house just before his brother, Wyatt, calls to tell him that his sister-in-law is in labor. Since Casey is a doctor and has just arrived in town to fill a position at the local clinic, she and Emmett brave the elements and walk to Wyatt's house to help deliver the baby. There's an instant attraction between Casey and Emmett, but he is reluctant to get involved with her because he thinks she feels sorry for him. And he doesn't think a blind man has anything to offer a woman. But Casey is determined to prove him wrong, no matter what it takes. Heartbreaking, heartwarming, and full of spicy love scenes, this one is a keeper. The characters are both realistic and endearing, like old friends, and you just can't help rooting for Emmett and Casey. *Hindsight's 20/20* will make you cry, make you laugh, and warm you all the way through. ~ *Regan Murphy, The Review Team of Taylor Jones & Regan Murphy*

# HINDSIGHT'S 20/20

## HEIDI SPROUSE

*A Black Opal Books Publication*

GENRE: FAMILY SAGA/ROMANCE

HINDSIGHT'S 20/20
Copyright © 2018 by Heidi Sprouse
Cover Design by Jackson Cover Designs
All cover art copyright © 2018
All Rights Reserved
Print ISBN: 978-1-626948-73-0

First Publication: FEBRUARY 2018

Published by Black Opal Books **http://www.blackopalbooks.com**

"If love is blind,
then maybe a blind person that loves
has a greater understanding of it."
~ *Criss Jami*

# CHAPTER 1

Choking smoke, blaring noise, and too much of a crowd made Emmett Henry's head start to pound. His body ached from taking a beating at work. All he wanted was to finish his second beer, pay the tab, and go home. A few more swallows—that's all it would take.

An ungodly shriek filled his ears and had him glancing across the packed room, unable to process what his eyes were trying to tell him. A brute of a man was using a young girl's hair for a rope, reeling her in without mercy—and then the unthinkable, bouncing her head off a table.

Emmett saw red, erupting from his seat, knocking over the chair and table. Beer, pretzels, and napkins spilled all over the floor. He closed the gap in seconds, his fist connecting with a poor excuse for a human being before offering aid to the stunned girl. Emmett turned his back on the slob for an instant, and his head exploded with pain, about to be lifted clear off his shoulders.

෴

He awoke with a jerk in the farmhouse where he was born—home to four previous generations of Henrys—sitting by the fire. The heat seeped into his bones, making him go loose. His eyes drooped closed as his heart gradually slowed, leaving him to stare at strange pictures painted on the inside of his eyelids.

The old house moaned, shivering with the cold, blanketed in snow. Bottled up tight, Emmett was snug and cozy in the family room, trying to fool himself that it was enough. The problem was no change of scenery in his life since…hell, since the cold set in nearly two months ago. The feeling of being trapped, claustrophobic in a six-bedroom house, was making him at odds with himself.

Outside, January's wind howled, the temperatures plummeting as the snow drifts mounted with no sign of stopping. Typical New York weather, upstate style. In rural Charlton, a best kept secret outside of racing's Saratoga, residents hunkered down and bucked up with the prospect of spring's return. Although the New Year was young, everyone else was feeling a sense of rebirth, second chances, and hopes reborn, Emmett couldn't move forward. He was still in that bar.

A creak and a bang of the door announced his big brother, his only brother, Wyatt. Coming in without knocking, stomping the snow off his boots, shaking it off his coat, hair, and hat, making a ruckus, as usual—a daily occurrence. Emmett couldn't help but smile in affection for him even when aggravated by the intrusion. After all, what were brothers for but to annoy the heck out of each other? *Gotta love them.*

കൗരൗ

"Man, it's quite a Nor'easter brewing out there. I came to check on you, make sure you have everything you need. I see you haven't moved from that fireplace. Don't mind if I do." Wyatt made a beeline for the substantial hearth of his old homestead, a place that had been the heart of the home growing up and still drew him on his routine visits. Small wonder that Emmett favored the comfy recliner placed front and center.

He gave his kid brother's arm a squeeze and stood in front of the flames that cast shadows on the wall and made them dance. The wood crackled and popped, sparks shooting up the chimney. "I wouldn't get so close if I were you. That cherry is burning like a firecracker." Emmett warned, turning toward his brother, who had brought a whiff of fresh air and bite of the cold with him, clinging to his clothes. "How much snow have we got?"

Putting his back to the flames, Wyatt wiggled his toes to get the circulation moving. He'd tromped through the woods about a quarter mile from his place as the roads were too nasty for driving. "Oh, there's a good foot out there and no signs of stopping. I called you, but you didn't answer, so Samantha made me come. She'd be with me if the baby wasn't going to drop any day. Like a mule, she is. I promised her I'd check on you personally, the only way the woman wasn't strapping on snow shoes and bringing a blanket in case she had to give birth under a pine tree. Why didn't you answer the phone? You know it makes me nervous when you don't answer, Emmett."

A wall came up between them in the crossed arms and stubborn set to his younger brother's jaw. "I'd answer if I needed anything. You know that, Wyatt."

The two were stamped of the same mold, carved deep by their father, Jackson Henry, a man who left his mark. Both were broad of shoulder and muscular, topping off at over six feet, sturdy like the oaks that grew on the surrounding land. Both had inherited Jackson's full head of sandy hair that called to mind a rich oak stain, streaked by sunlight in the warmer months, gone darker in the winter.

Their eyes were a point of difference—Wyatt had what many considered slate, blue skies tinged with gray on a cloudy day. Now, Emmett—his were the brown of sweet honey, as golden as autumn leaves or light shimmering on the surface of the water. They used to be filled with warmth and happiness as bright as his personality, but now only managed an empty stare.

For all his life, minus going solo until age two, Wyatt had seen the light in those eyes, caught it, found it infectious, been a moth drawn to that golden glow. He couldn't bear it to see it snuffed. He closed the gap between the two of them, knelt down and gripped the younger man's thigh, applying pressure.

"Emmett, come to our place. Stay with us until…please. It's eating me up inside having you here all by yourself, especially this time of year. I worry about you and…I'm afraid, Em." His throat thickened and he bowed his head.

A hand hovered in the air and rested on his damp, tousled hair. "Wyatt, what good would it do, having me rattling around there, and you about to have a new baby and all? You don't need me underfoot."

The bitterness was welling up. It took an effort to turn off the tap and shut it down, but supreme willpower was one thing Emmett Henry had. Otherwise, he wouldn't still be here at the ripe age of thirty-two. "And you make it sound like it's only temporary. This isn't changing, and there's no sense in you thinking otherwise, no cause for worry or fear. I'm blind, and I've come to accept that. You need to do the same. I can manage. Look around. Anything amiss?"

Wyatt lifted his head and scraped a hand across his cheek, dashing away a stray tear. He hadn't come to terms with what happened to his brother, would be damned if that was ever going to happen. A quick survey showed the house was neat, too neat, as if no one lived there.

"No, it's fine, but that's what I'm afraid of. You're not living, Emmett. Ever since the accident, you're in this chair, holed up in this house. Enough is enough. You need to get up and moving, get out. If I need to drag you back to our house to make sure you don't wither away here, I'll do it. I'm bigger and stronger—"

"Accident! Will you quit calling it a blasted accident? That bastard in the bar hit me with a chair. I don't call that an accident. That's blunt force trauma!"

In a blur of movement, the recliner was empty, and the sightless man had crossed the room, hit the closed door to a closet, and pounded it with his fist. The wood was solid and unforgiving, like the sense of pity and self-loathing that had been with him ever since the day the lights went out. Emmett turned, chest heaving, and raised his fists, wearing a fierce scowl.

"I'd like to see you try and take me, Wyatt. Before this, I was a nice guy, but I've learned nice guys finish last. I tried to keep a sweet, little, innocent girl out of trouble and look what it got me. So if you really want to try and bring me home, have my sunny personality gracing your place, you'll have to come and get me. I promise it won't be pretty."

He raised his chin, thrust it outward, lowered his stance. Their father had taught them well when it came to holding their own in a fight. If only the guy in the bar hadn't cheated.

Wyatt cleared his throat and took slow, measured steps toward his brother, announcing his approach. When he was within reach, he put both hands on Em's shoulders. Human contact was more important now than ever before, proving there was that vital link between them.

"I'm not making you go anywhere. What do you say to a drink before I get back?"

Anxiety crept up in his voice. "I really can't leave Sammie long. She was having cramps earlier—if this is it, I don't even think I can get out to the hospital with this monster of a storm. I wanted to hang around to keep an eye on her, but she ousted me with a broom, said I was being impossible what with worry gnawing at me for her and for you."

Emmett exhaled hard and pulled Wyatt into a bone crusher of a hug. "I'm sorry I'm such an ornery cuss. I just get so...*angry*...and I feel sorry for myself—not a good mix. Come on. We'll have that drink, and you'd better get going. Can't have my new niece or nephew born without getting an eyeful of your ugly mug first thing."

He pushed away from the wall and headed toward the kitchen, his hands raised slightly, but there was really no need. The blueprint of this house was imprinted on his brain. Hitting the kitchen, he mentally counted his steps, found the right cabinet, and took down a few shot glasses. A few steps more and Emmett was rummaging in the liquor cabinet, skimming his fingers over the bottles and pulling out Southern Comfort.

"Oh yeah, I'd say this baby is just what you need before you head out in the cold, Daddy." A little bit of finagling and keeping his finger hanging over the brim helped him measure out the right amount. He handed a glass to his brother, held his own up until they clinked, and slugged it back fast. "Mmm, should have a fire in your gut now, tide you over until you're in the warm and willing arms of your wife."

The other glass thumped on the counter, and the bottle clinked, sliding back into place in the cabinet. Hands, rough with work around the farm, were on his shoulders once more. "All right, I'm going, but so help me, if you're in trouble and don't call me—"

Emmett had a tenacious hold of his brother's elbow and walked him to the door. "If I need anything, I'll call. If that baby comes, you call me, and I promise that I'll answer unless I'm incapacitated. I'm sure I can be good for something for a wee one. I can hold the little tyke, manage a bottle, sit by the crib, give you guys a breather. Changing the diaper might get messy, but I'll give it a go." He felt for the hook by the door to hand over his brother's coat, fumbled on the floor, and found the boots, still wet.

"Here's my hat, what's my hurry? Have you got a girl coming over or something?" The door was open, and Wyatt got a little push on his back, between the shoulder blades. "All right, I'll quit procrastinating. Good night, little brother. Stay safe—be well." He made to go, turned back and gave Emmett a hug that stole his breath away. "And Em, you're still a nice guy."

Laughing, trying not to sound sour, Emmett gave his brother an insistent nudge. "Get going, will you? Sammie will kill me if I keep you. I'll be fine. Thanks for coming, Wyatt." One more hug and footsteps stomped off into the distance.

Emmett stepped outside, heedless of the chill or his lack of winter wear. No coat, no gloves, no hat—nothing between him and the elements. He tipped his head to the sky and let the flakes dust his hair and his face, savoring the wash of cold air over his body, the sensation of snow spitting at his skin, wind tugging at his hair, whipping it around his head. Filling his lungs, winter's bite made him feel alive, made him want to wander on his own, keep going and never stop.

If he opened his eyes, there were shadows. If he closed them, there were more. It made no difference and kept him from navigating through the night that was always his companion. Confined to the small patch outside his door, the murky glow of the outdoor light showed him the way back in when he was good and ready.

His teeth started to chatter, his body quivering like an autumn leaf hanging on a tree branch in the wind. *Not yet, you got that? I'll go when I damn well please.* In his mind's eye, he was a kid again, the whole world looked like a giant snow globe, and Emmett was about to go sledding, flying down the hill past the barn, all the way to the pasture...

✧❃✧

Crap! The car would have to die in East Bumble in the middle of one monster of a blizzard! Her father had always told her to be prepared, stock the trunk with blankets, a parka, food for a week, a first aid kit, water, tools, a hardware store, flares. What did she have? Her purse, driving gloves, and a coat with a hood. *Big whoop. Oh, and don't forget a cell phone with a dead battery.* Dad was probably laughing his butt off in heaven saying, "I told you so," with great glee and satisfaction. '*You've got book smarts but no common sense, Case.*'

Casey Mitchell looked in the rearview mirror and saw her father's gaze, down to the same exasperation that would taint his moss-green eyes, giving them the spark of an imp. She blew her dark bangs out of the way in frustration. *I know, Dad—I know—no common sense and no sense of direction either. I have got to break down and buy a GPS.* The little village of Charlton couldn't be that hard to find. She'd done it before. In the daylight. Without a snowstorm.

She got out of the car, stomping crossly. *Act your age, Case. You're twenty-eight, not two. You are a sum a cum laude, nationally board-certified doctor, capable of managing this minor crisis.* There was one bright spot, literally, a light from a house not too far off, a quarter of a mile maybe. Nothing for it but to start walking. She trudged through the drifts, cursing her wet feet from her stylish, impractical boots, shivering, longing for a warmer coat.

Casey had misjudged the distance. Had to be closer to a half mile with another quarter mile down the long lane to the sprawling farmhouse. A Currier and Ives kind of place. One to be appreciated in better circumstances.

The door was ajar, casting a warm glow on the front porch and snow, pinning a man in its light. His arms were flung open wide, his head tipped back, sandy hair wild in the wind. Something was wrong with this picture, the way he stood motionless in nothing but jeans and a flannel shirt, snow coating his hair, lashes, and shoulders, with the face of Gabriel come crashing down to earth, beautiful yet so haunted.

At the crunch of boots in the snow, he turned her way, revealing a tower of a man with broad shoulders, impressive height, and golden eyes beyond compare. "What's the matter, Wyatt? Lose your way home?" Teasing, his lips curved up playfully as his eyes searched the darkness, proving to be blank.

Thrown off guard, Casey hesitated until his forehead creased in confusion, prodding her to speak. "Ah, no, I'm not Wyatt. My name is Casey Mitchell, and my car broke down about a half mile...mile...God knows how far, away."

She blew out an aggravated puff and continued. "Plus the battery in my cell phone is dead. Obviously, I never learned the Boy Scout Motto about being prepared. Must have missed out on that day in Girl Scouts too. Could I come in for a few minutes, thaw out, call for a tow?" She balanced on her left foot, then her right. Her toes were cold, and she couldn't help being a tad anxious.

The grin on his face was contagious, spreading to her lips and making them reluctantly travel in an upward direction. "Don't feel bad about the phone," he said. "The service is really lousy around here. As for the tow, Fast Eddie won't come out in this. I'm Emmett Henry. My brother might be able to give you a hand. He lives just down the road. Come on in and get warm."

He turned toward the door and gestured for her to precede him. Casey slipped past, inhaling the wintery, spicy scent of him, and felt a ripple of pleasure in the pit of her stomach. Emmett followed, hit an icy patch on the step, and would've pitched head first into the entryway if she didn't reach out to catch him.

"I'm all right, thanks." He jerked away, crimson streaks staining his cheeks, an angry glitter in his empty eyes as he closed the door with a little more force than necessary. A few steps into the living room, and his head was down, his hands on his hips.

"Sorry. My manners are rusty, and it stings my pride, stumbling, falling down." His chin lifted, beautiful eyes of liquid gold searching, and his hand came up, a peace offering.

"But we all fall down sometimes, Emmett. The hard part is getting back up, and you managed quite well." Casey accepted the offer, firmly pressing her palm in his, and the heat streaked up her arm, all the way to her heart, giving it a kick start. *Easy, Case, or you're going to start hyperventilating.*

Emmett held on for the space of a heartbeat and another before breaking away, clearing his throat. "You must be freezing. Your hands are like ice. Make yourself comfortable by the fire, and I'll put on some tea or coffee?"

A little breathless, she answered weakly, "Tea," and watched him head off to the kitchen, his steps sure, no need to feel his way in the place that belonged to him. Casey pressed her hands to her cheeks, glad he couldn't see how they burned or the way his touch set her to sizzling. God, but the man was a fine specimen, rugged, hair tousled, fire sparking in those golden eyes. His stance, the jut of his chin, his squared shoulders—all said *Go ahead world, throw anything at me. I can take it.*

Stepping up to the mantle, absorbing the welcome heat of the hearth, her eyes were drawn to pictures of her host—riding horseback, playing baseball, messing around with a man so similar it had to be his brother, standing as best man on his wedding day. The glow in Emmett's eyes snatched her breath away. Whatever had taken his sight had come later in life. Casey was grateful for one reason—she could stare at him forever, and he'd never even know.

# CHAPTER 2

Emmett's heart was tripping, heading for an eruption. He'd thought going blind had killed his attraction to women. Judging by his current state, that part of him was very much alive. He was getting light-headed, dry-mouthed, with a fluttering feeling in his stomach, his innards liquefying.

*Damn. Wish I could see her.* Her voice was like milk chocolate, warm, sweet, and rich, her touch soft as velvet. He gripped the kitchen counter and breathed in, held it, let it go. God, she even smelled good enough to eat.

Rattled, he concentrated on the task at hand, taking down cups, tea bags, the sugar bowl, and spoons, putting on the kettle. "Sugar?" he called out, her response of "Two, please," ringing in his ears. Digging the spoon into the bowl, he lightly skimmed his finger over the teaspoon to judge if it was full and dropped it in, even though she didn't need any additional sweetening.

The kettle whistled, and he caught up the handle, resisting the sudden urge to go in the next room, grab hold of her, kiss her, and see if she tasted as good as she sounded. "Holy *Mother*—"

Emmett bit off the rest of a colorful string of curses as the boiling water washed over his hand while filling the second cup. Keeping his mouth clean was a habit, ingrained from childhood after having his mouth washed out with soap too many times, although he'd tended to slip more since life knocked him on his butt.

*Stupid idiot! You've got to keep your head!* Down on his knees, fumbling for the edge of the sink, his fingers snatched the towel to swab up the puddle on the floor. *Right, fool. Scald yourself some more, why don't you?* The offended hand was screaming, his eyes stinging, and she was there, smelling like brown sugar, vanilla, and his mother's homemade cookies, all rolled into one.

"Let me see." There was a brief pause, cool, gentle hands cupping his. Her breath, hinting of something minty, skittered along his cheek. "You need to get that under cold water."

The water was gurgling, his hand was doused under the chilly flow, and the ice maker was running on the fridge. An instant later, a cold, lumpy bundle wrapped in a kitchen towel was placed on the burn. "How about I carry the tea cups?"

Emmett's face twisted with the applied pressure then smoothed with a conscious effort. A short nod, and he held back a curt response. "Sure. Thanks. Sorry, but I'm relatively new to being helpless and hopeless."

Quiet laughter was his response.

He followed the sound of her damp stocking feet, slapping on the floor, and the clink of mugs on coasters. Judging by the squeak of the chair, she'd settled into the recliner to the left of the fire. His hand brushed her shoulder, felt her quivering—from the cold? Or was she feeling the same pull, like quicksand, dragging her under? "Let me get you some dry socks and a blanket." Ignoring her protests, he navigated his way to his bedroom, grabbed thick socks, an extra pair of slippers, and the quilt from the foot of the bed.

"Thank you. You're a sweetheart." Her voice was

practically a whisper, a throaty sound that turned up his internal temperature gauge to mercury-bursting levels. He pulled out a smile and retreated to his chair, maintaining a safe distance to avoid throwing himself at the woman.

❦❦❦

Plying her with tea, bringing her tidbits to make her comfortable, opening his home to a stranger—no easy feat for someone in his position—inching his way into her heart. Casey snuggled in the quilt, an intricate affair—probably a family heirloom—and buried her face in the steaming mug, taking her fill of Emmett Henry as unseeing eyes reflected the flickering flames of the fireplace. *Wouldn't mind sharing that chair, some body heat, warming up all the way with him holding me.*

"So, Miss Casey Mitchell, what brings you to these parts? Just passing through or do you plan on staying awhile?" Uncanny, the way his honey gaze was level with hers as he shifted his focus away from the fireplace. *Drip some more liquid gold my way. Let me get lost forever.*

Her wandering mind had her gulping her drink too quickly and sputtering, while his eyebrows sprang up inquisitively. Casey waved at him, remembered his situation, and managed to choke out, "Swallowed the wrong way—sorry." Another sip, this time at the proper pace, and she could continue. "I'll be staying. My job and apartment are all rolled into one place. I've switched gears from city emergency room to country bumpkin. I'm going to be the new general practitioner at the clinic."

Her companion's face darkened with a storm of emotion for a wrinkle in time. A hesitation and his shoulders straightened, a smile finding the way to his face. "Ah, a city mouse turned country mouse. Congratulations. We were wondering who would take over for Old Doc Smith. I'd say you're a bit of an improvement in appearance, judging by the sound of you. Of course, he was older than the hills. Welcome."

ᶜᵔᵓᶜᵔᵓ

Doctors. They left an awful taste in his mouth, bitter, hard to swallow. Emmett had an overdose nine months ago when he'd been hurt, with too many follow-up visits. The hospital. Wyatt dragging him to every specialist within a reasonable radius—he would've canvassed the country if Emmett had allowed it. Doc Smith had been a weekly visitor, checking up on his progress for Wyatt's peace of mind. Until the stroke killed the old physician.

*Maybe you can arrange some house calls with this one.* A mental snort and Emmett forced himself to be cordial, babbling something about being an improvement, a pathetic attempt at welcome. "Guess you landed yourself in a pretty good spot tonight. You're only about two miles from the clinic. Let me call my brother. Wyatt might be able to get you towed home once the storm quiets down."

Pushing out of his chair, crossing the room, Emmett could swear he felt the pinpoints of her stare between his shoulder blades. Forcing himself to concentrate, no easy matter in present company, he punched in the numbers. His brother picked up and screaming in the background made the hairs on the back of his neck stand up. "Wyatt, what in the world is going on over there?" His stomach began to churn, his heart thudding painfully in his chest. It sounded like someone was dying.

The sound of his brother's voice, cracking on the verge of panic, only made it worse. Wyatt never lost his cool. "It's Sammie—she's in labor. I don't know why, but I had a feeling this was happening today, had it hanging over my head all day. The contractions started soon after I left for your place, and she couldn't do anything about it. There's no way we can go out on these roads. I won't risk it. It's coming on hard and fast. What do I do, Em? I've delivered calves and colts, not babies."

*Talk him down from the edge. Steady as she goes.* "Wyatt, take a deep breath now. Breathe. Now, tell Sammie to breathe her way through each round. Stroke her, gentle her like those horses, get her through the contractions."

He turned in the direction of his guest, running a hand through his tousled hair, hoping she didn't see it shaking. "You won't believe this, but I've got a doctor in the house. Doc Smith's replacement broke down and found her way here." Footsteps approached, and a hand grabbed his, her whisper in his ear offering assistance. "I'm sure she can help."

The wave of relief washing over the line almost pulled him under. "Oh, thank God! But Emmett, I don't know how you'll get here. There's no driving in this, not even the old truck in the garage, and I can't come to show you the way."

A hard swallow and a straightening of his spine gave him ammunition. A resolve of steel didn't hurt any. "Don't worry. I'll get us there. Make sure you put the outdoor light on."

A click of the receiver and Emmett was already across the room, feeling for his coat, fumbling with his boots and laces. Footsteps followed, and Casey knelt down beside him, her fingers brushing his and making quick work of tying his boots. "Thanks," he grumbled, reached out, found her hand, and gave it a squeeze. "Sorry, it's still hard accepting with grace. Not part of my make-up, being on the receiving end."

Then he was up on his feet, and his hand ran along the shelf over the coat hooks to find his hat and gloves. "Take anything you need off the shelf. I'm sorry to take you back out in the cold, but my sister-in-law is having her first baby, and my big brother is on the verge of a breakdown."

"That's no problem. I'm happy to do anything I can." There was a swish of material beside him as Casey quickly dressed for the elements. She took his hand, and they stepped out into the blustery night. A barrage of flakes hit Emmett's face, and a gust of wind snatched his breath away as he pointed himself in the direction of his brother's place. "Wyatt lives over to the right. It used to be my grandparents' place. When they died, it was left to him. Made it easy to decide who would get each place."

*You can do this, Em. How many times did you and Wyatt walk—no run—to Gram and Pop's, day and night? Your feet know the way, can take you there with your eyes closed.* His mouth twisted at that one until he realized Casey was waiting on him, her hand tightening its grip.

"Sorry. Haven't done this in—a while. Can you make out the stand of pines? There's a pathway running down the middle. Dad used to have us shovel it out when we were kids. Said it built character." He couldn't stop the grin from creeping up. "I think it was to get us out of his hair. Are we headed in the right direction?"

"Yes, you've got us off to a good start." A few steps forward, the wind tugging at their hair and clothes, doing its best to knock them back, and the doctor was breathless. "Can't say I'd mind this being shoveled out now." She pushed on beside him for about five minutes and came to a halt. "Whew! Can we take a break? I haven't hit the gym for a while."

*Unbelievable! There's got to be at least three feet out here.* Emmett didn't mind taking a breather, even though the snow was up to his knees, soaking through his jeans and creeping into his boots. God, he hated that feeling. Judging by the wet sensation brushing his face, there was no sign of the storm abating. Not the kind of night to be out and about.

He reached out, grabbed air, finally hit something solid yet soft at the same time, Casey's arm. "A little bit farther, and you should see his outdoor light through the trees. Go that way, and we'll be at his place in no time."

They resumed their arduous journey. *Soon, we have to get there soon.* The words were one track stuck on re-play, turning the urgency and anxiety up to the max. Had to do this for Wyatt and for Sammie. Emmett had never heard her sound that way, scared out of her mind, his big brother not far behind. Wyatt was like Atlas from Greek mythology, tough enough to bear the world on his shoulders. Nothing shook him—not their mother's death when they were young boys, not Dad's accident two years ago, nor Emmett's blindness.

But Sammie—she was his everything, his air, his earth, his water, his heart, the one thing he couldn't live without. What if something happened to his high school sweetheart? *Don't you dare go there.*

Casey grabbed hold of his arm and shook it in her excitement. "I see it! This way, come on!" A forceful tug and she picked up the pace. Emmett let her take the lead, fast forward, towing him along until they hit the porch. "Watch the steps. Up one, two, three. Sorry, you probably already know this."

Emmett waved her off, stomping off excess snow and getting the circulation going on the way up.

A creak of the porch door opening and they burst in-side, peeling off all their outer gear, fighting with wet boot laces, and throwing everything in a heap on the floor. Following the sound of the screaming to the bedroom, Emmett's heart hammered harder the closer they came to their destination. *Cut it out. If she can do this, you can do this. Suck it up, Henry!*

∾∾∾

Casey's mind was on overload, awash in a flood of impressions, taking note of everything as they stepped into the room. It was like a sauna, a space heater turned up to the max in the corner, a basin of steaming water, towels, scissors, twine, along with other odds and ends lined up on a dresser. A dog was whimpering under the bed, nose buried in its front paws.

The last scream trailed off, followed by panting and the soothing sound of a man's voice, dropped low, murmuring softly. A woman, with hair like sunshine and eyes as blue as the sky, fell back against the pillows, taking a brief respite from the wracking pains of the contractions. Her skin was wind burned, perspiration drenching her face, pasting wet tendrils to her cheeks, forehead, and neck, the hand that held her husband's chapped from doing farm chores.

Emmett's brother was very similar to the blind man in features, sharing his height and the same head of wavy brown hair. He glanced up, slate-colored stare locking with hers. A whisper in his wife's ear and he crossed the room, nearly crushing Casey's hand with his big, rough, work-hardened grasp. There was such relief lighting his eyes, a storm abated, his smile like sunshine after the rain.

"Thank God, you're here. I'm Wyatt. I knew I should've brought her to the hospital earlier today, taken a precaution, what with the weather. Sammie was fractious all morning, testy to no end, fighting cramps. Stubborn woman didn't want to pester me with the fact that she'd been in labor all along. She figured there was no sense bothering me until they got close."

He drew Casey to the bedside. "They got close in no time. A little over a minute apart now. No going slow for this one. She's always been a full-speed-ahead kind of girl. Sam—" Wyatt's voice softened, and his hand cupped her cheek. "—the doctor's here, honey. You're going to be all right."

"I'm Casey Mitchell. Don't you worry. Babies tend to take care of coming on their own. We just help as the cheering and clean-up committee." She took the young woman's hands, marveling at the strength in such a small package as her fingers were nearly ground down to the bones by the next round of contractions.

Another shriek followed by a strong gust of breath and the laboring woman managed a weak smile. Only a blink or two passed and her face was scrunching up again. "Oh, Lord—I feel like I need to push. I've got to push!" Her voice was rising again to ear-splitting decimals, a terrifying sound for anyone who wasn't familiar with the sounds of delivery.

Casey had been present for many births, sometimes as an observer, at other times as the acting doctor in her ER when there was no time to get to the maternity ward. This one didn't sound like anything out of the ordinary. God willing, all would go smoothly.

She washed her hands in the basin of water on the dresser, moved to the foot of the bed, and threw back the sheet. "All right, Sammie. You're looking good down here. On the next one, go ahead, give it that push!" A stool was pushed behind her, catching her legs, and Casey winked at the harried father, taking her position. Let the waiting game begin. Blowing a strand of hair out of her eyes, she took a deep breath. *All right, Doc. Get ready to put on your catcher's mitt.*

ᔇᔐᔇᔐ

Hanging back, feeling a need to step up, Emmett peeled off his flannel shirt, sweating to no end in the plunge from frigid to heatwave, and dropped it on the chair in the corner of the bedroom. He felt his way to the heart of the action—to a bedside chair—to offer his sister-in-law an anchor, although the sounds of labor acted like a homing beacon.

Sam latched on to his hand with an amazing strength, making the muscles in his arm bulge as his hand tightened around hers. He leaned forward, his free fingers gently touching her belly, skimming upward to her hot, sweaty cheek. Brushing the dampened hair out of her face during the lull, he pressed a kiss to her flushed skin, touched his forehead to hers. "Well, little sister, this is it. Showtime. Ready for the grand finale?"

Sam snorted loudly, followed by a grunt as her whole body tensed, shaking the bed and nearly detaching his arm from his body. How did one relatively small woman have such strength? Emmett leaned forward and braced himself, intent on giving her everything he had. There was a disruption and some jostling.

Judging by the sound, Wyatt had climbed up behind his wife and was taking on the role of coach, shouting, "Come on, baby doll. You can do this. You're the toughest woman I know. Let's bring this baby home!"

ᔇᔐᔇᔐ

Preparing for the arrival, watching the mother's belly tightening up with each ripple of her contracting uterus, seeing the body begin to open wider, Casey was concentrating on being in the right place at the right time. Another part of her took note of Wyatt Henry—hair wild, clothes rumpled, barefoot in a T-shirt and jeans—digging his fists into his wife's back to help her through the pain, talking her through it.

The mother-to-be bore down, gritting her teeth fiercely, pressing back against him with incredible force, and he did not falter. Impressive. When he realized the hospital was not an option, the man prepared, his knowledge of birthing animals coming in handy. Most importantly of all, Wyatt gave his support, one hundred percent. No skimping, no shying away.

The same could be said about Emmett. The man had his forehead pressed to the mattress as Samantha dug her nails into his skin until it bled. Again, no shirking his duty for this one. The contraction let up, and he had his face turned his sister-in-law's way, wearing a smile even if he didn't want to, offering words of encouragement.

Casey brushed hair out of her eyes with her forearm and cleared her throat. "Okay, okay Samantha. You're doing fine. Rest now while you can because the baby's about to crown." She sprinted to the dresser to grab a few towels, some as padding beneath Samantha, some for the little one about to arrive. Sam grimaced, and her whole body became rigid once more.

Casey pushed her legs back to help her with her position and shouted, "Now, Samantha! Push with everything you've got!" A scream ripped through the night, the dog began to howl piteously, and a thin wailing joined the chorus. The tears came. Casey could never hold back when the beauty of a new life arrived.

"He's here, Mama! You have yourself a boy, Daddy!" Wiping the baby with fingers that trembled, she swaddled him in a towel, laid him down, and snipped the umbilical cord. The afterbirth came next, gentle pressure on the new mother's belly expelling the placenta to be wrapped in a towel. Finally, the new little boy could be handed over to his eagerly-awaiting parents.

He nestled in his mother's arms, Wyatt was still behind her, holding his wife, and the tears were streaming down both of their faces. Casey's cheeks hurt from smiling so hard until she looked at Emmett. His forehead was pressed against the bed, his jaw clenched, both hands fisted in the covers. A shudder ran through him, and then he shook it off, sitting up and putting on his game face. Casey couldn't shake the fleeting impression of a man in torment.

# CHAPTER 3

E m, would you like to hold him?" Samantha said tenderly, voice hoarse from her exertions.

He nodded. Casey had been amazing, a whirlwind of activity, completely organized and under control. With his brother's assistance, she'd rounded up clothes from the nursery and bathed the baby.

Sitting at Sammie's bedside, holding her hand while she rested, Emmett could hear the water splashing, the new father's hushed wonder, the doctor's quiet, efficient instructions. In a matter of minutes, the little guy was transferred to his waiting mother, and then it was the new uncle's turn.

A soft, warm, surprisingly light bundle was placed in Emmett's arms, hitting his nose with the aroma of baby lotion and powder. Reflexively, his hold tightened to secure the precious package against his chest, causing a quiet mewling and the slightest stirring. He eased up and brushed his lips against a plump, velvety cheek.

Shattered. In that moment, cradling the next generation in the Henry line in his palms, Emmett was like spun glass decimated to powder. Everything he experienced was intensified by his blindness, Samantha's pain; his brother's anxiety; Lucky the German shepherd's fear as he hunkered down below; the lighthouse of Casey's competent hands guiding them all through the storm.

Hope for the future was born in this room, and a feeling of love beyond compare scattered all the pieces of his soul, leaving him unsure of ever putting himself together again. "Uncle Emmett, meet Jackson Emmett Henry." Wyatt's bear hug took him from behind, his voice filled with affection and pride. Yet he trembled, shaken as well.

The waterworks turned on, no stopping them, and Emmett didn't even try, simply scraped at his cheeks "That first name is perfect, Dad would be proud, but Emmett? You trying to torture the poor little man? I mean, *we* had to suffer the penalty of bearing Dad's brothers' names, but why pass on the burden?"

The hand that clamped on his shoulder was a thread, weaving him into his past, present, and future. Wyatt's voice dropped down to a whisper. "We needed a name for someone who would be strong like the mountains— someone who would not crumble, no matter what life threw at them. We chose the names of the best men I have ever known." A kiss on the cheek and his brother moved away, leaving Emmett rocking back and forth with his nephew.

ᡜᠵᡝᠵ

Emmett was stretched out on the couch before the fireplace, an arm over his eyes, beaten down from the trek in the snow and the tension of the past few hours. Wyatt covered him with a blanket and rested his hand on top of his head, wearing an expression of such tenderness and love, Casey had to look away. Rounding up a shot of Jack Daniels, Wyatt dropped down in a chair flanking the fireplace and picked up a picture off the side table.

It was one of his favorites, snapped by their father on a day when all was right in the world, an image of the brothers taking a break from working the farm, leaning against a fence with a horse in between them. Bonnie, a great, black Clydesdale with a white star on her forehead, had been nuzzling his kid brother's neck, making him laugh fit to bursting at the seams. Both brothers wore smiles as big as they come, and the glow in Emmett's eyes was bright enough to hurt.

Wyatt scraped at his face as his eyes began to sting, when a hand rested on his shoulder and gave a reassuring squeeze. "Your son is beautiful. He's sleeping like an angel with Sammie right now. She's out too."

Wyatt found Casey's hand and interlaced his fingers with hers. Choked up, emotions close to the surface, it took a moment to find his voice. "I just wish he could see him." He nodded toward the slumbering form on the couch.

Casey walked around the chair to kneel in front of Wyatt and take his hand. "I'll tell you something. Your brother must feel everything more strongly. When you put Jackson in his arms, you did not see his face. I think that he sees your little man better than you or I."

Wyatt managed a smile, shaky but genuine, and leaned forward to kiss her on the cheek. "Thanks, Casey. That's exactly what I needed to hear."

He pushed off his armchair, went to his brother, and spoke hoarsely in his ear. "Little brother, come on, time for bed." Groggy, Emmett unfolded his long frame from the couch, allowing his brother to put an arm around his waist and lead the way to a spare room. Boots off, covers pulled up, down for the count. The doctor watched, propped against the doorway, until Wyatt showed her to the room next to Emmett's.

So tired he could barely see straight or put one foot in front of the other, Wyatt hit the lights and braced himself against the doorjamb. "Here you go, Doc. I dug out one of Sammie's nightgowns for you. There's a new toothbrush and a comb in the bathroom across the hall. Anything you can scrounge up in the kitchen is free game. If you need me, you'll probably have a better chance waking the dead, but you're welcome to try."

She patted his back and moved to duck under him when Wyatt pulled the young woman into his arms, planting a kiss on the top of her shining black hair, causing surprise in a blur of green eyes. "Thank you. God, thank you, Doc, you don't know how much we thank you for getting us through this night. I might've managed— no I *would* have managed, but not nearly as well. Having my most precious gifts in such good hands is all I could ask for tonight. You sleep well."

Casey mumbled goodnight, and Wyatt shut the place down, locking up, turning off lights, pulling the grate in front of the fireplace. By the time he found his way to his bedroom, his body was ready for a fall. Good thing there was a soft place to land in the nest of blankets, swapped for clean, fresh-smelling linens by the ever-competent Casey Mitchell, the angel of mercy that landed on their doorstep. He pressed himself, spoon style, next to his wife, draping an arm over her hip to rest his hand on his son. Didn't even get his boots off.

&#8498;&#9674;&#8498;

*Head fuzzy. Throat scratchy. Went to bed much too late, but babies come on their own schedule. Feisty little cuss.* Loud wailing coming from his brother's bedroom brought Emmett to the surface, pulling him from dreams. Jackson Emmett Henry definitely had a healthy set of pipes.

Scraping his hands over his face, pressing his palms into his eyes, he rubbed his eyelids and opened them wide. Always hoping for a miracle, Emmett ran through the same routine each morning. *Slept too late too.* He could tell, judging by the lightening of the shadows. The sun had to be turned up on high, flooding through his open curtains, making slight headway through the murkiness.

Made him out of sorts when he wasn't up with the dawn, having become a creature of habit. He found comfort in finding some measures of control in his life to combat that which was beyond his control. Another squawk and Emmett couldn't help grinning. *Babies—one of those things you can't control. They control you.*

Sitting up slowly, working out the kinks, the scent of fresh-brewed coffee drifted in, speeding things up a bit. The prospect of a pot, hot and ready, was a luxury for Emmett. Many a morning would find him groping his way to the kitchen, propping himself against the counter, fighting to remain in an upright position while he waited for the electric coffee pot to cycle through. *Have to get one of those one cup things, have it in a minute.* Today, he'd have his first cup sooner than that, the sooner his butt was in gear.

Throwing off the covers, he climbed out of bed and slowly made his way across the room. It had been a long time since he'd spent the night in his bedroom at Gram and Pop's. Memory served, helping him put the knob in his hand. Emmett gave it a good pull and ventured into the hallway. *Just a few steps to the right, forward, and you're at the bathroom.* Wham! He stubbed his toe hard against the molding and started cursing up a mean streak.

There was the creak of a door opening and a cheerful voice—way too chipper after a night like they just had—called out. "Hey, you all right?" Footsteps came his way, leaving him no room for escape.

Hands on his hips, head down, eyes closed, Emmett

hissed, "Yes. Just let me finish counting to ten, so I can keep my temper in check." *Take a deep breath. Hold it. Slowly let it out.* "Things aren't where they're supposed to be. I'm used to home, you know? Anyplace else, I feel like a bull in a china shop."

He raised his chin, pasted on something resembling a smile, only to feel the real deal happening when Casey moved in close. She smelled incredible, all damp and warm, clothes clinging to her skin—must've taken her shower already—and put her hands on his shoulders.

"You need to make an adjustment in your calculations. Turn to the right—" Her hands shifted him that way, and her breath skimmed his neck, starting a fire in the pit of his stomach. "About two steps and you'll be there." A gentle push and she let go. *Good thing she didn't hold your hand. Might not have been able to control yourself once you got in there.*

Murmuring thanks, he followed directions, shut the door, and leaned against it, waiting for his temperature to come down to normal limits and his heart to stop skyrocketing. A hard swallow and he nodded to himself. *That's it, Em. Hit the shower and make it a cold one. That coffee will have to wait.*

A solid fifteen minutes, give or take, and he joined the womenfolk at the table. A quiet suckling told him the little man was having his breakfast too. A coffee mug was pressed into Emmett's hands as he sat down, and he trailed his fingers upward, following the hand to the arm, to the shoulder, to the cheek, then pulling back shyly. *Most definitely not Wyatt.* "Thank you, Casey."

A press of his shoulder and a chair scraped beside him. "You're welcome. Do you want some toast or eggs? I'm chief cook this morning. Samantha's got some other things to attend to." Her warmth rolled over him, giving him a bright spot, and he gravitated toward the sound, tilting his head her way, feeling a smile grow.

"No, thanks. Stomach's got to wake up first." Turning toward the quiet smacking and sucking from the tiny, suction machine, he reached out, and Sammie's hand took his firmly in her tough grasp. "What are you doing up already, little mother? You must be beat."

A squeeze and she let go. A patting sound ensued, accompanied by a small burp that made everyone laugh softly. "You know me, Em. Can't sit still for long. Besides, when Casey said she was cooking, that did it. I'm doing okay, all things considered. Sore, but I suppose that's normal."

"I'd say. It's not every day you push a bowling ball out of your body." Emmett shook his head, inhaled the life-giving properties of his cup of coffee, and took a long swallow. A few more and he set it down, listening to Casey bustling at the stove, then the sink, washing up, good at multi-tasking. His forehead creased in thought. *Something's missing. Scratch that. Someone.* "Where's Wyatt? Don't tell me he's still in bed."

"No, he's out clearing driveways. We got about a foot, and your brother is insistent everything is clear in case Jackson and I need something." Long-suffering patience clearly colored her words. Emmett could hear a hint of exasperation as well. "He's set on clearing us out, and Emily's too. Joey Sammons stopped by, worried when he didn't see any movement around here. He volunteered to do your place."

Emmett pushed back from the table and fished in his pocket, pulling out a twenty-dollar bill he'd shoved in there, just in case. He laid it on the table. "You make sure Joey gets that, okay? He's a good kid."

The chair shifted beside him, and an arm was wrapped around his neck, the scent of baby powder blended with mother's milk coming with the familiar touch. "Em, you don't have to do that. We can pay Joey. He's doing a few more for Wyatt today, too, as a favor."

Emmett reached up to pat his sister-in-law's cheek and spoke gruffly. "Yes, I do have to do that. Now, how about you let me get an armful of that little man?"

Without hesitation, the tiny bundle was set in his arms, giving him instant gratification. He tucked Jackson in close in the crook of his neck, relished the little puff of air on his skin from that itty-bitty mouth. Amazing.

Casey cleared her throat, and if he wasn't mistaken, there were tears in that voice. "I hate to be a bother, but I have to get to the clinic today. It's my first day. Is there someone I can call for a lift?"

Moving with the utmost care, not wanting to disturb his precious cargo, Emmett stood up. "Here, Sam, you take the little guy." He managed to get in a hug as they made the transfer, turning next toward the doctor's voice. "Listen, if you're up for the walk, we can head over my way. Joey might be able to give us a lift if we catch him. If not, we'll round up someone."

A light kiss brushed his cheek, leaving a scorcher on his skin and sending his heart haywire. "You are the sweetest man. Will you be all right on your own, Samantha?"

"Oh, yes. You two go on now, and thank you again, Casey, for everything. We're forever in your debt." With orders from the doctor for the new mother to behave and take it easy, and Emmett's insistence that she lie down on the couch before they left, they pulled on their winter wear and headed outside.

"Which way do you want to go? Woods or out to the road?" Emmett waited at the bottom of the steps, ready to go whichever way his companion chose. It was cold out, but not unbearably so, and the sun was warm on his face. The walk would do him good. He hated being penned up for too long, stuck inside his head too much as it was.

"Woods. It's absolutely beautiful, everything coated with fresh snow. When I was little, I called it the snow palace, and I was always sad when the new snow fell off the trees. It's like that Robert Frost poem." They turned to the left and Casey took his hand, guiding his steps in the right direction.

"'The woods are lovely, dark and deep. But I have promises to keep and miles to go before I sleep.' 'Stopping by Woods on a Snowy Evening.' I always liked that one, all his stuff. I imagine the farmhouse he lived in was a lot like these parts. He had a place in New Hampshire. I always meant to go see it…" Emmett's words drifted off, resentment threatening to darken his mood. Chalk up one more thing he couldn't do. Shaking it off, he pushed harder through the snow, figuring work would burn off the anger. "It is gorgeous around here, isn't it?"

The trip went much quicker in the daylight without being buffeted by fierce winds. The sound of an engine and a plow scraping the pavement announced the presence of the neighbor's teen, still clearing the drive. There was a screech of brakes, the door slammed, and a hand grabbed his, pumping it enthusiastically. "Congrats, Uncle Em! Can't believe the little bugger decided to come last night. You must be the doc! Sam and Wyatt told me all about you. I'm Joey Sammons. Is there anything I can do for you two this fine morning?"

The kid spoke so fast he nearly sent Emmett's head to spinning, being accustomed to silence and the thoughts on his own mind most of the time. "Yeah, actually, you can, Joe. Will you drive us up to Casey's car, see if we can figure out the problem? Otherwise, she'll need a lift to the clinic."

"No problem, no problem at all. Get you fixed up in no time." Joe took hold of Emmett's elbow, guiding him toward his pick-up. "Now watch the door, Em, and watch your head getting in. You all right now, Em?"

The kid was anxious as all get out, treating him like he was fragile or something, and it set Emmett's teeth on edge. His hand shot out, found the teen's arm, and grabbed hold, hard. *Ease up, Henry. Ease up.* That meant working to throttle down his voice to a reasonable tone as well. "Joey, stop treating me like an old man. I'm not going to break. If I get a few extra bumps and bruises, I'll live."

"I know, Em—it's just, well—I'm not used to—" The kid was starting to stammer. *Good job, Emmett. Embarrass him, why don't you?* Emmett cut him off and hooked a hand at the nape of his neck, as if grabbing a young pup.

"I know you're not. Neither am I. It's a learning curve for all of us. You can learn not to coddle me, and I'll learn to accept a hand up with a little more grace, okay?" His eyes started to sting, and he patted the young man on the back with a resounding thump. "By the way, thanks for the driveway. I left twenty dollars over at Wyatt's for you. Don't let that wily brother of mine short you."

He couldn't help but smile to himself as he pictured the kid ducking his head and blushing, starting to stutter some more as he gave even more attention to getting Casey into the passenger seat.

Emmett didn't have to see to put two and two together. There were two parts to the equation—a healthy teenager with raging hormones and a young woman which led to only one conclusion: the doc was hot.

A bumpy ride out, slip-sliding a bit with the exuberance of the young, and Joey pulled over just a short piece down the road. "Can I have your key, ma'am? I'll see if I can figure out what's what."

A jingling noise proved she produced the item in question. The door opened and slammed shut, shaking the cab. Emmett sighed and shook his head.

"Eager one, isn't he?" There was a hint of laughter in the doctor's voice. Luckily, she found humor in the situation, not annoyance. "Well, that didn't take long. Joey's on his way back already.

The teen climbed in, huffing and puffing a bit with his haste. "Not too complex, ma'am. You just need some gas." Everyone got caught up in the giggles as he revved the engine, did a three-point turn, and rumbled back to the Henry House. There was a filled gas can in the barn—on hand for just such emergencies.

Joey left the truck idling, moving to open the barn when Emmett squeezed his shoulder. "Listen, Joey. I know you've got more driveways to do, and I can use some fresh air to clear my head. It was a long night, you know? I'll walk with Casey to the barn and to her car, let you get back to work." The passenger door creaked as it swung open, and he heard the thud of feet touching the ground.

His driver chuckled and gave him a hearty slap on the back. "Sure." Leaning in closer, he whispered conspiratorially, "Want some alone time with the doc, do you? I'm telling you. She's a babe."

# CHAPTER 4

Spinning tires and the impression of speed had Emmett bowing his head with his hands on his hips. "He's fishtailing right now, isn't he? Kids today—" That set him to laughing. "Sound like my father. Sometimes I forget I was one of them once, not that long ago. Come on. We'll get that gas, send you on your way."

He held out his elbow, and Casey set her hand in the crook of his arm, leading him to the large, red barn. Her hand was on his, setting his palm on the knob and Emmett took it from there. Remarkable. She knew how to guide him without making him feel like a cripple.

They stepped inside, hit immediately by the sweet smell of straw and horses, their footsteps echoing in the cavernous space. "See the stalls on the left? There's a gas can and some other supplies in the first one."

About five paces and his hands hit the swinging door. Emmett pushed it open and nudged the area with his foot until he tapped something with a little give, something that sloshed. Reaching down to pick it up, he heard Casey's long, low whistle. "Wow! You have a lot of empty stalls. Did this used to be a working farm?"

Emmett's face twisted in contempt as he gripped the door of the stall on the way out, setting it in motion, leaving it squeaking on the hinge with its swaying back and forth. "It was a full house and more in the stable out back. Horses. Mainly Clydesdales, but other breeds as well. Whatever whim caught my dad's attention. After this—" He waved at his eyes. "—I couldn't do it anymore. Couldn't care for them or exercise them. They're at my brother's now."

The exit was calling him. Had to get out of this place. Too many memories. Casey rested a hand on his arm, and it took an effort to let go of the tension he now felt in the barn.

"You miss it," she said.

His bark of laughter was without humor. "What good is being a farm boy through and through, fifth generation on my family's land, when I can't do the only thing I ever wanted or knew? The horses were what nearly killed me when this happened. I love to ride but couldn't anymore, and there is no way, no how, I'll have someone leading me around out there. Not fair to the horses. Those animals are meant to be ridden, used to me taking them all out one by one, every day."

They'd made it outside by this point, his feet stomping the ground hard with the barely banked fury that was never far away. "I thank God every day my father didn't live to see this. Oh, I got a good settlement from the...*unmentionable*...who did this to me, that and the insurance money from the bar. They didn't want to be put out of business, so I'm set for life."

He couldn't help but sneer, biting off the last words. Emmett stopped, squeezed the doctor's arm. "Sorry, I'm still a tad bitter. Just tell me to shut up when I mouth off too much."

Her silence was telling. *I'd say it's time to shut it.* There was a lull between them—after non-stop excitement from the moment Casey showed up at his doorstep, this was their first quiet moment, and they became awkward, neither knowing what to do with it.

Conversation turned to the inconsequential—the scenery, the neighbors, the cardinals, jays, and chickadees dressing the trees. "Well, here we are," she said. "Lean up against the car, and I'll give it a go." The doctor was a little breathless, probably tired from their hike or anxious to be on her way.

The walk was longer than Emmett thought. *Probably should've let Joey drive us.* There was some rattling, the sound of liquid swishing around and being poured, the strong smell of gasoline filling his nostrils. After being out for a prolonged period, the cold was setting into his bones, making him shiver. He could hear the key scraping in the lock, the creak of the car door, and metal finding its way home in the ignition.

One turn and the engine roared to life. "Woo, woo! We have lift off!" Casey's arms were around him, and she planted a quick kiss smack dab in the middle of his mouth before grabbing his hand and pulling him around to the passenger side. "There. Let me drive you home, and I'll get to work."

A minute later and she rolled to a stop, the heat starting to come up in the car. That was nothing to the crackle the touch of those full lips left on his, socking it to him in the pit of his stomach with sudden impact, making it hard to catch his breath.

Emmett opened the door, stepped out of the car. Every part of him wanted to climb back in and slide up close to her, like a second skin. He pressed a hand to the roof, kept himself on his feet, barely. "Listen, you ever need anything that I have to give, you'll know where to find me. I don't go far."

He extended a hand to her in farewell, and the girl set him off balance when she grabbed hold, slid across, and gave him one more brush of those fine, full lips.

Breathlessly, he bid his goodbye, "Nice to meet you, Miss Casey Mitchell," and stepped back.

Emmett stood stock still, wind ruffling at his hair, tugging at his clothes as the sound of her tires and engine receded into the distance. Turning toward the house, he felt drained dry. It was all he could do to put one foot in front of the other, get inside, and get his boots off, butter fingers fighting him.

Once down on the bench by the door, getting back up again was a challenge. Leaving his coat on the seat, crossing the room to build a fire was a near insurmountable obstacle, and his head started to throb. *That's a no brainer, idiot. Didn't eat. Didn't sleep well. Overdid it, trying to be the Lone Ranger for the pretty girl. God, I wish I could see her face!* The last log tumbled out of his fingers as the pain bloomed, driving him back into his recliner, leaving no room for anything else.

୧⤀୨

"Shoot! You'd lose your head if it wasn't attached!" Casey didn't make it half a mile when she glanced at the seat beside her and slammed on the brakes. A quick scan of the rest of the car proved to be useless. Her purse wasn't there, something that could wait except that the key to her apartment was buried in its mysterious depths. Counting to ten, forward and backward, she blew her bangs out of her eyes and turned the car around.

*Here we go again.* Not that she minded going back to Emmett Henry's, not in the least. She'd love to look at that tall, dark and handsome, staring into those golden eyes with no risk of him catching her drooling or tripping over her tongue hanging to the floor. The problem was he'd think she was a scatterbrain!

There was nothing for it but to get over herself and

go back in there. Casey parked the car only to smack herself in the forehead. *How about his gas can, Mitchell?* She'd set it in the trunk after filling up her tank. She tossed the keys in her coat pocket, popped the trunk, and grabbed the red can. She debated only for a moment, then a quick jog ensured it was put in its rightful place in the barn. A stitch had her pressing a hand to her side by the time she rapped on the door to no answer. Maybe he was taking a nap. A quick pop in and she'd be on her way.

Casey pushed the door open to find a figure sitting by the fire, palms of his hands pressed into his eyes. He was nearly bent in half, face twisted in pain. Her own discomfort forgotten, she hurried to his side and knelt down beside him. "Emmett, what is it?"

He shook his head slowly, hindered by the thunder in his brain. "It's nothing, just a headache. Ever since my injury, they hit me hard sometimes. I guess a chair to the head will do that." His words were slurred a little, his eyes darker. He tried to smile encouragingly, but the attempt fell flat.

Casey moved behind him and massaged his shoulders and the rigid column of his neck, giving extra attention to his temples. "Better?"

"A little." He winced when she hit a particularly sensitive spot, then his face smoothed—from her touch or willpower.

"Why don't you lie down?" Casey wrapped her arms around him, whispering in his ear. "Come on, Em. Let me give you a hand."

He nodded, moving his head gingerly, showing the amount of pain the man must be in. The moment Emmett stood, he started to sway. "Sorry, I'm really dizzy."

"That's all right. Lean on me." There it was, that lingering reluctance to accept help. He stiffened for an instant until she pressed against him, her arm around his waist. An arm draped over her shoulders, and they took the steps slowly to his bedroom.

Casey pulled back the covers and helped him climb in. "Be back in a minute. I've got some pills in my purse that will help," she said, thankful for the small medicine cabinet that traveled with her, *Because you never know.* She grabbed the packet and a glass of water and took the stairs two at a time.

Emmett was curled into a ball, gripping a pillow with knuckles gone white. Still hurting. Really hurting. She ran her fingers through his hair, down to his cheek, and let her palm rest there. Warm. A little too warm. Head-aches could do that sometimes, especially migraines. "Sit up and take these. They're pain killers, strong stuff, with sedatives. They'll knock you out until it's gone."

Fighting back a groan, Emmett came up slowly, leaned against her, and took his medicine. "Good boy," she teased before he dropped back down to the pillow. "I'll be downstairs if you need anything. I'm not going anywhere until I know you're okay." That he didn't pro-test told her Emmett Henry was in hurting status.

ഇരുന്നു

Pacing in front of the fireplace, watching the strange images that danced within the flames, she waited for someone to pick up the phone. *Calling in on your first day. Great way to make a good impression.* "Charlton Clinic, this is Angie speaking. We're closing up shop. Do you have an emergency?"

Casey pulled up short. "Angie, this is Dr. Mitchell. What's going on?" She moved forward to pick up a photo off the mantel. Graduation day, Wyatt's arm hooked around his brother's neck. Emmett too handsome in cap and gown, ready to take on the world, the future shining in his golden gaze. Her eyes squeezed shut, and she forced herself to pay attention to the receptionist.

"Oh, hi, Dr. Mitchell! We've been trying to reach you, sweetie. What with all the snow, everyone has been canceling. We figure there's no sense in staying open today. We'll try again tomorrow. Did you make out okay in the storm last night?"

Casey set down the frame and sank into Emmett's recliner, haunted by the thought of him perched before the fire with his empty stare. Shaking the memory, she concentrated on the phone call and the chipper receptionist on the other end. "You won't believe my night! My car ran out of gas, I lost my way, and I stumbled all the way to the first farm house I could reach. I just started to thaw out when the phone rang. The guy's sister-in-law was in labor! Next thing you know, we're trekking through three feet of snow to deliver a baby! Whew! I'm hoping things will slow down when I get to work."

"Delivered a baby! Well, I never would have imagined—who are the lucky mama and papa?" There was a snap of chewing gum on the other end. Angie Donaldson was a hopeless addict with several flavors in her purse and on her person at all times. If Casey wasn't mistaken, she heard fingernails tapping on the counter. Angie was also hooked on nail salons.

"The Henrys. Samantha and Wyatt—they had a baby boy, Jackson Emmett. I'd say he was about eight pounds, a healthy, little tyke. I'm sure they'll be in to see Sharon and Paul as soon as they've had a breather or when enough snow melts, whatever comes first." Sharon Matthews was the OB/GYN at the clinic while her husband, Paul, was the pediatrician. Between the three of them, all the town's needs would be taken care of efficiently.

The gum snapping and nail tapping stopped long enough for a shriek as Angie hollered the good news to the other doctors and staff. "Oh, my! Another Henry boy! Seems boys run in that family. Must be those strong genes." There was a pause and the flashy, feisty woman on the other end toned it down, speaking gently. "How is our Emmett? We see him very little these days."

*Our Emmett.* Said in that proprietary way of a small town, where everyone knew everyone and felt ownership. Casey's eyes began to sting and her throat to tighten, a lump forming in her stomach as she pictured the man upstairs, her unlikely hero.

"Oh, he's all right. Stubborn, isn't he? The man made me tea, insisted on guiding me to his brother's place, stuck it out for the delivery when most men would turn tail and run, and made sure my car was in order today. He's upstairs sleeping off a headache right now. I think he might have a migraine kicking his butt. Could be from pushing too hard."

There was a sigh on the other end. "That's Em. Never was one to take the easy way out. You say hi to him when he wakes up. I know he's in good hands. Don't worry about a thing here. Tomorrow is another day." On that note, the line disconnected.

Casey shook her head at the receptionist's babble, wondering if the girl's tongue ever wore out, and set down the phone. The strain of the past twenty-four hours catching up to her, she stretched out on the couch and pulled the afghan off the back. *Might as well get a little shut-eye while* things are quiet—

*Crash!* A loud thud overhead had her tossing the blanket on the floor and taking the stairs two at a time once more.

⸎⸎⸎

Hindsight was crystal clear, a cruel trick—dreams

that could be seen so vividly, in elaborate detail. He could smell the fog of tobacco smoke. Taste the stale pretzels. Hear the crowd cheering on the football game and the dull roar of conversation ebbing and flowing in the bar, the echo of Wyatt's laughter filling his head. The beer tasted really good going down, the classic combination of barley, wheat, and hops—a cold rush to his gut.

A just reward was their due. They'd worked hard, breaking in horses all day. *Breaking in the people, more like. I'm so damned tired. Should've stayed home, gone straight to bed, do not pass go.*

Wyatt tipped back his head and took a last swallow, laying money on the table for the tab when a woman's shrieking pierced the air. Emmett turned to see Mindy Allen, the preacher's daughter, over in the corner with some low life wrapping her hair around his fist like a blonde rope and pulling hard. *What in the world? What's she doing here? The girl can't be twenty-one yet.*

That train of thought crashed to a halt when the scum banged her head on the table, and Emmett saw red. The pretzels were overturned, his beer mug knocked over—*a shameful waste of good alcohol*—his chair hitting the floor as he crossed the room. His mind was on auto pilot, set on one goal—taking the jerk out.

Mindy was crying, blood running down her face, when Emmett gave the guy a good jab in the midsection and then the head. Emmett took hold of the distraught girl's hand, wincing at the sight of her nose. *Broken, no doubt about it.* His hand fished in his back pocket, and he handed her his bandanna.

"Minnow, I don't know what you're doing here, honey, but you get on back to the bartender, and he'll make sure you're taken care of, you hear me?" She nodded tearfully and moved to go, dabbing her nose, adding more red to the crimson cloth.

"Em, behind you!"

Wyatt's voice rang out, sharp with fear, and pain bloomed on top of Emmett's skull, Mindy's china blue eyes wide with terror as her hands came out to catch him.

The world went dark...

⌒⌒

Emmett came to with a crash, knocking the lamp off the bedside table with his thrashing. Shaking, covered in a cold sweat, the lights still out. Covering his eyes, avoiding the inevitable, he tried to get up and go when strong arms wrapped around his middle.

"Oh, no, you don't. You're staying put until you get your feet back under you." Casey. Warm. Sweet-smelling. Solid and real. Here, by some small miracle. Slowly his heart stopped tripping although breathing was tough for completely different reasons as the doctor's fingers brushed his cheek, continuing on to run through his hair. "There," she said. "All right now, want to tell me about what just happened?"

Emmett fell back against the pillows, an arm shielding his eyes, not that it mattered. He could sleep with them wide open. Wouldn't make a whit of difference. Lids were for show now. "Just had a visit from the past coming back to bite me in the butt. I don't luck out like old Ebenezer Scrooge with an all's-well-that-ends-well kind of story. One thing we have in common—there's no changing what was. Have to hope what is will be enough to deal with whatever will be." He clammed up, waiting for the eruption of resentment to die down. "Sorry. Probably sounds like gibberish. I just dreamed about how this...catastrophe...hap-pened. Pretty mean making me watch it all again, and ironic. I can see perfectly in the dream."

The mattress sank down as Casey sat beside him and took his hand in hers. "What did you see, Emmett? What happened to you?" How tempting to lean in closer, let her catch him, never let go.

The words came haltingly at first, then in a rush, spitting out the beginning to the end—waking up in the dark, finding himself in a hospital bed days later, brought out of a medically induced coma due to swelling in his brain caused by a chair upside the head. He laughed, because crying or being mad at the world wouldn't change anything. "They've told me that Wyatt threw himself at the guy like a linebacker, went completely berserk, took him down hard. Too late. Everything happened too fast."

Casey's fingers were gentle, stroking his hair, trailing down his cheek, cool to the touch. Her voice was soothing as well. "Wyatt did everything he could. Just like you and your doctors, I'm sure they did the same. If you could go back, do you think you would've done anything differently?"

Emmett mulled that one over, chewed on it a while, and the doc waited. Except for the sound of her breathing and her touch, he wouldn't have even known she was there. He shifted, pulling himself up to a sitting position, and propped his elbows on his knees. "Maybe I would've handled it in a different way, made sure it went down differently—but no, I wouldn't have dodged. That's not part of the Henry code. Besides, someone else might have been hurt. It could've been Wyatt—and Wyatt, he's a daddy. My brother needs to be whole for his boy. No, my father would say what is meant to be is meant to be. Guess that says it all."

Casey squeezed his hand and took him by surprise, kissing him on the cheek and leaving a scalding spot that most likely turned scarlet. "Hold that thought." She walked away, leaving him in the cold, warming him up again with her return. "Take these." More pills and a tall glass of water. "Drink it—*all* of it."

"Yes, Mom." Emmett did as he was told, found the table with his hand to set the glass down, wincing at the bare spot. "Did I kill the lamp?"

A little bit of finagling and Casey picked the lamp up, allowing Emmett to run his hand over the surface. "It survived, no worse for the wear. Must be made of tough stuff, like a Henry."

Emmett snorted. "I'm not so sure about my being all that tough, but I'll do." Heading a sigh off at the pass, he let his fingers do the walking until they found the woman at his side, and linked with hers.

"Thanks, Doc, for everything. It's nice to know we've got someone who will make house calls. I might need to cook up some excuses to get you out here for some more visits." He pulled a smile out from somewhere, tried it on for size. It fit. "Now, what do you say to some lunch…or dinner before you hit the road?"

# CHAPTER 5

Casey chose Charlton because it was the farthest thing from Albany that she could get, figuratively speaking. A sleepy, quaint, Christmas-postcard kind of town, where life moved at a snail's pace, dotted with historical markers from Revolutionary and Colonial days. The place took a person back to a simpler time. The perfect do-over kind of place.

Her first day at the clinic didn't disappoint. Run of the mill. An ingrown toenail. The flu. Strep throat. Gaps in between that had her wondering if the clock even moved. No knifings. No gunshot wounds. No domestic abuse nightmares involving adults or children. *No fathers lying on the kitchen floor, the life spilling from their eyes.*

"Casey? Hello! Are you in there?" Sharon Matthews, the resident OB/GYN propped a hip against her desk and slid her glasses down her nose, shaking their newest doctor from her reverie. "Ah, there you are. Honey, it is quitting time. How was your first day?"

Short and curvy, the bleached-blonde woman presented a pretty package with her bobbed hair, batting long lashes that covered an amused gaze of cornflower blue. *Hmmm...looks more like a Playboy Bunny than a member of the medical profession. Small wonder husbands love to accompany their wives for appointments.*

Shaking her head at the ramblings rattling around inside her mind, Casey shut down the computer and stood up to stretch with her hands high over her head. "It was good, but is it always *this* slow?"

Casey walked around the desk, Sharon hooked an arm around her waist, and they headed through the door.

"Well, most days, although some will make your head spin. I thought you had enough of emergency room pacing in Albany." Sharon slid her a sideways glance, putting her on the spot for an answer. No skipping out on this one.

Casey grabbed her purse from under the reception desk, waved to Angie, wincing at the fluorescent yellow get-up she was wearing. It really clashed with the fiery red curls straight from a bottle. Making a beeline for the door, Casey followed her colleague out to the parking lot.

Sharon's husband, Paul the pediatrician, waved from the car, brushing fair bangs out of shamrock eyes. Compact and muscular, he looked more the part of a surfer. Impatient to go home, he beeped the horn, interrupting efforts at conversation. Casey tilted her head his way. "I think beach boy is ready to go home. Are you sure you two don't belong in California? You really look out of place here."

Sharon laughed and gave her a wink. "Sweetie, looks can be deceiving. We've lived here all of our lives." Shivering dramatically, she pulled up her coat and gave Casey a quick hug. "A tropical climate does sound appealing, though. Get on inside before you turn into an icicle. Glad your day went well, Case." She flitted across the parking lot, blowing a kiss and calling out, "Toodles!" before hopping inside the car. Casey couldn't help a pang of longing as the two doctors bridged the gap between them in the front seat, latched on to each other, and proceeded to kiss with such skill the windows started to steam up. To have someone hold her that way. Make her toes curl. Emmett Henry's face surfaced in her mind, and a swarm of butterflies broke loose in her stomach.

Feeling like an intruder, she turned back to the clinic. What used to be a two-family home had been converted. Doctors' offices and labs were downstairs, a full apartment upstairs. Taking the entrance to the left, she climbed the steps, relishing the creaking that gave them character, like all old houses. Jangling her keys in the lock, she let herself in.

The place was cozy and looked lived-in, thanks to the "Moving In" party the Matthews and Angie had thrown when the U-Haul truck arrived. Everyone had pitched in, staying from early in the morning until evening, making sure everything was unpacked and in its place. Pictures were hung; curtains dressed the windows; knickknacks arranged; and housewarming gifts presented in the form of potted plants, chocolate, and wine. At the end of the day, Casey's new friends even made sure to feed her, a pot luck supper already in the fridge. Thinking about their generosity of spirit still brought tears to her eyes.

This evening was the opposite of that festive day. Quiet, too quiet after all the excitement with the Henrys and work. The silence was especially oppressive for a girl who had lived with her parents, saving money with all those college loans. *Who you kidding, girlfriend? You weren't ready to leave the nest.* Until everything fell apart. *Not going to go there, Case. No feeling sorry for yourself anymore, remember? You promised. Think about Emmett.*

Giving herself a good, mental kick in the seat of her pants, she turned on the radio, put on her flannels and fuzzy slippers, and tried a book for a while. When her stomach started to rumble, she made popcorn. *No fun cooking a big meal for one.* Her father had loved her cooking, praised it up and down, wondered why she didn't become a chef. Shying away from those thoughts, she made a yogurt smoothie for dessert, figured that would supply some health benefits. She slurped the cold treat down, curled up under a blanket on the couch, a movie filling the hours. Time to hit the hay.

Casey climbed into bed, shut off the lights, and stared into the darkness, replaying the events of the past few days, holding up vivid snapshots in her mind of Wyatt and Emmett. She couldn't help but linger on the latter. *Sound like cowboy names,* she thought fuzzily until sleep took her under—and straight into Emmett Henry's arms…

❦❦❦

The wind was howling outside, buffeting the house and making it shudder. Snow was spitting hard like the night she bumbled into Emmett's life. Here, in her bed, the man was a furnace, making covers unnecessary as she tossed them aside and pressed herself against the sculpted, hard planes of his body.

No extras on Emmett, a honed work of art. Moonlight spilled through the window, casting him in silver, making his eyes glitter like starlight, taking her breath away. She could stare at him forever and not be interrupted by self-consciousness from him sizing her up. No whittling her down, as men were wont to do.

Emmett's talented fingers were skimming over every part of her, learning her body more intimately than any other man ever had, better than she knew herself. Sending sparks flying. Traveling from the tips of her toes. Brushing her heels. Running over her legs. Skimming her hips.

Hugging her abdomen. Cataloguing each rib, every ounce.

He lingered, passing over her chest, dancing along her collarbone and her shoulders. Finally, his fingers wandered back in an upwards direction. Emmett dedicated extra time to exploring her face before threading his hands through her hair. He rose above her, his mouth devouring hers, and she burst into flames. The ashes fluttered down on his skin in the form of kisses, and she consumed him.

ↁↁↁ

"Oh my God!" Casey woke up with her cheeks on fire, entangled in her covers, gasping for breath. She escaped her bed and flung herself at the window, yanking it open and sucking in deep, restorative breaths. Pressing her forehead and palms to the cold glass, she stared outside at a landscape caught in the throes of another fierce, winter storm. Closing her eyes, the only thing she could see was Emmett's golden gaze, calling to her for another taste of honey, and the flames flickered in the pit of her belly. *Girlfriend, you have got it bad.*

ↁↁↁ

Wyatt made Emmett feel like a dog, said he had to take him out, get him some fresh air. Next thing, Emmett would need to hang his head out the window and let his tongue dangle. His brother ought to buy him a collar and a leash.

Mouth twisting in frustration, he crossed his arms over his chest and tapped his foot. *Feel like a fish out of water or some exotic display, sitting in this blasted room while they visit the pediatrician. Sammie didn't need me tagging along.* His jaw set and his shoulders straightened, back pressing against the chair. *Nobody needs me tagging along.*

Listening to the muzak, the typing of the receptionist's keys, the murmur of conversation in the waiting room, the drone of news on the television, Emmett hated being out of his element. All he wanted was to be back at the farm. Puttering around. Doing his housework. Walking the fence line, a source of daily exercise because he could find the way back. To be anywhere but here. He especially hated doctors' offices.

Except for one doctor. Wouldn't mind spending some time with Casey Mitchell, tucking himself into a locked room and her capable arms. Sealing his lips on hers, giving artificial resuscitation a practice run. Could never be too knowledgeable, mind you. Running his hands up and down her body, discovering unchartered territory and claiming it for his own.

He closed his eyes at first then remembered it didn't matter since lids were an accessory now, and let the fantasy take him. The cool, smooth material of her lab coat, shedding it like an extra skin, taking whatever she wore underneath and removing unnecessary barriers, running his hands through the curtain of her hair, a place where he could lose himself for a while. A scent drifted his way, something real, something familiar, a blend of brown sugar and vanilla, snapping him back to the here and now. Emmett straightened and cleared a throat gone dry as shoes tapped his way. "Doc?"

જીજીજી

Casey walked into the waiting room for her lunch break to see a familiar figure in a chair, emanating reluctance, arms crossed, jaw clenched, golden eyes staring straight ahead. Anyone who didn't know him would think the man was being downright cantankerous—until his head turned her way, his eyes homing in on her with amazing precision, and a smile bloomed—blinding sunshine after the rain. "Doc?"

Remnants of last night's dream flashed through her mind, making her thankful Emmett could not see her face. She crossed the room, sat beside him, and touched his arm. "What brings you here? Not sick are you?" A stab of concern poked her. That headache had been bothering her, making her wonder if there were more serious implications. Head injuries were sticky. One could never be too careful.

Emmett shook his head in aggravation, grumbling down low in his chest, "It's my brother. Thought I should get out for a spell, said the change of scenery would do me good. Like I'm a pet that needs to be aired and exercised, or something. As for the scenery—" He waved a hand in front of his eyes and laughed bitterly. "—no change there. Sammie's getting the baby checked and I won't be surprised if Wyatt bullies her into getting her own check-up. We should be here a while." He let out a gust of air, blowing his bangs out of his eyes, clearing the way for a good look at his golden amber gaze that could entrap any woman.

Casey couldn't help but chuckle. Emmett looked like a sullen little boy. Thrust out his bottom lip, and he'd have a good pout going. "What do you say I spring you a little while and take you to lunch?" she asked.

A grin was growing, lighting him up from the inside out, making his eyes shine. He stood, crooked his elbow for convenient hand placement, and flipped out his collapsible cane. "Lead the way. God, I hate this thing. It just shouts 'Here comes Mr. Hopelessly Helpless.'"

They headed in the direction of the entrance when

Emmett pulled up short. "Oh, wait." Far from helpless, he turned back and skimmed his fingers along the wall, counting the doors along the way, tapping on the second on the left. Wyatt yanked it open, wearing a grin like a cat that caught the canary when his brother's hand found his flannel shirt and grabbed onto his shoulder. "Hey, Wyatt. I'm here to inform you that *I* am going to lunch. With a live woman. Don't send out the search party. Or the dogs. Or the police."

Boisterous laughter followed them all the way to the coat hooks by the door as they shrugged into their winter wear and ventured out. The frigid wind pinched Casey's skin and snatched her breath away the instant she stepped outside, making her hold tight and press closer to the man beside her. *He really is a furnace!* That thought had the heat flooding her face. A glance at Emmett and she saw his cheeks were stained crimson as well. Interesting.

Steering clear of dangerous waters, Casey concentrated on the matter at hand, warning Emmett of the step at the curb, an icy patch, when the door was near. He pushed ahead of her, feeling for the knob, and held it for her, a true gentleman. Sonny's Side Up Diner was the only show in town for casual meals. Otherwise, there was the Old Inn and Tavern, a more upscale kind of place. A welcome wall of warmth wrapped around them, accompanied by the cheerful hum of conversation during the bustling lunch hour.

The cook manning the grill left the kitchen to personally greet the latest arrivals. A big man, with a heart to match, his face was wreathed with an ear-to-ear smile. His bald head gleamed in the sunlight, chocolate eyes warm enough to melt a heart of stone on the coldest of days. "It's about time you showed that sorry face in here, Emmett Henry! The place hasn't been the same without you, and your brother...well, he's like a dog without his bone, completely lost whenever he comes around."

The man gave him a bear hug, slapping him on the back hard enough to make the younger man wince, and a meaty hand came up to give him a firm squeeze at the nape of his neck. "Don't you be a stranger anymore, you hear me? You come in with Wyatt or this pretty lady."

He let go to extend his hand in greeting. "Pleased to meet you. You must be Doctor Mitchell. A town this size, we know everything. I'm Sonny Olsen, the owner. You ever need a good meal, you've come to the right place. Enjoy and make sure you pry that boy out of his hidey hole more often." Casey stammered a greeting and let Emmett's insistent tugging draw her into the dining area. The crease between his eyes and the jut of his chin suggested he wasn't happy.

ເຈເ

*Hidey hole? Why can't Sonny leave his nose where it belongs?* Small wonder Emmett didn't come to town often. In a place the size of a postage stamp where they all knew everybody's business, he felt like they were all poking him on a slide under a microscope each time he set foot off the farm. People knew him since diapers, until his life ground to a halt in a barroom brawl.

They were curious. Pitying. Callous in their thoughtless observations. Take now, for instance, the whispers or the telling silences as people shut up. God, he hated being stared at, felt it on his back as the hairs rose up. Nothing for it but to grit his teeth and push through it, like all the rest life had slammed at him.

"Can you help me to a corner booth? I like corners." *Hidey holes?* The voice in his head mocked. *Shut up, why don't you?* Emmett growled back, beating down panic as Casey spoke softly, indicating a seat. He flicked his cane, snapping it back into its compact form, and tucked it into his back pocket.

He sank down, and his hands ran over the table, making a mental map, finding equilibrium. Napkin, silverware, placed the way he liked it. Salt. Pepper. More napkins. Menus. His fingers drummed on the table as he resisted the urge to cross his arms. *You can do this, Emmett. A meal. Out. With a girl. Breathe.*

A high-pitched squeal made him want to cover his ears as rapid footsteps came their way and a kiss was pressed to his cheek, water glasses thudding on the table next. "Em! God, it is good to see you. You look great, too. High time, farm boy, high time. I'm Cindy Johnson. Em and me, we graduated in the same class."

"It's nice to meet you, Cindy. I'm Casey Mitchell. I'm the new doctor at the clinic. What do you recommend for lunch today?" Amusement colored her words, making the knot in Emmett's stomach begin to unwind. He flicked a hand out, aiming for the water, misjudged, and sent it over with a bang.

"Crap!" He shot up quick to avoid a flood in his lap and a thorough dousing in an extremely embarrassing area. Cindy was dabbing at his leg, apologetic beyond belief, Casey adding her own efforts to the mix, swabbing at his seat, and he could hear the twitch in her mouth. *The woman wants to laugh. Can you blame her?*

Emmett pinched the bridge of his nose, took a deep breath, and silently counted to ten. "Will you stop with all the bother? It's water. I'm not made of sugar. It will dry." Cindy squeezed his hand. He pulled her in close, gave her a clumsy peck on the cheek, and tossed in a smile. "It's all right, Cinnamon, really. Now, back to business. What do you suggest today?"

While the waitress rattled off the selections, he was running through his options. Picking a meal was no longer a simple task, another thing Emmett had taken for granted in his past life. Had to narrow the selections. Nothing complicated, no cutting, no soup. He tended to dribble and drool, not appealing. Missed sometimes as he fished with his spoon, and food tended to slip around on his plate, trying to get away from the knife. Might as well stick with a sandwich, chips. Easy. The doc ordered turkey and rice soup with a club sandwich. That sounded so good on such an icy day, made his mouth water, but it was too messy. He went with a Reuben. At least it was hot.

"Not that it's an option here, but have you learned braille?" Casey asked casually, out of curiosity or perhaps for a conversation starter, her spoon clinking her bowl with the speedy delivery of her first course. That soup smelled out of this world.

Emmett's shoulders stiffened at the topic while his stomach growled. *Quiet down there!* "I don't have much call to use it, but I suppose I'll get around to it sometime, maybe. I use audio books, a program on the computer—I get by." Their sandwiches arrived next, a distraction, and more water. Casey's hand crossed to his, guiding it, letting him place it on the cool glass to avoid a repeat performance. "Thanks," he murmured gruffly and dug into his sandwich, tucking it away, self-consciously dabbing at his face from time to time. *Try not to wear it, Em.*

Casey slid her plate to the edge of the table. "That was really good. I don't think I'll be brown bagging it." As she leaned forward, he caught another whiff of her perfume, body spray, whatever concoction it was that women used to torment men. The girl probably had no idea what she was doing to him. Nearly a year of self-imposed exile didn't help. *Getting dizzy here.*

A lull in conversation fell between them, and Emmett had a need to fill it—with her. His hand reached out, brushing hers and latching on. "What do you look like? It's been eating at me, the not knowing. I've formed a picture but God, I really wish I could see you, find out if I'm even close." No fair really. He knew everyone else around these parts, held them in his memories. Not the doc. She was a blank, a voice and a touch with no mental photograph.

She laughed nervously, and her hold on his hand tightened. "I have green eyes and dark hair. Nothing to write home about."

His hand broke free to float in the air and hovered. "May I?" he asked. There was a pause, probably as Casey nodded. It was such a habit, most people didn't realize how often they did it. Her answer came when she clasped his hand to her cheek and bobbed her head up and down. She allowed him to run his fingers over her skin, and his palm cupped her cheek. "Now, really tell me, make me see you," he whispered softly.

Another pause. A collecting of her thoughts? He heard her swallow audibly, take a shaky breath. "I have my father's eyes, the luck of the Irish passed down, green as emerald stones flashing in the sun—his words, not mine," She laughed softly, but beneath was a strong current of sadness. An unhappy ending somewhere along the way. "My hair is my mother's, nearly black it's such a dark brown, from her Native American roots. It's straight as straw, and I've got a bit of a sharp nose, thanks to her too, plus a tad of a slant to the eyes."

Did he hear a hint of annoyance at those features? That would never do. Bent on changing her mind, making her see herself the way he did, Emmett set both his hands to the task of revealing her true beauty. His fingers crossed the entire surface of her face, her closed eyelids, and threaded their way into her hair. He felt her shiver, a bow strung tight, about to release. Something answered within, a delicious thrumming, and his insides pulled taut, but this time nerves weren't to blame.

                              *ᴇ⁄ᴐᴇ⁄ᴐ*

    As he had no need to shield them, the sunlight hit Emmett's eyes, set the gold to glowing, honey gleaming in a jar, and made Casey suck in a quick breath. He might not have to look away, but the light in his gaze was nearly blinding her. "Your hair is like black silk I bet." His hands, competent as any doctor's, were running through the long strands, down to the ends that were hanging loose at her waistline, settling on her hips, and she was quivering. *I am a firm believer in spontaneous combustion. Touch me much more, and I'm a goner.* "You've been blessed with the kind other girls would kill for." His hands were on the move again, skimming her shoulders, running down her arms, taking her hands. "You're what, about five-five?"

    She nodded for the second time and mentally kicked herself. *He needs a voice, idiot!* "Yeah, I'm the ordinary size all around for height and weight, not too big, not too small—average."

    Emmett shook his head, and that grin was teasing at the corner of his mouth, tugging it upward, transforming him into something so much better than those sullen moments. "There isn't anything average about you, Doc." He brought her hand to his lips, brushing his mouth across her knuckles, a heat wave running through her before letting go.

    She was contemplating a trip to the bathroom to run her head under the faucet when the man surprised her once more, fishing out his wallet. He began pulling out bills, each denomination folded in a particular way, laying out a twenty and a five on the smooth, oak surface. "That ought to cover it, right?"

Another nod, and she actually stamped her foot in annoyance. "That's plenty. You've got a pretty ingenious money system, but I invited you. I didn't expect you to pay. This was supposed to be my treat."

Emmett shrugged. "In my world, a man does the paying to show his appreciation for the gift of a woman, her time, her company. As for the money, Wyatt or Sammie help me. They come a few times a month to do banking, bills, fold my money, take me grocery shopping. At least they don't have to wipe my nose or my butt."

There it was, that bitterness welling up once more in the twist of his lips and the darkening of his eyes. He shook off the cynical tendency, his laughter bubbling up. "There were health aides for a brief time, supposed to get me on my feet, watch me, keep me from bodily harm or something. Once they left, my brother and sister-in-law humored me when I asked for help to create an insanely anal system of organization. My clothes, my kitchen cupboards, the fridge, the medicine cabinet—talk about obsessive compulsive." He shook his head and leaned against the seat, draping one arm over the back. The longer they sat, the more relaxed he became—a gradual unwinding to the true self beneath the controlled exterior.

"I can understand that. It's a way to make sense out of crazy. I did the same thing. When I ran my shift on the floor of the ER, everything was just so. All my staff knew my system, how things worked when I was in charge. Even now, my office is organized beyond belief, down to the slant of the paperclip holder and the stapler."

Emmett listened patiently, a skill most men didn't have, only to take her by surprise when the flow of conversation ran out. "I've really enjoyed this today, Casey. I'd like to get to know you better. How about dinner my place, Friday night? Give us a chance to get into all the nooks and crannies. I'll try not to scare you off, scout's honor." He crossed his heart with a boyish grin, making anticipation blossom within.

"I'd really like that too. It's a date." As if on cue, he stood and eased his way out of the booth. Lost in concentration for a moment, tuned in to his surroundings, he flicked out his cane once he knew the coast was clear. A bit of struggling, nothing being as easy as it was for the sighted, and his coat was off the hook by the bench and on his back. He fumbled with the zipper, and Casey had to resist the urge to step forward and do it for him. *Right. Treat him like a child. That will go over like a brick balloon.*

Filling the need to stay occupied, she slipped into her coat and, giving into curiosity, closed her eyes and tried zipping. Her tongue poked out like it did when she was thinking hard about something. Emmett cleared his throat beside her, making her eyes snap open, her cheeks burning since she felt like a child caught with her hand in the cookie jar.

His face was turned toward her, questioning. "Ready?" He held out his elbow, and she took it, listening to the friendly farewells of the staff as they made their way outside. A few steps carried them back to the wooden stairs and porch of the clinic. With loud, echoing thuds, they crossed the distance, and he found the doorknob once more, taking pause and stepping in front of her before he opened it. "Thank you, Doc. That felt really good. I haven't done that in a long time. Too long. This either." He moved in close, and his hand found the way to the nape of her neck, strength held in check as his fingers kneaded at the delicate bones. His breath kissed her skin and then his lips were on hers, a quick, sweet taste and he pulled away, latching onto the door as if it was holding him up. "Have a good day, Casey. I look forward to seeing more of you."

There was humor in Emmett's smile and his honey eyes as he opened the door and let her inside. Casey's knees shook all the way back to her office, her heart beating like a bird seeking to be set free. She had a feeling Emmett Henry could open the cage.

# CHAPTER 6

*A*n *unlikely set of Musketeers,* quipped Casey's inner voice as Sharon caught her at the door, looped an arm in hers, tucking the other in her husband's. "We're going to the Old Inn and Tavern to have a couple of drinks, splurge on some appetizers. They're half price until nine." She wiggled her eyebrows and bumped hips. "What do you say, Case? It's in walking distance. No worries if you get intoxicated."

Paul winked at her and leaned over to give his wife a smooch. "I won't let this one get out of hand either. Come unwind with us." The couple was very sweet, extending invitations often to their newest member at the clinic, never making her feel like a third wheel. After lunch with Emmett, Casey wasn't ready to go home to be alone with her thoughts, not yet. They might be too X-rated, even for her mind.

"Sounds good." The stroll to the Old Inn and Tavern was only three buildings down. A timeless, brick building with red doors, white trim, and white dormers, graced the corner at the intersection. The stately structure, lovingly preserved by the Howland family, had seen the birth of a nation, staff serving up meals and spirits since 1700 to the present day. Currently, Sarah and James Howland were the proprietors, rolling out the welcome mat for residents and visitors alike. The moment Casey walked in, surrounded by woodwork, soft candlelight, and plenty of windows to let in sunset's pale pink glow, she had a sense of homecoming.

Paul took their coats and hung them in the cloak room, allowing Sharon to install their guest in a snug booth in the back of the tavern section. Cozy and homey, the room was filling in at a steady pace, the hum of conversation rising and falling around them. "Three glasses...no make that a bottle of your house wine," Sharon nodded as she tapped the menu lying on the table. "And an appetizer sampler. Anything else, honey? No. That will do."

Paul slid in next to her, brushing snow off the top of his head, doing the same in turn for his wife. She pecked his cheek and smiled brightly as he poured from the newly arrived bottle, its contents a ruby red in the candlelight's glow. "Some night, you'll have to join us for dinner in the dining room. It's classy. Maybe you could bring Emmett." Sharon hid her grin as she buried her nose in her glass but couldn't hide the mischief in her patch of sky blue eyes.

Casey sputtered, nearly choking on her wine and pressed a napkin to her mouth, the blood rushing to her face. "How do you know about—*Angie*! That girl can't keep anything to herself, can she?" Taking another sip, she attempted to keep her cool. Only the whole glass would do the trick. A few more swallows, and she didn't flip her lid.

Sharon caught her hand and gave it a squeeze. "Actually, it wasn't Angie this time, even though that is a sensible assumption. You can blame Wyatt and Samantha with their wild speculations when Paul was examining the baby. Their tongues were still wagging when the new mother came in to see me next. Now don't go getting your nose out of joint." Her gaze softened as did her tone. "They mean well. They love Emmett and want to see him happy."

Paul looped his arm around her shoulders, allowing Sharon to prop her head against him. "We all do. We've known Em and Wyatt since preschool. I graduated with Wyatt. My better half finished high school with Emmett. As the old saying goes, the Henrys are salt of the earth, good people. They'd do anything for you, no matter what their own circumstances are. Emmett's getting hurt would've broken a lesser man, but they've had practice dealing with tough." His gaze turned inward, and he clammed up. "Enough said."

"You ought to be able to relate, Case." One night, Sharon had come up to the apartment for coffee, and somehow Casey's own sob story had leaked out. *Don't go there tonight or you'll be worse than those guys who are always crying in their beer.*

Side stepping the topic, her colleague drained her glass and gave them both refills. "One thing's for sure— that boy is easy on the eyes." Paul stiffened beside her, making his wife take hold of his collar to plant a kiss. "I just like to look, Paulie. I won't touch. I chose you to play with, didn't I?"

His body went loose, and they drifted in close together, Paul's hand coming up to cup Sharon's head. Intimate contact was on the way, but first—they were caught up in each other, as if the rest of the world went away.

Excusing herself quietly, Casey slipped to the bathroom and splashed cold water on her face. Staring at her reflection in the mirror, palms pressed to flaming cheeks, the scene in the tavern kept replaying in her head with a key difference—Emmett was in the booth with her and nothing else mattered.

Emmett snorted as he sang the lyrics to "I Walk the Line" by Johnny Cash softly under his breath. Dad had loved Johnny Cash, the Man in Black, and played his stuff all the time. The country crooner often kept Emmett company during his trek along the fence line.

Restlessness, feeling caged—that was what shoved him out to the pasture day after day. Couldn't get out of his head, couldn't get away from the darkness, but moving, breathing hard, pushing the envelope helped. Damn near got him killed in the beginning. Sheer stupidity, really, meandering into the middle of a forty-plus-acre stretch. Thought he'd never find his way back, forced to go down on his hands and knees, pawing the ground to find his own tracks. Crawling up his porch, filthy, nails broken and worn down to the quick, palms and knees skinned raw. Talk about terror, lost in his own field.

Being sensible today. Had a thermos of hot coffee in his pocket and he was bundled up until moving was stiff. Didn't like being covered up so much, blocked his senses, made it harder to be aware of his surroundings, but Mama would be proud, seeing her boy dressed for the elements. He'd picked up the fence line that began behind the house, at the gate with the family name carved on it, and moved to the left from there.

Two hours at it, thinking about three. Knocking fear flat on its butt, finding out how far he could go. Henrys were made of strong mettle. Pretty hard to make him cave. Eventually, he'd go the full distance. Keep on going and never stop.

"What the hell do you think you're doing?" Wyatt's voice, angry and fearful at the same time, bit through the silence and carried over the field. Heavy steps jogged toward him, accompanied by puffing and gasping. A hand locked his arm in a grip that was hard as a vice.

*That'll leave a mark.* Couldn't see it, but Emmett could feel it. Didn't care.

"Do I need to get your head examined again? Em, it's below zero with the wind chill, and here you are wandering aimlessly—" His brother's frustration hit the boiling point. *Mount Vesuvius, move over.*

Emmett cut him off, yanking out of his grasp, continuing on his walk with jerky motions. "I've got a fence as my guide, gives me a sense of direction. I've been doing this every day, Wyatt, two hours, at least. What? You think I'm going to wait for you to walk me, be my seeing-eye dog?" The words spit out of his mouth like something sour.

His gloved fingers flailed, found the fence, pulled him along, away from confrontation, even while his free hand curled into a fist. *Don't lose it. He's your brother, for God's sake. Besides, swing at him, and you're on the losing end of a fight. All Wyatt has to do is step back.*

"But in this cold? You'll turn into an icicle, be a frozen block in a snow drift." Wyatt's exasperation was clear, slicing through the air. The stomping of his footsteps came closer. No losing him. He definitely had the advantage.

Emmett shrugged. "Hey, I'm tough. Do the postal service proud. Rain, sleet, snow, and ice, I'm out here. I've been doing this since the beginning. You can thank your wife. She told me to get out, stop sulking. I still sulk, by the way, but not for as long or as hard."

He concentrated on getting to the next fence pole. And the next. And one more.

"Well, you scared the crap out of me. Don't do that again. You're making me go gray before my time. You can't see it, but trust me. What do you say we go back now?"

Emmett set his jaw and kept on going. A whisper of movement, a whoosh, and something smacked him in the middle of his back, knocking the breath out of him.

"Wyatt, no fair. I can't see to hit back." Emmett listened for his brother's breathing, the crunch of his footstep in the snow, used his instincts, knew what moves Wyatt would make. All his other senses were hypersensitive to compensate for the one he lacked. Packing a sizeable snowball between his palms, he let it fly.

Bull's eye, judging by the grunt and then impact as his brother tackled him, taking them both to the ground. A wrestling match ensued, gloves flying, fingers lodging into coats, rolling in the fresh powder, kicking, grunting, dodging each other's fists and elbows. Finally, lying breathless in the snow. Emmett imagined their breath taking shapes like the clouds drifting overhead. God, he missed finding shapes in the clouds. He missed clouds, any shape, any color.

Stay still too long, and the chill was settling into their bones. Getting wet, getting cold, sapping strength. Emmett gained his feet, shivering, swaying a little, and extended a hand. "Come on. Let's get in. It's freezing out here. Making you cranky. What are you doing out here anyway?" His lip was twitching. He had to bite down on it to keep from laughing.

Wyatt accepted the peace offering, welcoming a hand hold for leverage. "I must need to get *my* head examined. I can get you there faster if we cut across the field," he said, trying not to whine, his teeth were chattering, making him sound pretty pitiful.

Emmett decided not to keep his brother hanging. "Go for it." He latched onto his brother's arm, inwardly balking at the need. A burning desire welled up, to walk freely, unguided once more. Clamping down on that line of thought, he concentrated on keeping pace, not dragging them down. Probably an hour or so passed when they stomped their way across the wooden floorboards of the porch, stepped inside, and the warmth of the fireplace was like walking into a wall of heat.

Peeling out of his gear, fighting with frozen laces, Emmett rounded up flannel shirts and heavy socks. Wyatt made a beeline for the fireplace and stoked the fire, creating a crackling blaze that snapped and nearly burned them as the brothers sat in the recliners that flanked the hearth. Emmett rested a minute, soaked up some heat, and then busied himself in the kitchen. He went about the business of brewing a fresh pot of coffee, rubbing his hands together and breathing on them to thaw out while he waited for the percolating to stop. "Need a hand?"

Apparently, his brother had left his post. Had to go poking his nose in again. God, Emmett hated that. "Do I look like it? I'll be right out, Wyatt." Emmett's hands gripped the counter so tightly his knuckles cracked, and he gritted his teeth. A forceful exhalation, and the spoon clanged hard against the mug. Good thing he didn't break it. Liked that mug, Lord knows why. A few more deep breaths brought his blood pressure out of the danger zone and made it possible to carry the cups into the living room. He nudged his brother's chair and handed off his coffee, settling himself in his own chair and taking a long draw of the hot brew. *God give me strength.*

"So, every day, that's why you're in this chair whenever I come in. You're warming up or thawing out. I wondered why you weren't getting soft."

Emmett shook his head, unable to tuck his grin into hiding at his brother's teasing tone. Making quick work of his drink, he crossed over to Wyatt and gave him a light punch in the stomach. "I'm harder than you." Collecting coffee cups, it was back to the kitchen to prepare a snack. Nothing fancy. Ritz, peanut butter and jelly, load on the peanut butter. Stick to your ribs and the roof of your mouth, a kid's staple.

Turning his head, Emmett called over his shoulder. "I know you're following me. I can hear your heavy breathing back there. Get in here." At the approach of footsteps, he slid the plate down the counter, set the knife in the sink, put away the jars. Methodical. Organized. Had to be. "So, I'm glad to know Sammie and little Jackson are doing well. How about you? How are you holding up, *Dad*?"

"It's the toughest job I've ever done. Sammie, she's amazing, like she was born a mother, but me? I'm learning as I go. I hope I'll be good at it, passable at least."

Emmett could hear the uncertainty and a smidgeon of fear in his voice. He found the wall that was his brother and climbed his way to the nape of his neck, getting a reassuring grip. "No sweat, Wyatt. You've had lots of practice with me, especially in this past year or so. You'll do. Hands down, you are one of the strongest people I know."

It was Wyatt's turn to squeeze Emmett's neck in a reversal of roles. "No, that would be you, little brother." He brought him in for a hug and proceeded to give his back a pounding. "Love ya, Em. You know that, right? That's why I drive you crazy. It's part of my job description."

ভঙঙ

*Dinner at Emmett's.* For three days, Casey alternated between a state of sweet anticipation and jitters, thinking about an evening at the Henry House, minus the distractions and drama.

She had the day off from the clinic, it was about three or so, and the sun was on its downward slope what with night coming earlier in the winter months.

Snow was falling, a good six inches accumulating on the ground, but she had safe passage, thanks to her new car. It was the one indulgence to herself, thank you very much, when she was hired at the clinic. A good set of studded snows crawled up the lengthy stretch of driveway at Emmett's house without a problem. *See, Dad. I remembered something that you taught me.*

Laughter filled her head and a familiar voice, affectionately sarcastic around the edges, started pecking. '*But why that Japanese crap, girl? Should be American-made.*'

Casey knew her father was right, but the Toyota Camry had been a steal, a leftover on the lot, and the Clearwater Blue Metallic caught her eye. Her little Bluebird sang to her from the instant she pulled into the dealership. Easiest sale that guy made all day, he'd told her.

Rolling to a stop by the house, she allowed herself to truly study the place for the first time. On a night fraught with upheaval and an arrival after dark, her main impression had been feeling like she was caught up in a tumultuous blizzard, emotionally and weather-wise.

Today, the property took her breath away. From the sprawling, white farmhouse, still dressed with a great pine wreath and a festive bow in red for the holiday season, its wrap-around porch gracing all sides, to the traditional red barn and outbuildings, everything was kept meticulously. Stretching beyond to fields as far as she could see, surrounded by a fence line, an expanse of pristine white reached to pines standing guard at the border. Rising above were gently rolling mountains, Vermont's Green Mountains or the Adirondacks, she wasn't sure which, her sense of direction leaving something to be desired.

Casey stared out at a brilliant, blue sky dripping

down to a canvas of white, kissed by sunlight so bright she had to slip on her sunglasses. Beautiful, but something was missing. The pasture should have been filled with horses, with one great steed carrying a long, lean, rugged form on its back.

Emmett Henry belonged out there, broad shoulders filling out his Carhartt coat, jeans like a second skin, wearing his work boots, doing the job that he loved. Riding her way, a cloud of breath hovering around him as he swept her up behind him, allowing her to press herself against his hard body and drink in his warmth, his scent, to wrap her arms around him and—

She wrenched her mind from that particular train of thought, struggling to get her breathing under control. A glance in the mirror revealed cheeks stained crimson, emerald eyes that glittered too brightly, and a pulse beating wildly in the hollow of her neck. Letting out a deep breath, Casey switched her focus to the real landscape and gasped. *Silly fool! Have to admire the man though*, she thought begrudgingly. He might feel sorry for himself, aggravated to no end by the limitations of his disability, but he pushed his boundary lines, fighting hard against their restraints.

The subject of her fantasies was turning up the temperature and getting her blood pumping for an entirely different reason as she watched Emmett walk the fence line. He was a good distance out, probably over a mile, a pinpoint in a knit cap, gloved fingers holding on to the wood from time to time for support, using it as a compass, a white puff hovering around his head with each exhalation.

There had to be at least three feet of snow out there! Quite a workout, ensuring that tan Carhartt would keep him warm enough. All well and good until he had a nasty fall or some other mishap befell him. What then? All they'd find would be a frozen corpse sometime after the thaw.

Yanking on her hat, pulling on her gloves, thankful she'd worn good boots, Casey hopped out of the car and slammed the door. Trudging in Emmett's direction, she passed the path to the house and pulled up short once more. The driveway might not be plowed yet, Wyatt probably occupied and in no rush, but his brother had managed to clear the walk, his trusty, red shovel propped by the front door. Talk about obstinate and independent! Emmett couldn't have let his brother do it. No sir.

Pumping her arms. Faltering. Going down in the powdered fluff. Coming up again sputtering. Casey's body heat definitely made up for the cold by the time she finally closed the gap between herself and her host, on the homeward stretch. Breathing hard, a stitch in her side, she marched up to him and gave him a none-to-gentle poke in the chest. "Just what the heck do you think you're doing, Emmett Henry?"

A look of confusion, tinged with annoyance, turned to amusement as his golden eyes homed in on the source of her yammering. His lips turned up, their full curve a momentary distraction. "Why does everyone keep asking me that? It's pretty self-explanatory. Taking a walk. What's the problem?"

"The problem? The problem?" Her hands came up, both this time, to ram against his chest with enough force to shake him to his boots. "The problem is no one knows you're out here, and if you get hurt, you're a heck of a long way from help. You might not be able to get yourself out of the elements, and then you could die of hypothermia. I've seen what hypothermia does to a person. It's not pretty, idiot!"

He took a step forward, a dangerous flash in his eyes and then his hands reached out. Emmett found her, pulled her close, and his mouth came down hard, brushing her jaw first before making the way to its final destination, planting a fierce, hungry kiss on the lips that lit a fire in her veins. He set her heart to tripping. She would've fallen if his strong arms weren't holding her up. Her hands came up around his neck, and she gave herself to the kiss, let it have her.

Just when Casey was sure she'd have to come up for air, Emmett broke off and pulled back. "Let's get one thing straight. No one calls me an idiot, except me. Stubborn mule, okay. I'm touchy about stupidity." The smile was back, any anger dying down, and he moved in closer. "You know, you're a darn, fine kisser, especially all hot and bothered. Let's try one on the cool down." And this time, he took his time, yanking off his gloves so he could thread his fingers through her hair, the cloud of their breath floating around them as they exhaled. Time spun out, no beginning or end, and she went loose under his gifted touch.

*Must be a source of pride, being capable of reducing a woman nearly to liquid in his hands.* His fingers shifted to the nape of her neck, kneading the muscles, releasing the tension. "Now, why don't we try starting over? Hi, Case. How are you? It's good seeing you again."

Her laughter bubbled up and his joined hers, sweet music, spilling out and running over, warming her to the heart.

# CHAPTER 7

Strange, having something to look forward to. It would take some getting used to. He'd taken to the field again, after Wyatt left, too restless to stay inside, waiting for Casey to get there. The fresh-fallen snow put him to work on his walkway, but the brief exertion involved in shoveling the path wasn't enough. When it came to tackling the lengthy driveway, Emmett decided he wasn't a glutton for that much punishment.

Sticking close to the fence, burning off a slight chill with each step, in his mind's eye, he mapped out the landscape. He pictured the scene the way it had always been, setting each detail in place, like building a wall brick by brick. He was surrounded by horses—his favorite, Bonnie, walking by his side, nudging him to get back on, ride some more, only to prance off with the others to find her mate, Clyde. Emmett's hands were still tingling from direct contact—helping Casey down off the horse, and his backside was still warm from her body pressed against his. She was graced with soft curves in all the right places, that midnight curtain of hair drifting to her shoulders, with eyes greener than springtime leaves looking his way.

He had to have her, couldn't get her soon enough. Emmett kept walking, her hand tucked in his. Headed for the stand of pines at the edge of the field and the shelter beneath their branches, he didn't even make it that far, taking her down in the snow. There should have been a cloud of steam rising around them as the heat of their bodies melted everything down to a bare patch on the ground. Plenty warm enough out here. Might even have to shed a few layers.

"Just what the heck do you think you're doing, Emmett Henry?"

Reality took him by surprise, he'd been so lost in the fantasy. Casey was beside him, up close and personal, her hands ramming up against him and giving him a charge like a defibrillator. He muttered a rebuttal, couldn't even remember what, his brain clouded by a red fog.

Anger flared, sputtered, and died, replaced by an ache so fierce for her. Emmett locked his lips on hers before any thoughts crossed his mind. *Deal with the consequences. God, it has been way too long without the touch of a woman. If she slaps you, it will be worth the sting.*

She didn't fight him, paving the way to another kiss that had his insides in a tangle and his legs turning to jelly. Holding on tight was as much for his sake as hers. His fingers got a good grip at her neck even though he wanted to bury his hands in the sleek mass of her hair, breathe in the scent of her, wear her like a second skin. Reluctantly breaking away, he came up for air. "Now, why don't we try starting over? Hi, Case. How are you? It's good seeing you again."

Immersed in her laughter, Emmett couldn't help but allow his to float to the surface. It felt good to laugh again, to feel that bubble of happiness swell up anytime that she was near or she crossed a mind that had been barren for much too long.

Casey moved in close, and her hands traveled up his arms to his chest, her gloves grabbing hold and reeling him in one more time. By the time they broke apart, she was shivering. "I'm all right, Em, and I'd have to say you are equally talented in the kissing department. Do you think we could head back now? I'm freezing my butt off."

His hand moved to the area in question, skimming the surface and making her squeal. "Oh, we couldn't have that, not with such a perfect caboose. Lead the way. I'm sure we can find some ways to warm up when we get back to the house."

She didn't hesitate, taking his hand in hers and drawing him alongside her.

*The girl must be really cold.* The deep snow didn't even slow her down. They both were breathing hard when they hit the porch steps. The heat of the fireplace wrapped itself around them the moment they stepped inside, and Casey let out an audible sigh of appreciation. Emmett could hear her peeling out of her outer garments and itched to help her. When her hands rested on his, untying his laces, the sizzle between them almost made him pull back—or dive in.

"Let me...I'll go get us something hot to drink. You take advantage of the fireplace."

The living room had always been the heart of the home. Emmett saw no reason to end the tradition simply because his life had been sent into a tailspin. Heading off to the kitchen, he briefly considered hammering down something tall, strong, and cold to head off vaporization.

Upon his return with coffee, the room was quiet. Too quiet. "Casey?"

"Hmm? Oh, sorry. I was almost out. The combination of this chair, throw blanket, and that fireplace is hypnotic. I bet you spend a lot of time out here." Emmett navigated her way, placing a cup in her hands, wrapping his fingers around hers to make sure she had a firm grip.

*Right. You just want to touch her some more.* Unwilling to cross over to his own chair, he sat down cross-legged on the floor, soaking up the warmth of the hearth. Head propped against the bottom of the recliner, eyes closed, feeling mellow. Until her fingers found their way to his hair.

Emmett's shoulders stiffened, and his mug nearly crashed to the floor, his body quickening with a fierce hunger that had not been fed for too long. Not trusting himself, he gained his feet and forced some light banter. "Way too much time. I practically live out here. Must be why they call it the living room. I'm going to get dinner started. You chill." His lips began to twitch. "Or…liquefy. Whichever you prefer."

Back in the kitchen, he pressed his palms flat on the kitchen table and bowed his head. *What are you doing, Henry? She's come for dinner, nothing else. Give her a glimpse of how you're feeling, and Casey will head for the hills, never come back.* "What can I do?"

*Great. Another babysitter.* And there it was, all he needed to get his back up. "I *can* cook. I'm not completely incapacitated, believe it or not." Emmett smacked his hand against the refrigerator door, rummaged inside, and began slapping ingredients on the counter. The knife jangled, the jar of sauce nearly shattered, and the foot tapping beneath it all could not be missed.

"Sheesh, sure are touchy, Em. I thought you were thinking about accepting with grace. People help each other all the time, appreciate it even. It's this human kind of thing, developing a cooperative spirit. Don't mind me, though. I'll clear out."

Her footsteps started to retreat, and Emmett moved quickly, darting across the room, reaching out, and caught her arm. "I'm sorry, Case. You're right. It's just— I get so ticked off about the things I can't do independently, I'm bound and determined to do all the rest on my own. I hate having to rely on someone else for anything."

She was standing in front of him, her breath a soft fluttering against his face, and her forehead rested against his. "Let me tell you a secret, Emmett. We all have to let go sometimes and lean on others. Otherwise, we're all alone. I don't know about you, but I don't like alone."

A hard swallow and he cleared his throat. "You're right. Wyatt tries to tell me the same thing. Come on back to the kitchen. Why don't you do the salad? I'm still a tad dangerous with knives." He held a palm up as a truce. She accepted and took his hand. Stepping back in the culinary hub of the home, Emmett pointed to the counter. "Everything you need is over there."

With the cheerful sound of chopping underway, he filled a pot with water and placed it on the stove, another pot of sauce joining it. "Don't go cutting yourself, now. First aid is *not* my strong suit." A wheeze of laughter from across the room had him smiling, a definite improvement in mood. "So, how's life in the fast lane?"

Casey snorted, her chopping put on pause. "Slow, pitifully and blessedly slow. Sharon and Paul said I shouldn't get too complacent. It's still a major improvement over Albany. There was no such thing as a slow day there, and lucky me, I worked the night shift—nearly had a breakdown."

Something else, something more happened. Emmett knew if he picked at the thread long enough, the full story would unravel, but he didn't pry. Casey would confide when she was good and ready. "I can understand that. Working nights is a nightmare. There were times Wyatt and I would be birthing foals, up all night. That was enough to cure us of taking a third shift job. Good thing you came here. We seldom need any medical care after dark. You'll feel like you're sinking in quicksand some days or watching paint dry on a wall, this place can be so sleepy."

The chopping had stopped again while Emmett grabbed a large colander, plunked it in the sink, and carefully dumped the pasta overboard. The steam rose up, hit him in the face, and forced him to take a step back. Bumping into Casey, he swung around and found himself in a tangle with no wish to get out. "You're pretty good, getting all of that pasta where it belongs, not burning yourself. Sounds like you really are grown up. What about that bread on the counter? You want me to slice that for us?" If he wasn't mistaken, the girl practically purred.

Breathing the same air, sharing space, standing close, Casey almost went to his head. *Forget what's cooking on the stove. What about what's going on between us?* Mentally giving himself a shake, Emmett nodded. *Wait—what was the question? Right, something about bread.* "Sure, go for it."

He listened to her rattling in the cabinet, setting a platter down, eventually heard the knife sawing through the crusty loaf. Since her hands were too busy for him, he occupied his own, tossing red peppers, olives, bits of chicken, and mushrooms into the pot of sauce. The heady aroma set his stomach to rumbling. He plunged a spoon in and held it out in what he judged to be the right direction. "Come taste this, tell me if it passes muster."

A few footsteps his way, a whiff of her perfume, and her hand was on his. Electricity! Emmett was sure Casey felt the same jolt with the quiver in her touch as she sampled the sauce, letting out a little moan of pleasure. "Mmm. That's really good. You'll have to tell me your secret." *Right. As soon as I get the picture of your luscious mouth locked on that spoon out of my head.* Pretty hard. When the mindscape was the only thing you saw, the imagination became really vivid.

"This was my dad's recipe. The main key isn't in the ingredients which are basically the same every time. It's the cook. You add what you like to your preference, a little more of this, a little less of that. Add a dash of the unexpected, and, wa, la—you've got pasta surprise." He couldn't help chuckling as his hip propped against the counter, arms crossed. "Actually, Dad was notorious for doing too many things at once. Raising two hellions on his own, taking care of a farm and a household, you couldn't blame him."

Emmett caught the scent of her once more, felt weakness in the knees coming on. Best to keep moving. He turned and felt for the appropriate cabinet, pulling out dishes. "Anyway, he'd forget what was in the sauce, add doubles. Sometimes, he'd get bored and toss something new in—or one of his rapscallions would."

"I bet you gave him a run for his money." Behind him, a cabinet opened and shut. He sensed a shadow tailing him around the kitchen table, setting down glasses while he laid plates. Some more clanging and silverware clunked down on the table. A whoosh of cold air brushed past him with the opening of the refrigerator door and something else thumped nearby.

"Wow, this is nice having a personal kitchen genie." Emmett pulled out two, large serving bowls, carefully dishing out the spaghetti and the sauce respectively. "Would you grab the dressing, please? There are a few bottles on the inside of the refrigerator door. Oh, there's a bottle of wine on the top shelf too."

*Wine? You sure about that? Either one of you has too much, and it could make for a dangerous combination.* Ignoring the voice of caution, he set the bowls down and rummaged through a drawer to find the corkscrew.

He caught the butter dish, hit the radio on the wall—something soft, old time, classic—and finally sat down.

Emmett had to resist resting his head on the table. Entertaining took a lot of work. He was out of practice. "Please, help yourself." He was reassured to hear dishes moving and silverware pinging off the glass, giving him time to get the bottle of wine open. A pop and the aroma arose on the air.

Casey was inhaling deeply across the table. The picture of a lovely woman, with a full flow of dark hair framing a startling gaze of green, filled his head. He imagined she sat with eyes closed, cheeks flushed, head tilted back to reveal the pure, pale skin at her throat. Emmett wanted to kiss her right on that mad fluttering of her pulse. To cup her face in his hands, lock their lips together, and bury his hands in that glorious head of hair…before losing himself in her—

"Emmett? Hello, Emmett? Are you in there?" Her glass made a bell-like sound as it tapped against his. "Why don't I pour the wine? You seem to be having a moment." There was a gurgling, and then Casey's hand was placing the cool glass in his, wrapping around his fingers in a move that mirrored Emmett's upon their escape from the cold.

"You all right?" she asked.

He raised his glass and pulled out his shiniest smile. "What could possibly be wrong? I've got a good meal on my table and a guest to share it. Cheers!"

Their glasses clinked as Casey echoed his toast. A healthy swallow and it was possible to concentrate once more. Emmett filled his own plate, taking more time and care than he normally would to avoid any spills or embarrassment. *You're doing all right—for the shape you're in.* Smiling at the sarcastic voice in his head, his own Jiminy Cricket, he took a bite. *Passable. It won't kill anyone.*

"This is good, really good. You've got Italian down." Casey's fork scraped on the plate, and then there was the crunching of the crispy, Italian loaf, and her proximity was putting him on sensory overload. "So, you've given me a little, but not enough." Some more shifting and swallowing, wine going down the hatch. "Tell me some more about your family."

Like that, was it, sticking to small talk? All right then, he wouldn't rush her, even though digging much deeper appealed to him. As for putting himself under the microscope—he'd rather not. "Oh, well, Mama died when I was four and Wyatt was six, had an aneurysm in her brain—a nasty secret, of sorts. It happened in her sleep. A totally freak thing, out of the blue. I don't remember much about her, a blessing and a curse, I guess."

Another swallow and he leaned back in his chair, his fingers drumming on the tabletop. "I grew up in a household of men. My father, Jackson Henry, was a Paul Bunyan of a man, big as they come. His back was strong enough to hold up the world, tough enough to raise two boys with a love that had no bounds. Dad had his pain, wore it from time to time, but didn't wallow. When it was too much, we headed next door to Gran and Pops."

Laughter, ready and easy, came up again, brushing off the dust from childhood memories. "My Uncles Wyatt and Emmett were there, too. They were younger than Dad by a few years. They'd come over to our place a lot, helping out with the horses, with us. Taught us everything we had to know."

"It sounds like you had the best growing up years. So did I. What happened to everyone?" More casual conversation with more wine filling the glasses and an expectant silence.

Emmett became quiet, sipping at the dark, red vintage, trying to douse the hurt that was welling up. "Gran and Pops passed in my late teens. Uncle Emmett and Wyatt have their own farms, not too far off."

Another swallow hit the pit of his stomach, and the glass was empty. Not enough wine in the world to put out the pain. Might as well not try. "Two years ago, Dad was out mowing the field with the big tractor. The thing tipped and pinned him, another freak accident. Wyatt called nine-one-one, and we ran like hell. The two of us tried to lift the damn thing off him, you know, like in those stories when miracles happen."

The familiar burning in his eyes made him pick up his glass. Finding it full once more, Emmett gulped down the whole thing, fast. "I guess we ran out of miracles that day. We weren't strong enough. By the time help came, it was too late. To be honest, it was too late from the very start. We couldn't believe Superman died. I miss him every day. I tell myself to stop being selfish, I had him for thirty years. My father loved Mama something fierce. The way I see it, the one blessing that came from losing him is knowing he and my mother are together again. By God, it still hurts, more than anything else."

The words came to a halt, and he exhaled, hard. Time to redirect, toss the ball to her court. "Okay. I showed you mine, now you need to show me yours. What's your family story, morning glory?" *That's it, Em, try and be light when you just dropped a lead balloon.*

Her hand was on his, and he felt its trembling. "Oh, goodness, nothing so terrible as yours. I'm really sorry, Emmett. How awful that must have been." He waited. If he'd learned anything in a year of blindness, it was how to read the nuances of a conversation. Words and facial expressions could lie. Tone spoke only the truth and Casey was aching.

It was his turn to press her palm. She stumbled on. "I lived at home. My father wanted me to save money, get a jumpstart on paying my loans until I settled down with someone." Soft laughter trickled out, but it rode on sadness. "Not too many dating opportunities for a new doctor on the ER floor. Anyway, Dad died unexpectedly, and Mom moved to Florida. My heart wasn't in it to stay in Albany, so I headed out here. No major catastrophes."

Her evasiveness rubbed him raw, her false cheer throwing salt in the wound. "That help business you talked about earlier, Case? It's a two-way street, goes both ways. It was hard for me to talk about my mother, my father. The least you could do is pay me the courtesy of being honest about yours."

Emmett shot out of his chair, moving fast, probably too fast. He'd found from experience that was how accidents happened. Tossing dishes in the sink, he headed outdoors in nothing but slippers and a flannel shirt. His foot hit an icy patch, almost sent him flat on his back, but the porch post gave him something to grab hold of and skirt disaster.

The air had changed, the wind kicking it up a notch, another batch of snow whipping in. He filled his lungs, relished the sting. Stomping his feet to get warm, Emmett realized he wasn't cooled off enough to go back inside. Grabbing the shovel by the door, he started to clear the path. Plain. Simple. Uncomplicated.

The door creaked open and banged shut, followed by clomping footsteps and heavy breathing. "*What* are you doing?" Huh. Exasperated, was she? Try sitting in his head.

"Why do people keep asking me the obvious? I'm shoveling. I'm not completely useless, you know? Who do you think did all the shoveling before?" He turned away, moving in a flurry, running out of air, and ramming into something. Cursing under his breath, Emmett started over, only to get disoriented. He'd have to go back to the porch, prod the snow in the area, find his boundaries, something not meant for other eyes. Huffing and puffing, he leaned on the handle of the shovel and stared hard at nothing.

"My father died of a heart attack, in our kitchen! I was right there, standing next to him when he hit the floor. I'm a doctor, for God's sake, and I couldn't save him. Maybe—if I'd had the equipment, I don't know—I didn't even get to say goodbye. Like that, he was gone, snuffed out like a candle!" Her voice rose up in the night, slicing through the darkness, to the quick, revealing the hemorrhaging that had been concealed.

*Have to stop the bleeding.* Emmett dropped the shovel, letting it clatter on the slate walkway, taking great strides to reach the porch, get to her. His hands were frozen as he fumbled for her, found her, finally cupped her face in his palms. *Stupid! Didn't even wear gloves!*

Her breath drifted over his skin, and the sobbing began, tears raining down—shaking so hard, she was falling to pieces.

He had to hold her together. "It's all right. Come back inside. I'm sorry I bullied you into talking. Come in…" His fingers gently dried her cheeks, and he pulled her through the doorway. If only he could lock the pain outside and never let it back in.

# CHAPTER 8

Emmett kicked off his slippers and guided Casey to the living room, propping his back against his chair, and tucking her on his lap as if she were a child. Rocking her back and forth, his hands ran over her hair, over her back and her arms, gentling her. *No wonder he was so good with those horses. The man has magic in his hands.* His touch, his soft murmuring of words of comfort, his lips brushing her hair, everything was too much.

The careful control she'd clung to for the past several months slipped and came undone. Crying her eyes out, something she hadn't done since her father's death, since childhood, he let it happen and waited it out.

When she finally wound down, and his flannel shirt was damp from the burst flood gates, Emmett rested his chin on top of her head. "Okay now? You don't have to say anything more."

Casey shook her head. She pulled back, seeking a tissue. He pulled a bandanna from his pocket and handed it to her.

*Uncanny. A horse whisperer and a mind reader.* "That's just it. I think I do have to talk about it. I couldn't when it happened four months ago. I had no family, just a few relatives scattered far and few between, no one to confide in. I built a wall and hid behind it. So did my mother."

Anger and resentment, never far from the surface, threatened to boil over. Casey had to make a concerted effort to turn it down. "They'd been married thirty years, gone in a blink. She was hurting so badly there was no supporting me. Unable to deal with any of it, Mom packed her bags and headed to Florida. The only place I had was the ER, and I couldn't take it anymore. The pressure, the pace, how many of them died—and seeing my father over and over in my patients. I got out of Dodge, and I came here with my tail between my legs. I know. I must sound pitiful."

Strong arms wrapped around her and pulled her close, forming a harness that kept her secure and wouldn't let her fall. "Hush now. Stop being so hard on yourself. You needed a change, new geography. Everyone needs that sometime. Trust me, if I could get out of this head of mine, I would. I get stuck in a rut, and you really have to kick my butt to make me budge. A boot in the rear does us all good sometimes."

Casey ran her hand down the warm, thick flannel of his sleeves, reached his fingers, and began to play with them. Her thumb went round and round on the back of one hand, and he shifted beneath her, settling her in a more comfortable position. The heat of his body, knowing that he was solid and wouldn't cave, nearly did her in. "How do you handle everything so well?"

"Oh, I'm a good actor," he said. "On the outside, I've got this cool exterior, but the inside—that's a royal mess. I think I'm losing my mind sometimes and angry, God, I am still so angry. In the beginning, when I was well enough to come home, they had people here, nurses, therapists, working with me, teaching me *life* skills. I'd slip outside for a walk because I couldn't stand being inside with these…intruders! This was *my pain, my fight*, how dare they take it upon themselves?" His hand balled into a fist, his breathing getting harsh. "You don't need to hear this."

The tables had turned. What had begun as Casey's opportunity to express her pain was now Emmett's chance to set himself free. "Yes, I do. Anything you share might help me along the way." She turned to get a better view of her support system. His gaze was trained on the fireplace, the flames flickering in his golden eyes, shifting shadows dancing across his face. "Tell me, please."

He tilted his head her way, a small smile hovering but not quite making it. "I started with a little postage stamp of space in front of the house. Then I worked my way out to the four oaks on the front lawn and on to the driveway. I could tell the difference between the grass and the dirt of the lane when I worked back and forth with my cane. Finally, I hit the road and walked a piece. I'd count mailboxes."

Now there was a scornful twist to his lips, and Casey found herself taking his hand in hers, creating a lifeline. "They didn't like that, my babysitters, I told them, tough, I'd do as I please, that I wouldn't get far, now would I? After all, it would be a heck of a lot easier for them to find me. Two weeks of being chewed out, and I tossed them."

What had begun as a pep talk was now a purge, a tale he had to tell, needed to tell, and Casey listened. The room grew quiet. Emmett still gave her the impression of the archangel Gabriel, crashing to earth, or a fallen star, tortured yet beautiful, struggling with his transformation and limits. The words continued to flow, a slow, steady stream.

"Once they left me alone, I holed up in my room except for a brief foray to the liquor cabinet, grabbed a few choice selections, brought them in, and fought a panic attack of monumental proportions. This house, the place I grew up in and knew like the back of my hand, terrified me. I had to relearn it, all of it, and I wasn't ready to climb that mountain, wouldn't do it with prying eyes. I learned my bedroom *really* well."

Dry laughter and rueful grin were a poor attempt at humor. Emmett's eyes rested on her, giving the illusion that he was truly looking at her while watching the screen play of his life. "I went on a real bender. Good thing my bathroom is attached. I was real proud of myself—I never missed the toilet. I considered that an accomplishment."

The fire crackled, and Emmett carefully moved her aside, getting up to move the screen, add another log, and poke at the coals. Satisfied, he put everything back in its place and rejoined her. Casey's silence prodded him to continue. *Come on, Henry. You've left me at a cliffhanger. Finish the story.*

"On the second or third day, I lost track, Sammie came, found me on the floor, in a sorry state. She said to me, 'Do I need to clear out the liquor cabinet like I'm your mother?' No pity, aggravated as all get out. Looks can be deceiving. That woman is as tough as nails. I bit her head off, said she might as well take the knives, scissors, any sharp implements, the shot gun, the matches, the rope, and my ties. I told her to baby proof the whole, blasted place and wrap me in bubble wrap! Got myself all hot and bothered, threw up again. Nice, eh? She didn't have much sympathy since morning sickness had hit her every day. Pity, I brought it on myself."

Emmett shrugged, rolled his shoulders as if pushing off the weight of bad memories. "Anyway, she told me enough was enough, that they loved me. And my brother, wearing a rut in the floor in the next room, was chomping at the bit to get in there and get his hands on me. To shake some sense into my head. To fix me."

He fell silent once more. When he continued, his voice was hoarse with emotion. "Sammie and Wyatt, they're crazy about me—they'd have to be to put up with all of my crap. It's because I'm so crazy about them that I realized—when I hurt myself, I was hurting them. Wyatt lost my mother, my dad. I'd be damned if I'd let them lose me, even if they couldn't fix me." He shook his head as if that could do away with the unpleasantness, straightened his shoulders, and wrapped up.

"So. I came out. I promised no more binges on alcohol, practically had to make a blood oath on the cross of our Lord, and slept it off. After that, I learned my house, step by step, counted my way every place I had to go, memorized it. Ran my hands over everything, got down on my hands and knees, organized my cabinets, closets, dresser—everywhere. I recruited Sammie and Wyatt to help me create a system for everything—fridge, groceries, cleansers, papers. Talk about going overboard! I started venturing out more each day. I found if I walked the fence, that helped. I could go for hours and find my way back to myself. Baby steps pulled me out, and they'll do the same for you in this new life. If you need someone to walk with you, you've got a volunteer." He finally stalled, kissed the top of her head, and simply held on.

Casey sank into his touch and found herself letting go. Sleep took her down, took them both. When she came to, the log in the fireplace was glowing bright red, heat rolling off without a flame and they were sprawled on the floor, Emmett's arm providing a cushion for her head. His head was turned her way, a smile toying with his lips, and he looked younger without the crease between his eyes or tension pulling at his features.

She reached out with a tentative touch and pushed his bangs out of the way, even though they couldn't ob-

struct his vision. "Em?" He shifted, and his eyelids fluttered. "Em, it's pretty late, past midnight. Shouldn't I be
going home?"

He shook his head, his tongue flicking out to lick lips
that had gone dry, and she had an urge to get a taste when
his words caught her attention. "Hmm, what? No, it's too
late and probably snowing too hard. Wyatt won't plow
until morning. Stay put." Emmett was practically tripping
over his tongue, his words slurring with the heaviness of
sleep. "We'll have a slumber party. I'll behave, promise."

His finger crossed his heart, and he slowly rolled into
a sitting position, taking her with him. A moment later
and he was on his feet, not too steady until she joined him
and he looped an arm over her shoulders. "Thanks." He
brushed the top of her head with another kiss and took a
deep breath. "Too bad I'm dead tired because you smell
good enough to eat."

Forgetting herself, she wagged a finger at him at first
then let her tongue loose instead. "You promised to behave, Boy Scout. Let's go. Off to bed with you before
you lose your head. Upstairs?" At his nod, she steered in
that direction when his hand came out and hit the wall on
the way.

"Hold up. Got a few things to do first." Emmett
turned and worked his way through the house, checking
the screen in front of the fireplace, making sure it was
snug and holding his palms over the hearth to judge its
heat. Onward to the door, he locked it and flicked the
lights off, doing the same with the rest, except for one
light over the kitchen sink. Habit or for her benefit? His
hands ran over the stove, double-checking that everything
was off. Mentally checking off each room, he was methodical in his approach, probably did the same thing every night.

He caught her hand at the bottom of the stairs and

gave her a sweet, sleepy smile that called to mind a little boy, although there was nothing childish about Emmett Henry. "Okay, Case, let's go." They made it to the top with the satisfying moaning and groaning of the steps beneath their feet, an old house that withstood the test of time talking to them.

Emmett gestured to the right. "Your room is the first on the left. It used to be mine. Look in the drawers, and I think you'll find a T-shirt, some old flannel pajamas. They'll do. A bathroom is across the hall, and there's an extra toothbrush in the cabinet. You need anything, I'm in the last bedroom on the right on the other end of the hall." Flipping a hand to the left, he waved vaguely in that direction, suddenly appearing to run completely out of steam.

Casey stepped in close and gave him a hug, skimming his lips with a butterfly kiss. Anything more and she'd be tucking him into bed—then staying for the duration. "Thanks for everything, Emmett, especially for listening."

He pulled her in and planted another kiss, this one taking root and spreading tendrils of warmth through her body, making her heart take flight. His arms wrapped around her and her face pressed against his chest. Judging by the thundering of his heartbeat, his was ready to soar as well. "Like I said—it goes both ways. Thanks for the help, Case. You're right. Sometimes we have to give it to each other and take it. Have a good night."

Emmett let go, and she felt like a kite without a string. Watching him make the trip to his room, fingers brushing the wall for added security—that mind was a steel trap and catalogued every inch of the way.

He didn't need to hold on to anything—Casey had to grab on to a doorknob. Otherwise, she'd be floating along beside him, waiting for him to catch her and reel her back down to his arms.

⟆⟆⟆

The bacon was crackling in the pan, the fat popping and hissing while Mama tended the stove, keeping a close eye on the sunny side up eggs smiling from the pan next door. She pushed a strand of hair that captured sunshine behind her ear and tossed a sky-blue wink to her boys as they waited in their chairs, trying not to drool. Toast hopped up in the toaster, and she was right on it, handy with a knife, slathering on butter and sticking in two more slices without missing a beat.

Daddy snuck by and pulled a piece of cooked bacon off a plate, getting a whack from the spatula on the backside as a consequence, setting off peals of laughter from a wide-eyed Wyatt and Emmett. "Jackson, you cut that out, you hear? I need something to put on the table! Don't you see those starving children over there? They're beginning to wither!"

Their father effectively shushed her, his big, calloused hands hooking around her waist and shoulders, bowing her backward until her ponytail brushed the floor. His chocolate eyes could melt the hardest heart as he shook stray bangs from his face and pressed his lips to hers, breakfast snapping on the stove all the while.

Mama flapped her hands uselessly, finally latching them in his walnut hair. "*Jackson*, the boys are watching!" Her voice was weak as if it was hard to catch her breath, her cheeks flushed from cooking…and something more? Emmett might not understand everything, but he knew one thing—Mama and Daddy loved each other something fierce.

Daddy's smile stretched from ear to ear, and he

rained kisses all over her face. "Now, Elizabeth, we live on a horse farm. They're bound to learn about the birds and bees sooner or later." His laughter rolled out and carried her with him until they were a wheezing tangle of limbs on the floor, quickly joined by two, impulsive imps, and the bacon started to burn.

&#8477;&#8478;&#8477;&#8478;

Emmett awoke to darkness but realized it was morning, judging by the warmth on his face and the change in the quality of light. Only a dream but the scent of freshly cooked bacon, one of his favorites, *that* was real and all the more scrumptious because he didn't have to cook it. His tongue started salivating overtime just thinking about something he'd never had the patience for, especially now. He hated having to stand guard over the stove, invariably getting stung by grease jumping out of the pan. Patience—that was Wyatt's strong suit.

Pushing his legs over the side, he stood up and reached for the ceiling, listening to the pops his body made, wondering what sounds effects to look forward to in old age. The delectable smell from the kitchen reminded him of his house guest and kicked his heart up a notch. *Better hit the shower, Em, try and tame the beast.*

Collecting underwear, socks, a T-shirt, and jeans was easy, a few paces in familiar space. The hard part was stepping into a shower, an extremely hot shower to try and wrangle with the unfamiliar territory he was about to explore downstairs. A woman. In his kitchen. Cooking for him. Now.

The water rushed over his body, every part of him and its heat wasn't helping, only stirred the cinders and made them ignite. The sensation, the hot, moist gushing river running over his skin made him imagine Casey there with him, those hands, that hair, and mouth brushing against his skin. Emmett pressed his head hard to the wall, fighting the quaking that threatened to take over. *Come on, Em. Get it together. Can't stay up here forever.*

A heat wave met him on the journey down the stairs. *She stoked the fire.* That understatement made him grin. His sock feet carefully ran over each step, toes feeling for the edge. *Won't do to trip, not today—or any day.* Hitting bottom, his stomach did a little flip flop in anticipation. She was humming, something sweet and light. There was some kind of shuffling going on in there, interspersed with the sounds of cooking. Was she dancing? *God, I wish I could see her!* "Good morning, sunshine."

There was a clatter, something dropping on the floor. "Emmett! I didn't even hear you. You move like a cat!" The water ran in the sink, rinsing whatever had fallen, and her footsteps padded his way, bare skin on the kitchen floor.

She looped her arms around his neck and gave him a minty kiss. "Morning!"

*Mmm. Found the toothpaste.* Wishing to sample more of her, his hands moved down her arms to her waist, a little farther. *Found your T-shirt, too—and nothing else. God help me!* "I hope you're hungry. Breakfast is almost ready."

*Baby, you don't know how hungry I am.* He cleared his throat and slid into his seat. "I was dreaming about bacon, it smelled so good." Cautiously running his hands over his placemat, he found his coffee cup, the warm steam rising and hitting his palm, the sugar bowl, cream, and spoon waiting. The first, restorative swallow trickled down, and a plate was slid in front of his nose.

Something smelled good, out of this world. Picking up his fork, Emmett took a bite, and his eyes closed in pure ecstasy. "Scrambled eggs, home fries, *and* bacon—I am getting spoiled. No one cooks for me most of the time, and, when it's just me, I'm pretty complacent. I usually go with simple—cereal, oatmeal, might go out on a limb for toast. I could get used to this."

The chair slid out beside him, and another plate hit the table. A clink of a fork, some chewing, a few swallows, and bare toes were poking at his leg, making him sit up and take notice. "I could get used to this too, Emmett. Having someone sitting at the table, sharing my food, swapping stories, knowing I'm alive."

*Oh, definitely alive—not sure you can say the same for me much longer. Heart can't take it.* "Well...maybe we can come up with some excuses to do this more often." He continued to eat, even though his hands itched for better things to do, and they ate in companionable silence. Cleaning his plate, Emmett leaned back and patted his stomach. "That was the best breakfast I've had in a long time. Thank you, Casey." His fingers tiptoed across the way, found her hand and held on for a beat.

"You're welcome." A hummingbird kiss flitted over his cheekbone, and she was in motion once more, clearing the table and filling the sink. *Hmm. Shy this morning, are we?* He sipped his coffee, giving her time and a little distance, making her comfortable with him again. "Wyatt was here earlier, plowing the driveway." Her voice rose over the sound of running water and dishware hitting the drainer. "You should have seen his face when he walked in and found me here. He took a cup of coffee and went on his way."

Emmett couldn't help but laugh, although he heard an undercurrent in her voice. She wasn't happy to be discovered. "I'll set him straight, promise." He held out a hand her way. "Will you come here a moment? Let me thank you properly." She came, bringing the scent of home cooking and her body spray with her—irresistible.

A gentle tug and Casey was sitting on his lap, the lines of her body tense. That would never do. He thought of his dream, wished he could dip her to the floor, mirror the romantic moves of his father. Not having that familiarity, his hands stroked her arms, working to build that connection. Leaving one hand on her hip, he found her shoulder with the other, ran along her collarbone, ended at her neck. One pull forward, and their lips touched. Her body gave, and she rested her head on his shoulder.

"Emmett...I...you...I really like you, but we've only just met, and I don't want to take things too fast. I've been through a lot of changes. I'm still figuring out which way is up." Her heart was fluttering against his chest, her voice trembling. A little bit of fear there. He understood that. The unknown could be a scary monster, one that had to be dealt with every day on a personal level.

His fingers worked at the nape of her neck, moved to circle on her back, smoothing the path between them. "Darlin', I've had a crash course in change. It can knock you on your butt, but I'll help you to get up again. We can go slow as molasses, getting to know each other. What do you say we work on that a bit more right now?"

A giggle bubbled up, and her hands found their way to his hair, giving her something to hold onto when she planted the next kiss. Emmett finally discovered an advantage to being blind what with the way Casey filled his senses. The warmth and weight of her on his lap, her breath and hair brushing his skin and setting it to tingling, the pitter pat of her heart vibrating against his chest. There was something to be said for a blindfold and a woman. *Have mercy!*

# CHAPTER 9

Casey! Miss Casey Mitchell! Rise and shine, girl-friend. Get that butt out of bed!"

A cheerful but insistent voice rang through the apartment, accompanied by loud pounding. The woman under attack groaned and rolled over to crack one eyelid at the clock. The red numbers glared back at her. Eight a.m. On a Sunday. She had planned on sleeping later—much later. After sacrificing all her Sundays in the ER, having them back was a luxury not to be wasted.

"Casey, I know you're in there, and I'm not going away. Wakey, wakey!"

*Remember your oath. Do no harm. That means on the job and off it.* Scrubbing her hands over her face and running her fingers through her hair, Casey threw back the covers and stumbled to the door. The moment she opened it, Sharon breezed her way in, a tray of drinks in one hand, a paper sack in the other.

"Oh, it is a glorious morning! The sun is beaming, I tell you. It's downright tropical out there—thirty degrees. I woke up, took one look and said this is it, the perfect time for you and me to have a little fun. Drink your coffee like a good girl, eat your muffin, and let's get cracking!"

Casey accepted the gift of a tall cup of coffee, held it

in two hands and inhaled its strong scent as if it was a magical concoction. A kitchen chair caught her while she took the first few sips and began to feel alive, minimally. Propping her head on her palm, she offered up a weak smile to her chipper colleague.

"I don't know how you can be so awake. It's a battle of wills between me and the alarm each morning. Many an unfortunate clock has met its untimely end when I've smacked it or slammed it on the floor. And on a weekend? Unheard of. I forget I even own one."

Another long draw of java traveled through her veins and her stomach was ready for the muffin. One bite and her eyes closed in sincere appreciation. "This is heaven! Where did you get it? It tastes like grandma's apple pie!"

Sharon flipped her hands out and laughed, a bright sound that reminded Casey of birds singing or bells ringing at Christmas time. "Oh, just a little something I whipped up this morning. My apple crumble muffins are Paul's favorite, so I try to make them on the weekends."

She took a sip of her own coffee and stood up, beginning to pace, picking up one thing, peering at another, even though Sharon had been part of the moving crew. Did the woman ever relax?

Always a bundle of energy, she looked particularly vibrant today in a red beret, jacket to match, and snowy slacks that belled out at the ankle. Scarlet, high heeled boots gave her some height, while a splash of lipstick to match gave her a saucy smile. Cute as a button.

What Casey wouldn't give to have an ounce of that perkiness. A few more bites was all it took and the muffin was polished off. She swallowed down the last of the coffee for mental clarity and managed to muster some pep. "Sharon, I really do appreciate your visit, but exactly what are you doing here?"

"Oh, I forgot to tell you. I'm kidnapping you for a

girls' day, no arguments." There was a mischievous sparkle in Sharon's bright, blue eyes. The woman might be Casey's elder by a few years, but was much younger at heart. A wink and her firm grasp steered Casey to the bathroom. "Go on now, get gussied up."

Not sure what hit her, Casey decided that arguing was pointless against a force of human nature as strong as the woman outside her door. She turned the water on as hot as was humanly tolerable and climbed under the steamy stream. A flash of Emmett Henry came on strong, the man standing beside her, learning her every nuance with his sensitive touch, teaching her how to do the same. The experience was so powerful, she had to prop herself against the wall and let the water pound on her head.

Gasping for air, she turned the knob and stepped out on trembling legs that were weak as a kitten. "Sharon," she called out, her voice breathless. Squeezing her eyes shut and pressing a hand to her heart, she cleared her throat. Her voice was firmer on the second try. "Where are we going and what about Paul?"

"Don't you worry about Paul. The man is thrilled about being a lazy bones today, watching football and eating junk food all afternoon. We are going to the salon, the spa, to lunch someplace sinful with artery-clogging foods that are everything we advise against for our patients, window shopping, and you are going to spill it about your night at Emmett's."

Casey's heart started hammering even harder, and the heat rose up her chest, all the way to her cheeks. "Becoming a habit, isn't it, staying with those Henrys? I'm not worried about Wyatt—he's taken, hook, line, and sinker. But Em, that man is very unattached and what many would consider an eligible bachelor around these parts, even if he isn't so sociable these days. There are probably quite a few girls who are turning green with envy about your overnight."

The bomb dropped, and there was instant detonation. Casey yanked the door open, and the little blonde woman tumbled inside. Not the best place to prop herself up, perched cross-legged on a throw rug with her back against the sturdy oak.

"How did you know about that? *Nothing* happened, Sharon, not that it's any of your business. He made me stay because of the weather."

A cloud of warm steam hovered in the doorway, not even close to the explosion of temper on the way. Casey glared down at her friend, arms crossed, ready to take the rope from her robe and hogtie the little busybody.

"Hey, hey, easy, girl. Lighten up. I'm just teasing you." Sharon scrambled to her feet, rubbing her offended backside. Cautiously, she sidestepped the fuming woman beside her and inched her way to the kitchen. "As for my sources, I'll never tell." Her bottom lip jutted out in a pout, one that only made her prettier, and she sipped at her coffee to cover her consternation.

That pitiful expression doused the flames. Casey stepped forward and looped an arm over Sharon's tiny shoulders. "I'm sorry. I haven't had a lot of experience with guys, and I get touchy. I'm not an old, married woman like you. I still have a lot to learn."

"I'm not that old, but I can tell you everything you need to know and more. I'll fill you in on the drive. Now, get dressed so we can go." With a helpful shove in the right direction, Sharon was brightness personified once more, humming in the next room as Casey debated about her wardrobe.

Nothing stood out. The past ten years or so of her life had been dedicated to study and residency, leaving little room for something as trivial as clothes.

To be honest, what she wore had never been important to her. Why did it suddenly matter now with a man who could not see her efforts?

Settling on a black sweater, jeans, and tall, suede boots, she peered hard at her reflection and found it lacking compared to the pizzazz of the woman outside her door. A dab of makeup, a gold chain, and some dangling earrings didn't even come close.

"What are you doing in there? Painting the Mona Lisa? I'm coming in." Considering that fair warning, her companion stepped inside only to find Casey with her head bowed and eyes on the floor, crimson staining her cheeks. Sharon stepped forward and lifted Casey's chin, forcing her to meet an intense, blue stare. "What's going on in that head of yours, Mitchell?"

Casey shook her head. Mortified to find her eyes watering, she spun around and grabbed the comb, pulling it fast and furious through her long, dark locks, snagging it a few times. "I just can't compare next to you. No sense of style whatsoever."

Sharon stopped her, wrapping an arm around her waist. "Will you cut that out? Stop brushing so hard before you tear your hair out. As for style, you're wrong, sweetheart. Understated and simple works with a classic beauty like yours. Heck, you could wear a trash bag and a mop on your head and still bedazzle. I need all the extras I can get to maximize my potential. Now, get that chin off the floor and let's get a move on!"

With that, the firecracker was out the door and taking the stairs by two. Casey shook her head and grabbed her coat from the hook by the door. The horn started honking. "Let's go—*Now*!" No grass was growing under that girl's feet! "Come on, girlfriend!"

*ဢ*

Pampered! Something Casey had never tried before. Her skin was tingling from being buffed, her body limp and limber after a massage. Her hair had received an herbal treatment, cut, and style, bringing it to a high gloss that looked rather exotic the way it framed her face in a new way. Her eyes looked bigger, thanks to shaped eyebrows and the cosmetic expertise of the woman in the salon. Her nails, on her feet and hands, were transformed into something glamorous with a vivid shade of pink.

All in all, she felt like a new woman. Others were taking notice as well. There had been many appreciative glances coming her way during their lunch in an upscale café in Albany. Sharon had done well, choosing the right people for the job and was preening, thanks to her own treatment as well.

They walked arm in arm down the sidewalk, window shopping, admiring the finds in each boutique, when a shimmering, emerald gown stopped Casey and had her staring as she imagined wearing it to a ball, accompanied by Prince Charming in the form of Emmett Henry.

"Wow, will you look at the color of that dress? It would really bring out your eyes and show off that hair. You'd drive Emmett wild." Sharon cut herself off, covering her mouth. "Stupid me. I always forget how things have changed. In my mind, he's still the same, old Emmett I went to school with. I'm sorry, Case."

Casey's head was tipped, eyeing the gown, contemplative. "It's all right. I forget too, and I've only just met him. He's so good at making you forget. You know what? I think he'd like that dress anyway, and I know *I'd* feel good wearing it." Nodding, she turned and headed inside.

Finding the same gown on a rack, she ran her fingers over the brilliant fabric. "Yes, the material, see how it slides and it's so smooth. It would glide against my skin.

Look at this." She flipped the hem up to reveal what was underneath. "There's a lacy ruffle that fluffs it out. That adds another texture, and it will swish when I move."

Casey turned and glanced around the store. "And what about those stockings, the black ones with a stripe running down the back? Those satin gloves, too—oh, and a velvet jacket since the gown is strapless." She was gaining enthusiasm. "It's all about offering food for the senses when it comes to Emmett. I could give him one amazing date."

Sharon was catching on. She ventured to a counter in the middle of the store. "This perfume will drive him crazy. Paul bought it for me once, and I ran out of it in a month, he loved it so much. Dab some behind your ears, spray it on your neck, don't forget your shoulders and your chest. Add this necklace to fiddle with and earrings dangling when you kiss. Accessorize with this clip to hold your hair back so he can take it down, play with it."

Both women started to giggle at that one, cheeks turning bright red as they stared at their reflection in a mirror conveniently placed by the jewelry. Casey held out the armload of things she'd picked up along the way. "I never go overboard, but look at all of this stuff! I know it probably sounds crazy. I really want to ask him on a date now. He's had me to dinner. It's my turn, and I want to do it right even though he can't see me."

She handed everything over to the clerk and didn't even groan when the total was given. Casey wrote the check and accepted the bag, thinking of it as a present to herself to celebrate her new life. Sharon looped arms with her once more, and they resumed their walk along the sidewalk.

"You really like him, don't you?" Sharon asked.

They passed a bench, and Casey gestured to it, blowing her bangs away from her face as they both sat down.

Sharon perched beside her and remained still, a feat in itself for a woman who was constantly in motion. If it wasn't her body or her mouth, her mind had to be running at an incredible speed.

Appreciating the fact, Casey squeezed her hand and swallowed hard. "I can't stop thinking about him. That night we met, he filled my dreams. I wasn't sure what was and wasn't real. Ever since, asleep or awake, I keep picturing him, and I want to know him better, spend more time with him. I don't care that he's blind. In some ways, that makes it easier. I don't worry as much about him being disappointed in me." She stopped, bit down on her lip, pushed on. "I'm so afraid I'll mess this up. I don't want to hurt him."

"Honey, getting hurt is a risk we all take in relationships—it comes with the territory. If we didn't, no one would ever fall in love. I'll tell you this, though. They're always saying love is blind. Emmett might have one up on the rest of us."

Sharon rested a hand on her friend's shoulders and held on tight. "And the only reason Emmett would be disappointed is because he can't see how beautiful you are. Lucky for you, your insides are drop-dead gorgeous."

This time, tears came with the laughter.

છળળ

*She wants to go on a date?* Scared the bejezums out of him. Circumstance was a ruthless blade, slicing his life in two. Dating belonged to the before part. After meant rattling around this house, the fields, his head. Listening. Thinking.

Yet, Emmett told her yes, if it could really be called a date. She was coming here, bringing the evening with her. Making things easier on him after their lunch at the diner. That part was unsaid. The realization made him grit his teeth.

A woman like Casey Mitchell deserved a real date with a guy who could pull out all the stops. Getting a grip on the bitterness that threatened to choke him, Emmett raised his head and held his arms out to his sides. "Well? Do I look all right?"

Wyatt was sitting on the bed, tapping his foot, jiggling Jackson in his arms. "Yeah, sure. You look great, Emmett. How the heck do I know? My dating experience is pretty limited. I met Sammie in elementary school. We never got too fancy—flannel and blue jeans have always been my standard."

Sammie tapped on the door. "Hope you're decent because I'm coming in." The door creaked and clicked shut behind her, followed by a long, low whistle. "Oh, Emmett, you have got it." She stepped closer, and her hands ran over his jacket, brushing away lint, smoothing his collar.

A comb ran through his hair with a competent touch, taming it into some semblance of order. "So handsome, like your brother. Good thing I'm married or I'd be chasing you myself, give the good doctor some competition."

He could hear the smile in her voice and tucked her in his arms. "Thanks, Sammie. You, too, Wyatt. You're always there for me. I love you guys." His voice was rough around the edges and earned him a hug that was strong enough to squeeze the stuffing out of him. Further displays of emotion were avoided when the doorbell rang.

"Okay. Showtime." Pasting on something resembling a smile, he moved to the hallway, the entourage, in the form of his family, trailing after him. Counting the steps, pacing himself, Emmett set his hand on the doorknob and took one last, deep breath. Good thing. Breathing was about to become a luxury. "Good evening, Casey."

"Hi, Emmett," she said softly, her hand a caressing feather of a touch on his cheek.

A draft of frigid air blasted past him, carrying her scent, something amazing, and the floor nearly dropped out beneath his feet. Stepping back, he waved to the entry and her heels clicked past him. *Heels? This is that kind of date? That explains why her voice came from a different level.* Shutting out the cold, Emmett pressed his back up against the door and waited for his heart to get back on track.

"Hello, Wyatt. Sammie, you're looking great! I wouldn't know you had a baby a little while ago if I didn't see it happen myself, not to mention the little bundle of evidence. Looking good, Jackson."

"Casey you look…*amazing*…not that you don't usually look good, but that get up—I mean—wow!" Wyatt was practically tripping over his tongue. That was saying something for a man who usually had a talent for talking everybody's ear off.

"Get your jaw off the floor for God's sake, Wyatt." There was a sharp edge to Sammie's words, throttled down for the doc. "You look lovely, Casey. Don't mind my husband. He doesn't get out much."

Emmett's lips started to twitch as he took a step closer. He found himself wrapped in the sturdy arms of his sister-in-law, bringing the scent of baby powder with her and a smidgeon of envy. He could picture her skin turning green, her reaction to the doctor more telling than her husband's. "You have a nice time, little brother."

He nodded, kissed her cheek, and skimmed the top of Jackson's head that was nestled against her chest. Emmett wished the little man was in his hands, something to keep them occupied because a bad case of the nerves was setting in.

He was starting to sweat, hadn't felt like this since his teen years.

A hand grabbed hold of his shoulder and dug in. Wyatt. "Out of this world, Emmett. I'm talking universal. Hey, Sammie, can you get a dress like that? Maybe we should have a date night. Em will babysit, won't you? Sammie? Ah, good night, Casey."

The door closed with a thud, the music of a woman's breathy laughter following his brother's departure, proving his guest was nervous too. Were there butterflies stirring up deep down in her belly? His felt like a flock of chickadees had taken up residence in the pit of his stomach, batting around down there.

Emmett took a deep breath, pressing his palm against his middle, and pulled out a smile. "Hi, Doc. I've got to tell you. You smell like heaven." A step closer and she met him, her arms catching him. Lift off.

ⷮⷮⷮ

Casey made dinner. Steaks, cooked to perfection, and fluffy, mashed potatoes, a marvel in itself for a man who always ended up with lumps, even in the days from before. Stuck with baked most of the time. Simple was the name of the game for most of Emmett's cooking. Nothing complex, but it generally tasted all right. There was asparagus too, cooked in oil and garlic.

Laughing, she set a mint on his tongue after, said it would chase away bad breath and make sure everything got along in his stomach. Red wine, something sweet and fragrant, topped it off and made him light headed. Or was it the company?

Something soft and pleasant drifted in from the radio in the kitchen. The combination of good food, alcohol, music and this woman in close proximity had him feeling relaxed, maybe a little reckless. Emmett stood up from the couch, where they'd made small talk after dinner, and extended a hand to her. "Would you like to dance, Case? I haven't done this in a while, but I'll try not to step on your toes."

She accepted, and they began to sway in the living room. Emmett had never danced in the dark before. It was an intense experience as he savored the cool brush of her dress against him. The sound of its rustling and her scent combined nearly drove him over the edge. He held on tight to her waist—a little too tight—to steady himself and rested his cheek on her head.

"Thank you for the date. This is my first one since— I wish I could take you out on the town and give you your due, someplace where you could show off this dress and everything about you."

Her hands were resting on his shoulders. One moved to his cheek to stroke it with her thumb, and he could swear that the skin burned beneath her touch. "I'm game. Why don't we go out sometime, Emmett?"

His shoulders became stiff, and his jaw clenched, his body becoming still. "No, no, I couldn't do that. What's the point when I can't see anything? What good would it be to have you lead me around like a seeing-eye dog? That wouldn't be much of a date, and you deserve a real date, not someone shuffling around in the dark—"

She shushed him with a kiss, effectively stopping a full-blown rant, setting his feet into motion once more while the fire continued to crackle behind them and the music drifted their way.

"You don't know until you try. It might be an exhilarating experience. Think about it." She was quiet, but there was steel beneath her words, a determination to rival his own.

A few turns around the living room and her hand began to knead at the tense muscles at the base of his neck, loosening the knots in his stomach as well. "Getting out would do you good."

*Any place with you in it would do me good.* His forehead pressed to hers, and his fingers found the way to her hair, threading their way in, giving them something to latch on to. "You don't know the half of it. Getting out of this head of mine—now, that would be something. Can you do something about that?"

"I'll see what we can do." Their steps began to slow as their hearts began to trip. Casey took his hand and ran it over her dress, the jacket, the gloves, nearly pushing him over the brink. "You know—it's hot in here. Can you help me get these off?"

Smooth, soft satin was brushing along his face, fiddling with his hair. Emmett couldn't believe how sensuous it was to peel the gloves from her fingers. "And this?" *The jacket. Never knew velvet could drive me wild.*

The fabric slid off her shoulders, and his hands glided upward, caught on the necklace and toyed with it.

Emmett had to come in for the kiss, and the cool touch of her earrings brushed his cheek, made him fiddle with them next before his fingers migrated to her hair and discovered the clip. Tantalizing. Had to get it out, take her hair down. Threading his hands in smooth, fragrant tresses, his mouth landed on hers once more, and he was lost.

Casey found him, giving his hand a tug and they moved to the chair by the fire, her legs coming up in his lap, leading the way to the maddening stripe running up her stockings and something lacy at the hem of the dress, hinting of other mysteries. Emmett managed restraint, behaving himself, his hand returning to her waist, her arm, and the incredible, soft skin of her shoulder.

*Bet she's fair, like Snow White.* The fairy tale turned

real, in his living room, in his lap, in his arms. If only she could break the spell he'd been under the past year. His hand settled on her neck, and her pulse was fluttering under his thumb, her breathing strained. "How was that? Did I help you get out of your head?"

Emmett wheezed with soft laughter, his head nestling in the crook of her neck. "Honey, you've got me going completely out of my mind, ready to go anywhere you want to go."

# CHAPTER 10

Sonny, you've been doing this a long time. I'd think you would know better." Casey tsk-tsked, wincing at the sight of the angry burn on the cook's meaty hand. The owner of the diner had come in during the lunch hour after he went a round with a hot pot and lost.

The large man shrugged, looking out of place on her examining table, still in his apron, the top of his head shining with perspiration. "Oh, it happens to the best of us. I got careless. Rushing around, doing too many things at once, and I spilled a pot of boiling potatoes all over the place."

A grimace marred a face that was in the habit of smiling while Casey cleansed the burn with an antiseptic wash. The back of his entire, left hand was swollen and covered with angry red, blisters bubbling up. "The hot water, that wouldn't have been so bad, but the potatoes hit and stuck there a moment too long—" Sonny bit off the rest he was going to say as she treated a particularly, painful spot.

She stopped to press his arm. "I'm sorry. It has to be cleansed to avoid infection. I don't mean to hurt you." An antimicrobial gauze was next, wrapped loosely around the damaged skin without pressing against it.

The diner's proprietor managed a smile. "Honey,

that's all right. At least I've got a sweet, young thing like you to look at rather than that old codger, Doc Smith. He was a good doctor, but you're much easier on the eyes. You make the pain bearable." Sonny studied his hand, lifting it in front of his face and inspecting her work. A nod, a grin, and a glittering eye was turned her way. "So, have you seen our Emmett lately?" Casual, too casual.

Casey practically snorted. If she'd learned one thing about this small town, there were few-to-no secrets. They probably knew what color underwear she put on that day. "We had dinner the other night." *That's it. Keep him hanging. Give no extra information.*

"Good, that's good. We miss seeing him around, wish he'd get out of that house from time to time. Grocery shopping, that's about all he'll do, and half the time Wyatt does that without him." Sonny shook his head, and his face darkened.

"It's like having a prize stallion and keeping him locked up in the stable all the time. That man should be out and about. So what if he can't see? He doesn't realize how much we all miss having him around. He's a part of us. When that *bastard*, pardon my French, hurt Emmett, he hurt all of us, and Em only makes it worse, trapping himself out there."

Casey patted him on the back. "I'm afraid you're the one who might feel trapped. No using this hand for the next week. Come back and see me, and I'll let you know when you're back in action." She peered at his face intensely and shook her finger with a grin. "And don't even think about sneaking. Word will get back to me. I have eyes everywhere."

Rummaging in her pocket, she pulled out her pad and began writing rapidly across the page. "I'm prescribing an antibiotic to keep infection away. You can take ibuprofen for the pain. Change your bandage twice a day—it's antimicrobial and should ward off bacteria. If those blisters burst, rinse your hand carefully in cool water, pat it dry, and wrap it loosely in more gauze to protect it. If there's any sign of infection, you come back—pronto!" She stood up and tucked a strand of hair behind her ear. "Oh, one more thing. You need a tetanus shot."

Sonny made a face but was a trooper, holding steady while she made quick work of the shot. He stood up and extended his hand. "Thanks, Doc. I won't use this hand, but I've got to keep an eye on things. Think about what I said and get Em back to my place sometime."

"I'll try. Be careful with that hand and make sure you come see me in a week." A wave and the friendly giant was out the door. Casey shook her head and made an entry in the computer about his visit, noting the time, injury, and treatment, all the while thoughts of Emmett cropping up.

A pinging started on the glass and drew her attention to the view outside of her window. Great. Sleet or freezing rain. Pretty, but dangerous. That would mean more patients, especially those who were too foolish to stay in and ride out the storm. *Em will hate being cooped up.* She hoped the stubborn man didn't take it into his head to go walking in this. *Better go check on him once this clears.* Hopefully, Casey wouldn't be too late.

෬෨෬

Caged like an animal, Emmett was miserable. Recent weather had been a tease, a mild warm-up only to be hit with freezing rain. A step outside and the ice almost sent him on his butt. Creeping to the edge of the porch, his fingers found the shrub on the edge. It was completely coated in a thick layer that weighed the branches down and made them click together when the wind blew. The tell-tale pinging proved the garbage was coming down steady. There'd be no taking his daily walk. Too risky. One misstep and he'd be immobile, the last thing he needed. *Crap! Hate this! If I could see it, I could do it!*

Antsy, Emmett paced the rooms of his house, top to bottom, running his hands over everything, tidying a space that was already painfully organized, tempted to knock everything down, wreck it all, make a mess of the outside to rival his insides.

He was standing by the fire, hands on hips, soaking in the heat when a knock sounded on the door, and a voice called out his name. *Not now, Casey! Bad enough I can't get her off my mind, I'm not fit to do anything about it, and she has to show up, rub my nose in it.* "Come in," he called, trying to dig down deep enough to pull out some welcome.

There was the opening and closing of the door, a burst of frigid air streaming his way, the thud of boots being dropped on the floor, followed by a flurry of foot-steps. Hands like ice grabbed his.

"Hey, you. I've been thinking about you all morning. As soon as they treated the roads, I headed out. Thought you might have cabin fever, being cooped up in here all the time. I decided you have got to get out of this house! Get yourself dolled up, baby. I'm taking you to my place and making you dinner. After that, we'll occupy our-selves, somehow. We've managed before." Sweet shy-ness colored her words, drew him toward her even as frustration threatened to boil over.

A rushing river of chatter nearly had his head spin-ning, as accustomed as he was to sitting in silence. Em-mett nodded, giving her hands a squeeze, even as rebel-lion reared up inside of him.

*Where does she get off telling me what I need to do?* "What's wrong with you, not wearing any gloves? Stay here by the fire and thaw out. I'll only be a few minutes."

A walk up the stairs, counting the steps all the way, to keep his place and his temper, and he found himself in his room, back pressed against the solid oak door. *Go with her. You know you want to be with her.* That was the problem. His body wanted her while his mind was at war with his cravings, telling him to cut it out, that wasn't happening, he wasn't what she needed in his present mood.

Pushing off the door, he moved to the closet and ran his fingers along an assortment of shirts and sweaters that had been carefully arranged in some semblance of order. His favorite, a heavy brown one, was exactly where he expected, recognizable by the feel of the weave. Emmett pulled it over his head and finger combed his hair.

His palms, sweaty all the sudden, ran over his jeans. The pants would do. No holes. Hopefully no stains. A spray of cologne had it covered. Now to stop the thundering of his heart at the prospect of going out to dinner, even if it was just to her place. Emmett didn't do out anymore, hadn't since the incident.

Resolute, he stood at the top of the stairs and dusted off his courage. Casey Mitchell wanted to take him out, and, by God, he'd go. His feet carried him through the living room, to the bench in the entryway where he slipped on his boots and started fighting with the laces.

"Let me give you a…" Her words trailed off when he straightened up to glare a moment. Must have made an impression because she didn't offer again, sitting beside him to slip on her own boots.

*You need boots without laces.* Butter fingers lost the hooks several times, and he cursed under his breath when one of the eyes remained elusive, but he finally got the job done.

Emmett stood, his hand reaching out automatically

for the right place, thrown off when her coat was in the way.

"Oh, sorry. Let me get that." She stepped in close, her arm brushing against his, and he could've sworn her heat would singe his clothes. Casey smelled good too, like strawberries. Must have been the shampoo in that halo of hair he'd felt before.

Feeling slightly off balance at her nearness, Emmett caught the wall and leaned on it a heartbeat or two before grabbing his coat off the hook and shrugging into it. His fingers found the keys on the hook to the left of the coat hooks, everything placed in a calculated way to help him navigate a familiar world made unfamiliar without eyes.

A turn to the left, his hand skimming the small table for mail and he pulled his wallet out of the drawer. Tucking it away, he patted at his pockets and found his gloves. "There are more gloves in that drawer that pulls out of the bench if you need a pair."

"Aren't you sweet? Thank you, Emmett." Casey brushed his cheek with her lips, scorching in that casual touch, and he heard the opening and closing of the drawer down below. "Okay. All set. Let's go." She moved past him and let in an arctic blast of air with the opening of the door.

He shadowed her, took hold of the sturdy wood, and gave a little bow. "Ladies first." The doorknob offered support when her hand brushed the hair from his face and she moved down the walkway. Listening to her receding footsteps and the opening of a car door, Emmett took a deep breath. *Okay. Here goes nothing.*

His senses were screaming on the drive, filled with her. Her scent, the timbre of her laughter, the soft touch of her skin when her hand brushed his fingers.

Why did she have to keep touching him? Didn't the woman realize prolonged celibacy and blindness were not a good combination? Emmett began to fume, aggravated to no end that the woman thought she knew what he needed. By the time they took the second turn, only five minutes to her apartment over the clinic, it would be no surprise if steam was coming off the top of his head.

*Should have left me alone! I can handle alone. It's being with someone, a woman no less, that's too much!*

"We're here!"

෫෨෫෨

Wound tight like a coiled spring about to release, Casey could feel the tension vibrating in the confined space of the car. Emmett hardly spoke on the entire drive, giving the clear impression this was against his will. Getting out at her place, he flipped out his collapsible cane, the distaste for it clear on his face. She could get it. At home, the reprehensible object, a symbol of his disability, wasn't visible. But now, on unchartered territory, it was a necessary evil.

Coming up the narrow stairwell, he smashed his knee against the wall, only to ram his hip against the table next to her coat rack. Yanking off his boots with abrupt movements was a procedure made more difficult without a bench. It involved propping himself against the wall and balancing precariously on one foot until the job was done.

His cheeks were streaked crimson as he held out his coat. "Could I use your bathroom please?"

Emmett's words were clipped, his honey eyes flashing. *I bet he doesn't know you can still see anger in his gaze. Uncensored. Loud and clear.*

"Yeah, sure. It's right this way." Casey started walking, tapped herself on the forehead and stopped short. *Smooth, Case, really.* He knocked into her at her abrupt halt and exhaled sharply. "Sorry, I'm so sorry, Emmett. I guess I'm not too good at this." *This? What does this mean? Last thing he wants is special treatment.*

Taking a deep breath, she tried again. "It's straight forward, about twenty feet. You'll pass the kitchen on the right, and the bathroom is here on the left." She rapped the open door with her knuckles, giving him a reference. Reaching the doorway, Casey took his hand and gave a gentle tug. "Let me give you the grand tour. It's snug. Six steps in and here's the toilet, sink is next to it." She turned and extended his hand to the wall. "Here's the towel. I'll be in the kitchen making some coffee if you need anything."

A mumbled thank you and Casey slipped out of a room that suddenly became way too crowded, what with the feel of his hand on hers, the hammering of her heart, and the urge to kiss that clenched jaw.

Out to the kitchen, she rattled around enough to wake the dead, making herself a homing beacon. Her hands were trembling as she measured out the coffee, grounds scattering all over the place. Casey grabbed a towel and dusted them into the garbage, finally gripping the counter and practicing deep breathing exercises. *What on earth are you doing, Case? Did you bring him here for his sake or for yours?*

୧୦୧୨

He did his business, sitting down. Hated that, found it humiliating, one more indignity of blindness, but at least Emmett never missed. Sure to flush and close the lid, because women found those things to be important, he washed. Nearly sent the bottle of soap flying. Set it right with hands that shook. A quick splash of water on a face that burned and he buried it in a towel.

*Come on. Don't be a Neanderthal. So she brought you out of your comfort zone. Go make nice.* Finding the door wasn't hard. His feet remembered the way, and the kitchen was easy, the racket she made had him forcing a grin. A quick step into the room and his hip caught a heavy, kitchen chair. "Damn it!" He bit off the rest of the words, but a satisfying litany was streaming through his head.

"I'm sorry, Emmett. I should do a better job of making this place easier to get around. Have a seat. Your coffee's coming." She pulled out a chair, the scraping on the floor allowing him to home in on where to go.

Cautiously, rubbing his hip bone, he sank down, waiting to see if she would push him in like a child. Something in his face must have advised against it. There was a clatter, a saucer being placed on the table, and the clinking of a coffee cup. "Do you want cream and sugar?"

Emmett nodded, cleared his throat, trying to be pleasant, although he was still at a low simmer about being pried from his lair. "I can do that. Just set it by my cup and quit apologizing. I take some responsibility, you know. If I can't be patient enough to learn the lay of the land, I deserve whatever I get."

Nervous laughter was followed by the sound of something sliding across the table. A spoon was pressed into his hand, her fingers lingering for an instant, and he almost dropped it as if the metal were hot. *Get some self-control, will you?* He held the spoon in his right hand, took his time feeling around his coffee cup, taking care not to knock it, getting acquainted with the creamer and the sugar bowl.

Sugar was first, digging in, skimming the top. The creamer took a little more finagling, making sure he judged right as far as pouring and didn't go over the top.

Satisfied, he stirred and took a sip. All the while his hands were quivering. *Cut it out and get it together!* "How are you settling in here? Feel like home yet?"

ୡେ

Casey could swear Emmett was about to jump out of his skin. Was the man that uncomfortable out of his element? His foot was tapping, one hand drumming on his thigh, and there was a slight quaking in his hand when he drank his coffee. He was courteous, making small talk, but she was sure her guest didn't hear a word she said, his focus turned inward. If Casey said aliens had abducted her last night, Emmett would probably smile and nod all the while.

It was so maddening, smelling the scent of him, Old Spice, wood smoke from the fire, something unique to Emmett alone. Looking her way with those golden eyes, so handsome it hurt. She had to move, get up, put some distance between them. "So, what would you like for dinner? I've got turkey, salami, roast beef, and some nice, hard rolls. I could whip up some pasta. There's salad in the crisper…"

There was a clatter behind her, and the cup came down with a bang. Emmett shot up in a flash, kicking out the chair behind him, practically knocking it over. "Casey, look, I'm sorry, but I don't feel well. I think I'd better go home. Could you take me home, please?" His face was strained, gone white. His eyes glittered, as if by fever.

Instinctively, she reached out to touch his forehead, brushing hair out of the way as he pulled back, banging into the wall behind him. "Emmett! I just wanted to check your temperature."

Closing the gap, her hand skimmed his skin. It was

cool to her touch, and he jerked away from her once more.

"Okay, it's like that, is it? Yes, of course, I'll take you home."

Obstinate man. He set out before her, retracing his steps to the door. This time, Emmett didn't even bother with the laces on his boots. *Serves him right if he trips, the fool! What is the matter with him?* The anger began to well up as Casey shoved his coat into his hands none too gently and stomped down the steps, not even waiting to see if he needed guidance.

*The man never wants any help. Fine, I won't give it!* Going against the grain as a doctor, she made noisy progress to her car, the only assistance she'd offer. Emmett followed, running his hand from the hood to the door and settling himself into the passenger seat, expelling a forceful whoosh of air.

Five minutes later, they were back in his driveway. "Listen, Emmett, I wasn't trying to hold a pity party or irritate you. Believe it or not, *I* was lonely and wanted company. I thought you'd want the same."

His eyes were closed, his lips tight when Casey looked his way, seeking some acknowledgement. He turned to her, his hand skimming along her arm, sending sparks flying with his touch, finding her neck and holding on to the nape. With a steady pull, Emmett reeled her in, took a guess, and gave her a kiss that hit her jaw bone. Close enough. "I'm sorry, Case. I'm just not fit for socializing, not today. Thanks for trying."

He let go, making her feel like a junkie who'd just been cut off, the feeling of withdrawal was that fierce. Out of the car, tapping his way along the walk, fumbling with the key, and getting inside with a resounding slam of the door. *Case closed.* Leaving her shivering and alone in the cold.

# CHAPTER 11

*You're an idiot, do you know that?* Emmett flung his boots. It would mean hell finding them later but who cared? A scavenger hunt might do him good, would give him *something* to do. A toss of the coat and the keys to add to the self-punishment, and he stomped his way through the house, out to a cold living room.

*Great. No fire. You forgot to keep it built up on your way out.* A trip to the wood rack proved it to be empty. Further aggravation. He stormed out back, didn't even bother with shoes, his socks getting wet, his feet freezing, and grabbed an armload of logs. Back inside, shivering, he muttered to himself. The front door banged against the wall with a force beyond reckoning. He dropped the wood, one piece catching his foot and saw stars, letting loose some more colorful words. *Mama and Dad must be rolling in their graves. Better wash my mouth out with soap for good measure.*

"What the hell is your problem, Emmett Henry?"

More thudding, boots thrown on the floor, her coat and purse, too, judging by the jangle. Footsteps were marching his way. He caught that heady scent of strawberries once more, a breath of cold air clinging to her clothes and her skin, and Casey's finger was jabbing him in the chest.

"I'll tell you what your problem is. You're blind, and that's not changing any time soon. You stay here, holed up, licking your wounds, and it's time to rejoin the land of the living. You need to stop feeling sorry for yourself, get the hell out from time to time."

The words were sharp and fast, their bite strong enough to strip paint off his walls, not to mention a few layers of his skin, thinning it out. One more forceful jab rocked him on his heels. "And you know what else you need? You need to lose yourself, or find yourself, in a woman. Take your pick!"

✦✦✦

She was breathing hard. If he touched her chest, her heart was sure to be tripping. His hands came up and found her shoulders, taking hold in the grip of a vice. Emmett gave her a good shake. "Enough poking me, all right? You're right, about all of it, every word you said. There, does that make you happy?"

With that, he stepped in close, and his hand lodged in the thick curtain of her hair. His lips made their way home in a faltering, fierce trail of kisses. Once he found her mouth, all clumsiness was gone. He had to hold her, have her, all of her. His hands were moving up and down her arms, hers had hold of him, and she was whimpering.

Emmett wished he could pick her up like those classic old movies. Casey Mitchell deserved romance. *Have to make do.* Breaking away, panting like he'd run a race, Emmett tucked her hand in his and drew her along with him, up the stairs, to his room. He slammed the door behind them, pushing her up against it to get another taste of her. God, to get under her skin!

They took a step away from the door, and she was yanking at his sweater. One skilled tug and it dropped to the floor. Emmett took care of the rest, shrugging out of his T-shirt. Sliding down his jeans. Mentally counting to three and shucking his underwear.

There was the sound of an inhalation, and she wrapped her arms around his neck, devouring his mouth with her own. Her body was flush against his, her clothing rubbing against his skin, making the goose bumps spring up with sensory overload. His hands found the way to her blouse, some kind of flimsy thing. *Not winter clothes*, the practical voice in his head announced without notice. No matter, it meant easy access, lifting over her head and floating from his grasp. He let his fingers do the walking to the waistband of her jeans. A pop, a zip, and they were gone next, his thumbs hooking the undies along the way. *You do still know what to do! Guess you're not dead yet.*

"What about lights?" Casey whispered breathily, the words ending on a sigh as his mouth found her collarbone, her shoulder, and then moved south. She was humming in his hands, her body set on vibrate.

Emmett came back up to her mouth to plant a kiss, wearing a smile in his voice. "Welcome to my world. Won't need a light for what we're doing. Our bodies know the way."

Her hands worked their way up his body, velvet in her touch, starting at his hips and burning a trail up his ribs, to his shoulders, lacing into his hair. She latched on and pushed against him, forcing him back until his legs hit the bed and they were down for the count. "Case, listen. I haven't—this hasn't happened since I—not much opportunity for—"

Her mouth sealed his lips and stopped his words. "I want you to know something, Em. I don't do this casually either. There was once before, with another student in med school. We were both too tired, too lonely from the grind. A little too much wine, and we woke up scratching our heads, wondering what happened. I thought I'd wait until Mr. Right after that, and I think I've found him. Thought so since the day we met."

She buried her head in the crook of his arm and swallowed hard, emotions running high. Emmett's arms wrapped around her. Cradling her. Holding on tight until their bodies took over, proving there was no need for any more explanations.

Making love blind was indescribable. Everything was hypersensitive, his body turned up to the max to make up for the missing link. Her fingers, her body, her hair, and her breath brushing against his skin, made the banked coals at the heart of him burst into flames. They licked at his body, made him feel like he was incinerating. *This is burning alive, conscious of every sensation until the soul breaks free.*

Emmett was not sure where he ended and she began. When he couldn't take it anymore, her touching, her lips on his skin, her body pressed on top of his, the heat of her, he thrashed around. Flipping her over, he knocked the clock off the stand in a flurry of blankets, driven nearly mad with his famished body's response to her. Fighting to rise above her, pinning her down, driving himself to the edge, finding his way home. Lying with her in his arms, reduced to ashes, preparing to be like the phoenix and rise again.

❧❧❧

His eyes glowed, lit by starlight, his hair tousled in silver waves. His body was transformed to marble, painted white in the moonlight spilling through the open cur-

tains of his window. Emmett had no need to close out the
night or illuminate the darkness. Growing accustomed to
the shadows, what the moon gave was enough and she
was blessed with the gift of fully appreciating him without any self-consciousness.

For once, Casey didn't have to worry about *her*
physical appearance. With this man, it truly didn't matter,
a barrier shattered that no other man had been able to ac-
complish. She stepped in, helped him to shed her clothing, pressed her body against his. She wanted more,
wanted to take all, everything that Emmett had to give.
Wanted to wear him like a fine pair of leather gloves.

Becoming one. Beyond compare. Amazing, incredible, out of this world, like no other, having his fingers
roving over her body. After the first, fierce round, once
he had recovered, Emmett took his time. He learned every inch of her, from her toes to all the hairs on her head,
breath skimming over her along with his touch and the
heat and weight of him. *Good Lord, have mercy.*

They were caught in a tangle of blankets, bodies
pleasantly heavy, close to drifting off to sleep. Late. It
was very late, past midnight according to the clock he'd
knocked on the floor during his exertions. His chest rose
and fell slowly, his breathing even. Casey thought he'd
crossed over when his voice, hoarse as if having traversed
a desert, broke the silence. "You're the most beautiful
woman I've ever known." His hand found her hair and
began to toy with it while his other hand rested on her
hip.

She snorted softly and kissed his chest. "That's a
wonderful compliment, Em, but I'm going to let you in
on a secret. You can't see."

He let out a sigh and skimmed the top of her head
with his lips, shifting so that they were pressed closer together. "Case, I don't need eyes to know that about you."

One more deep breath and he couldn't hold back a catch in his voice, "But, God, I'd give anything to look at your face right now."

Casey rose up, saw a tear trickling down his cheek and she caught it with her finger before pressing her lips to his. "I wish you could, too, but maybe we're lucky. We both look with our hearts."

A laugh that was very close to a sob broke loose, and Emmett pulled her in close, burying his face in her hair, allowing himself to be lost in her arms. Her lips grazed against his shoulder, his neck, the sweet spot behind his ear. Set his body to humming, heart to hammering once more. She wasn't sure her body could take another round—but what a way to go.

# CHAPTER 12

His first cup of coffee. The counter held him up while Emmett cradled the mug in his hands, inhaled its rich aroma, and let the first sip hit his stomach. He might remain standing after all. The bacon was sizzling on the stove, eggs scrambling in a neighboring pan, and his body stood guard. No easy feat after a night in the capable arms of Miss Casey Mitchell. *Can't even keep my eyes open.* That thought brought out a snicker. Open or shut—no matter.

Footsteps were padding his way, light and quiet, making his heart pick up the pace in sweet anticipation. The scent of her came next, smelling like apples, sleep, sunshine and leftovers from making love, a combination that had the power to push him over the edge. Emmett gripped the counter with one hand, holding steady, and manned the stove with the other, dodging the smatter of grease for once.

Arms wrapped around his waist and her cheek pressed flush against his back. "Morning. What you got cookin', good lookin'?" Her chinned propped itself on his shoulder. "My favorite, bacon and eggs. Classic combination."

He turned around, skimmed his hands up her arms, mouth wrapped in a grin as he latched on to her lapels to take his fill of a good morning kiss. "Mm, you look good in my shirt."

His hands did some wandering, settled on her hips and drew her in close for another sample of that luscious mouth. Minty. She'd brushed. Anticipating his lips connecting with hers? His fingers traveled farther, cupped her bare bottom hidden under the tail of his shirt and his eyebrows crept up to his hairline. "Why you scandalize me, Doctor Mitchell."

It was Casey's turn to explore, her hands running under his shirt and over the smooth planes of his stomach, up to his chest, leaving a trail of kisses along his collarbone. His senses scattered, like looking through a kaleidoscope. She had that intense of an effect on him, disintegrating him, and he nearly crushed her in his arms, seeking an anchor.

Her cheek was pressed against his chest and her soft chuckle had heat flaring deep in the nether regions of his belly. *God, now is not the time for cardiac arrest, but I'll go happy.* "Your heart is beating a mile a minute, Em. Got you a little hot and bothered, eh? Do you need to sit down? Should I take your pulse and blood pressure, call nine-one-one?"

The crackling of the bacon on the stove was the only thing that restrained him from pushing her against the counter in a rush until they tumbled into oblivion. He cleared his throat and brushed the top of her head with his lips, inhaling deeply on the way, taking sustenance. "Let me—I've got to—God, woman, you've got me all in a tangle. Go sit so I can get this breakfast off the burner."

She laughed and gave his bottom a swat before obliging. A little distance helped clear Emmett's head, made it possible to fill the plates waiting on the counter, and carry them over. "That smells and looks divine, Emmett. You're spoiling me. My daddy loved to cook me breakfast. I miss that." Homing in on her voice, he placed the steaming dish before her, set down his own, and slid into his chair without mishap. He felt good. Competent. Like a capable grown-up.

He reached out, found her, managed to kiss her cheek. "Get used to being spoiled. It shouldn't be any other way with a fine woman like you." They both fell silent, forks clinking on their plates, giving into hunger. Casey's chair scraped against the floor, and she returned momentarily, placing his hand on a mug, already prepared, and Emmett didn't fight it. "Thanks, Case." A sip and his smile grew. "Perfect. Couldn't have done better myself."

"You're welcome. This breakfast really hits the spot. I don't know about you, but my stomach woke me up, protesting pretty loudly. You could probably hear it down here." Sunshine in her voice and words, warmth and light bouncing off him. The woman made him feel good, softened the sharp edges, filled the holes.

Setting down his fork, Emmett considered filling his hands with her. She must have been on the same train of thought because her chair slid out once more and Casey's fingers were playing with his hair. "You need a haircut." Her fingers ran over his scalp, became entangled, and she swooped down to take a nibble of his mouth. "I almost became a beautician." She moved in front of him, sat on his lap and went in for a deeper dip, her lips tasting like heaven. *Guess I cook better than I thought.* "I could cut it for you."

Concentration. Near impossible. Finding words, stringing them together, harder still. Casey Mitchell was stroke-inducing. *At least she's a doctor. You're in good hands.* "Hmm—haven't had much call for mirrors, but knock yourself out. Scissors are in the drawer on the top, far left over by the fridge."

She walked away, leaving a chill in her wake, but that shouldn't have concerned him because a moment later it was as if fire was coursing through his veins as her hands drifted through his hair and the snip of the scissors joined the sound of his panting. Her breath brushed Emmett's neck, set him to shivering, and his heart to tripping. He drew her into his arms with a tug, the scissors clattering on the table, and they were headed to the floor. Destination—vaporization.

こうこう

"To the right, Em. Hold the cart steady, that's it. Keep going. Stop. Hang on a minute. You want the garlic and herb sauce or the one with meat? They're on sale— buy one, get one."

Emmett gripped the handle and pushed his breath out hard while Wyatt deliberated over the culinary selection in the international aisle. *Who the hell cares?* "I don't know. Get one of each. I feel like a damned hamster in a wheel over here. Why do you have me do this anyway?" He planted his feet, crossed his arms, and leveled his stare in what *could* be his brother's direction. Someone brushed between them, murmuring apologies, and the heat rushed to his face. *I'm sure it's a person I know, seeing as I know everyone in this town.*

"Do what? Push the cart? Because I knock stuff over. Stop being such a grouch. Mrs. Miller, our first-grade teacher, looks like a bear just bit her, trying to get past you. What's got your panties in a bunch? Forward, by the way."

Emmett turned back to the cart and could hear his knuckles cracking, he held on so tight. His head was starting to pound. He despised shopping and banking day. If everything could be done online, that would be fine by him. "I hate this, making you and Sammie come out with me like my babysitters, having everyone's eyes on me, seeing how useless I am. Why don't you just sit me in the cart, push me around like a toddler?"

He missed his next set of directions, hit some barrier in the way, and rammed his hip into the cart. Mrs. Miller's ears would be bright red listening to the filth that spilled out of his mouth. *Get put in a corner for that one. You'd deserve it, too.*

Wyatt's hand clamped down on his shoulder, grounding him. "Will you cut it out? We don't mind helping out, but you need to give yourself a break. You do most everything on your own, stubborn mule that you are. Not only that, you need to get out some more." A pause and a forceful pat on the back came next, hard enough to set him to coughing. "You know what else you need? Some sweetening up. I'm taking you to the doc as soon as we're done. No arguments. Now, to the left and straight so we can get out of here. Jackson needs diapers, and Sammie needs a breather. I'm on Daddy Duty when I get home."

❡❡❡

Casey opened the door to find Emmett standing on the landing, a grocery bag in his hand, a disgusted look on his face. "Hey, you! Brr. Must be cold out there. You brought it with you. Let's get you out of this thing and warmed up." She latched on to his coat lapels, tugging him inside, taking his breath away with a kiss.

The bag slipped from his fingers with a thud to the floor, and his hands were threaded in her hair. He took a deep breath like a man drowning, on his last gasp. "God, save me. It was errand day. I can't stand errand day."

The pitiful expression on his face, the annoyance

plain in that golden gaze, made the giggles start bubbling up and they couldn't be stopped.

"Oh, you poor thing. Welcome to the human race. We all have things we have to do that we hate. I had to lance boils on an old man's back yesterday. Not pretty. Come in here and let's recuperate together." Casey picked up the bag and took his hand, destined for the living room and a big, cushy couch—and maybe the bedroom.

"Hold up. Almost forgot." Emmett started tugging on his boots, nearly falling over as he balanced on one foot. She ducked under his shoulder and steadied him. "Thanks," he grumbled, pulling off his jacket next and searching with his fingers for the coat hook, missing it until her hand gave him a little help. "Something else I can't do."

Casey darted forward and kissed his forehead, smoothing away the crease between his eyes. "Hey, no more pity party. Think about all the things you can do, like look gorgeous—drive me crazy—turn me on—make my heart trip—turn up my temperature—touch me in ways no one else can. You do not know the power that you hold in those incredible fingertips."

His arm snaked around her waist, and he drew her in close, kissing the top of her head as they moved into the living room.

"Okay, okay. Listen, you'd better get that in the freezer. It's fixings for sundaes." Emmett plopped down on the couch while she ventured off to the kitchen. "I forgot to ask. Is it okay that I'm here? Were you busy? Because I can call Wyatt or hitch a ride. Someone is bound to give me a lift. People around these parts tend to feel sorry for me."

Casey looked down at what she was wearing and considered her appearance. Old, holey pajamas. Mismatched socks. Hair yanked up on top of her head, un-washed. Not a lick of make-up. "I've been doing abso-lutely nothing, Emmett, except watching the day go by, lazy as sin. Want to join me?"

A return to the couch and his oh-so-able hands took hold of her, planting her bottom on his lap. "That is the best suggestion I've had all day. You take care of the watching end of things, I'll do the feeling because that's the easiest thing ever when I've got my hands on you. Now, what can you do to thaw out these frozen bones?"

As if in illustration, a shiver ran through his body and made her vibrate with him. Casey wasn't sure that reaction was a chill, not when the mere thought of his touch could start the quaking to hit her, head to toe, whether Emmett was actually present or not.

"Oh, I can think of a few things." She took his hands first, kissing every finger. Her lips traveled up his arm next, over his shoulder, and into that delightful dip be-tween his collarbone and his throat. "How about this?" Casey blew on his neck, watched the hairs stand on end. "And this?" Her teeth tugged on his ear, and a groan rumbled down low in his chest.

"No more. I can't take it. I'm liquefying here." His face was flushed, his breathing labored as if from intense exertion. His hands cupped her face, and a heat to rival the equator rose up from her chest all the way to her hair-line. "How about that ice cream?" Emmett's eyes glit-tered, pulling her in for one more kiss. *Now I know how a dragonfly trapped in amber feels.*

"Yeah, sure. Coming up." Back to the kitchen and the table held her up while Casey fought hyperventila-tion. This was the first time the man had been in her apartment since their near blow-up, bringing them to the next level in their relationship. That night—and morning after—in *his* kitchen, decimating.

That there was potential for more made her weak in the knees.

Footsteps sounded behind her, and his hands were on her waist, those amazing hands. It was her turn to shiver as the air left her lungs in a rush. Who needed to breathe when held by an angel? Close her eyes, and she was sure to feel his wings beating, poised to bear her aloft.

"Casey, you okay? I didn't hear any dishes out here. You're trembling. Sit down." Emmett pulled out a chair and settled her on his lap. "What's wrong?"

The fear in his voice made her take a deep breath and pull out a smile. *Lucky he can't see what's happening to me.* "Nothing. It's just you make me forget what I was doing and where I was headed. Why am I here?" She buried her face in the solid wall of his chest and felt him shaking, this time with laughter. *Can't beat them, might as well join them.*

"You came out here to make sundaes. Remember that? Ice cream, toppings, bowls, spoons? If you round them up, I'll help make them. I just need to warn you. Things could get a little messy around here." The goofy grin on his face was irresistible. Casey had to grab hold of his ears and give him a thorough kissing. He went loose beneath her hands. If she didn't move, the same fate would be hers.

Out of the chair, across the room, bringing out dishware and fixings with a tad too much enthusiasm. "Whoops!" she called out as a bowl slipped from her grasp and banged on the counter. Emmett was there once more, uncanny really, the way he always found his way. His hands were on her shoulders this time, and his lips brushed her neck. Casey's eyes fluttered shut, and she swallowed hard, leaning against him.

"Steady there, all right? Let's get started. How about you scoop ice cream, I'll do toppings. Just don't make it too fast sliding those dishes my way. We wouldn't want a repeat of that old 'I Love Lucy' episode. You know, when Ethel and Lucy make candy?" There was a bit of sadness darkening his gaze even as he smiled through it. Hard to talk about television and something he could no longer see.

"You've got it. Mmm, you picked my favorite. I love anything with peanut butter and chocolate." A few generous scoops and she set a bowl in front of him. Next, Casey took his hand and led him through the toppings on the counter. "Okay, you've got chocolate sauce, caramel sauce, nuts, and whipped cream. Have at it!" She returned to the task of filling the other bowl. Otherwise, those sundaes would be forgotten while sampling that delicious mouth beside her some more.

Emmett's tongue poked out of the side of his mouth, lost in concentration like a child. He was methodical, opening each container and poking a spoon in each jar first before getting started. A few scoops of chocolate made it in the dish, dripping down the side of the bowl. He caught it with his finger, his tongue flicking out to lick it off and the ice cream scooper dropped into the sink with a thud. Casey was sure the sound of her heart's pounding could be heard across the room. He turned her way, lips curving into a grin. "You all right over there?"

She nodded, forgetting herself once more, cleared her throat, and found some words. "You have to let me help catch the drips next time." That was all it took. He set the spoon back in the jar from the caramel and moved across the room. His hand fished for her, caught her, and reeled her in. Back to the counter and his finger dipped in the caramel before placing it in her mouth. Casey sucked it off and this time around his eyes squeezed shut.

Sundaes forgotten, Emmett's mouth found hers once more, blending chocolate and caramel, making her want so much more. When he finally broke away, his forehead rested on hers while his hand pressed against the small of her back. His voice went hoarse when speaking was a possibility. "My brother…and you…were right. I *do* need to get out more. Making sundaes is never this much fun at home."

That got them both going. Casey reached up to take his face in her hands and kissed his forehead, his cheek-bones, and his nose, keeping it light, fighting his pull—for now. "Let me help you finish up. If I don't, they'll be soup, and that would be a waste of some good ice cream."

He didn't fight her, moving back to the task at hand. Taking up the can of whip cream, Emmett shook it, took aim, and fired, getting the front of her shirt. "Emmett!" She shrieked, fought him for the can and a whip cream war ensued, ending up in his hair, all over the cabinets, the counter, and the front of them both. They were laughing so hard, they had to hold on to the edge for dear life. "All right—all right. I'm going to go change. I don't know what you're going to do."

Emmett gave her the smile of the cat who feasted on a canary or two, igniting a slow burn in her belly. His hands found her shoulders and turned her toward the doorway. "Don't you worry about that. I'll finish up in here." A little push and she was forced out of her own kitchen, cheerful whistling following her along the way.

Casey made it to her room and pressed her back up against the door, hand covering her heart as she felt it race and the blood rushed to her head, making her dizzy. *You can do this. Deep breath in. Deep breath out. Count to ten. Stop thinking about the unbelievably fine man in your kitchen.* A cold shower was what she really needed to stop the flames licking at her body, but there was no time.

Shimmying out of her clothes, she deliberated for a moment and slipped on a pale green negligee, something filmy that floated down to her hips. A trip into the bathroom allowed her to complete her inspection. Whip cream was in her eye brows, on her face, and her neck, her cheeks scarlet. *All Em's fault.* The shine in her eyes and the smile stretching from ear to ear proved she didn't mind. She wet a cloth with warm water to make herself presentable, pulled the band from her hair, and let it fall to her shoulders. A quick brushing of the curtain of long strands and a shot of body spray from head to toe would have to do. Squaring her shoulders, she returned to the kitchen and had to hold on to the door jamb or wind up on the floor.

Emmett had managed to clean up the kitchen, no small wonder without eyes to guide him. The toppings were cleared away, the bowls on the table. His shirt had been peeled off his beautiful body and was in the sink. His hair was wet. *What did he do? Stick his whole head under the faucet?* Whatever he did, the whole package looked impossibly good, jean-clad hip propped against the sink, empty eyes turned her way, mouth open in expectation. "What took you so long? The ice cream's melting."

She crossed the room, picked up the bowls, and set them in the freezer, freeing her hands for him. "Forget the ice cream. We'll have it later." Her fingers became ensnared in his hair while his danced along her body, and he sucked in as if punched in the gut, feeling the light, tantalizing material that brushed her skin.

"Take me to bed, Em. Second door on the left, past the bathroom." No need to tell him twice. He swept her into his arms, like knights of old and romance movie stars, his heart thudding against her, fit to leap from his chest. His feet carried them both down the hall without faltering, nudged the door open, crossed the room. "To the left two more steps. That's it. You've found it. Good boy," Casey teased lightly.

"I'm not a boy, Case. Thought you knew that by now, but let me prove it."

Laying her out on the bed, he knelt beside her and began to worship her body with his hands. Starting at the toes, working his way up and his mouth was next, kissing her skin. She started to writhe under his touch, reaching out to grab hold of him. His lips latched on to hers, and Casey saw a starburst behind closed eyelids. *Definitely, all grown up. No doubt about it.* Time to prove she wasn't a little girl.

# CHAPTER 13

Casey and Wyatt, two definitive sources in his life, said Emmett needed to get out. Okay, he'd get out. A step on to his porch proved the air was cold, not subzero. He was dressed appropriately, accompanied by his cane. *Good, old Trusty McGee,* Emmett dubbed his sidekick with a mental snort. Nothing for it then to get started. Time to stop hemming and hawing, go beyond the familiar to unexplored territory and the world beyond his backyard.

Emmett had it all figured out. Go to the end of his driveway, take a right on Hickory Hill Road. About two miles and he'd come to a "T." Go forward, and he'd end up in a snow bank. Take a right on Route 20, and it would turn into Main Street. Another half mile and he'd hit the welcome to Charlton sign, the sleepy village, three mailboxes, and the clinic on the right. Simple. Sketching the route in his mind, envisioning the times without counting when he and Wyatt had walked it or rode their bikes, Em was going to bite the bullet.

That was it. He'd go surprise Casey at the clinic, maybe take her to lunch at the diner. One last pre-flight check. Cane. Phone. Gloves, hat, coat, boots. Check. Suck it up and go. One thought nagged at the back of his mind. *You should tell someone what you're up to. Right, and they'd say you're out of your mind.* Pushing precautions and reservations aside, Emmett set out.

Not as easy as he thought. Being blind meant losing his sense of distance. His phone announced the time, giving him some idea of how far his feet had carried him, but nothing definite. Thankfully, the road was quiet this time of day, what with most people working. Emmett was glad no one passed him on the back-country road. He couldn't stand gawkers or people sitting on the pity pot, trying to cater to him.

There was no sound besides the wind rustling in the trees, occasional bird song, and his breathing. A spike in adrenalin made him aware of everything, kicked his heart rate up a notch. A few times his footsteps faltered, and he almost wrenched an ankle. One near miss had him gripping his cane at the edge of the pavement, jaw tight, eyes closed.

Beginning to wonder if this was so bright, Emmett reminded himself if he turned back, his mailbox would be waiting for him with the carved sign hanging underneath that he made in shop class for Dad. The one that said Henry. *Henrys don't quit.* Resolute, he kept going. His cane hit the T, finding pavement in front of him rather than the boundary of snow that corralled the road. Letting out a sigh of relief, his body turned right, gaining confidence, as if it knew the way instinctively.

*Not much farther. You've made it through the tough part, now for the home stretch.* His cane made a satisfying tap against the asphalt, driving him on when the sound of an approaching car, loud and fast, made Emmett jump to the side.

Heart in his throat, stomach churning, he felt the whoosh of air in its passing. *Close! Too damned close!*

And then *Thud!* A horrendous crunching sound, a horn blaring nonstop, and smoke clouded the air, filling his lungs, making him cough. Emmett pulled his scarf over his face and followed the noise, his heart fit to jump out of his chest the closer he got. *Please, don't let them be dead. Please!* Somehow, he found his way. Folding his cane and pocketing it, he ran his hands along the hunk of metal, wrenched at the door handle with a desperate surge of strength, finally yanking it open.

The piteous groan from its occupant proved a man was inside, slumped with his head against the wheel. Emmett peeled off his gloves and cautiously let his fingers travel over the driver's body, coming away slick and warm with blood. "Okay, okay, mister, you need to sit tight. I'll call for help."

He reached into his pocket, dialed nine-one-one and hit send. Nothing. The battery was dead. *Damn it! Why do you always forget to charge this thing?* "Crap! Okay. Don't move—I'll get help." Reaching across the car, satisfying himself there were no other victims, Emmett squeezed the man's shoulder and fought his way back to the road.

All sense of adventure gone, panic was rising, fighting for the upper hand. He beat it down, picking up the pace, jogging, sliding, stumbling, falling, wondering when this trip would end. Urgency pushed him on, and he hit the sign first, running his hands over the lettering. Nearly brought to tears, Emmett searched for the mailboxes next, turning into the parking lot of the clinic at last.

Hunched over with a stitch in his side, his breath coming in a sob, he heard someone call out, "Hey buddy, are you all right?" A car door slammed and running footsteps approached, a hand clamping down on his shoulder. "Can I help you?"

A good Samaritan. A stranger, no less, someone who didn't know him. Emmett gripped his knees and fought for air. "Just get me into the clinic, please."

A hand hooked the crook of his arm and drew him forward, giving quiet instructions, guiding him inside.

Emmett straightened and extended his hand, received a firm shake. "Thanks. I can take it from here." A flurry of protests and the man was gone. A few steps and Emmett's shout rose up over the soft music and hum of conversation. "Casey? Casey! Can somebody get Casey?"

More hurried footsteps and familiar, soft hands were on his face, wiping away blood that he'd smeared on his cheek. "Emmett, what happened?"

Strictly professional, Casey was wearing her doctor's cap, but controlled fear colored her words. He fumbled for her hand, gave it a reassuring squeeze.

"I'm fine. I went for a walk, but you have to call for help. There was a car accident back on—on Route Twenty, before it becomes Main. There's one man, the driver. He hit his head. I don't know what else. Just hurry." The words spilled out, leaving him completely drained.

Casey led him to a chair to and gave him a hasty kiss. "You stay put, you hear?"

Her hair brushed his cheek, and the scent of vanilla and brown sugar swirled around his head before she was gone.

"Angie, call nine-one-one. We've got a car accident on Route Twenty, not far from here. Tell my patients we have a delay, to reschedule if they prefer. I'm going to see if there's anything I can do." Her words were clipped, all business, heels clicking on the floor and the door slammed shut behind her.

Emmett shook his head, hands resting on his knees, following orders. Not hard, considering his body was shaking, and he was starting to sway. "Em? It's all right, Em. Put your head between your knees and take deep, slow breaths through your nose."

Sharon was there, her hand pressed to the nape of his neck, giving him something to latch on to until his head stopped spinning. Another hushed voice, Angie's, joined the gynecologist's and a cold cloth was wiped over his face, his wrists, and at the base of his skull. Gradually, the quaking stopped, and he didn't feel like toppling out of the chair.

"Better now? Sit up slow, no sudden moves. Looks like you were in shock, my friend. What were you doing taking a trip like that by yourself anyway?" There it was, the voice of reason chewing him out.

"Hey, I needed to shake things up a bit. Didn't expect it to be like this." The cloth was back, wiping at his hands, his face, dabbing at his clothes, and then his old classmate's lips brushed his cheek.

"You are quite a sight. Anyone seeing you would think *you'd* been in an accident. I've got to give Case credit for keeping a level head. If Paul walked in here looking like this, I'd be a blubbering mess. Do me a favor and sit tight where we can see you until she gets back, okay, Superman?" Her hand pressed his shoulder, and she kissed him once more, smack dab in the middle of his forehead. "Good to see you pushing the envelope a bit. Let's make it under better circumstances next time, okay?"

Her footsteps retreated, and Emmett leaned his head against the wall, closing his eyes and letting the comforting sounds of the clinic lull him to sleep.

⌒⌒⌒

"Come on, Em. Just a few more steps. That's it." Casey opened the door to her apartment, and the scent of lemon polish hit him, sunlight warm on his skin as she propped him against the wall and started undoing his laces. Emmett didn't know what was wrong with him. It felt like he was moving in a fog, struggling to string his thoughts together, unable to do the simplest tasks.

The doctor had returned, taken one look at him, and told Angie to cancel the rest of her appointments for the day. "Okay, slip your feet out. Now, how about heading to the bathroom to get you out of these clothes? There's blood all over them."

The journey down her short hallway felt like a mile. Emmett dropped down on the lid of the toilet and took her hand. "He's all right? You're sure about that."

A thousand possibilities had run through his mind before her return, and none of the outcomes were good.

Two cool palms cupped his cheeks. "He's going to be fine, Em. A concussion and some stitches. I talked to the doctor on call at the ER. They're keeping him over-night for observation, but the guy is out of danger. You did good. I'm going to turn on the shower and let you be. Paul sent over some pajama bottoms and a T-shirt. Towels are on the hook next to the tub. Give a holler if you need me."

The door creaked as it opened, clicking when it shut. Emmett shrugged his way out of his shirt, felt its stiffness from dried blood, and had to choke back nausea. His hand reached past the shower curtain, and the hot gush on his cold skin had him quivering, hard, fit to have him falling apart at the seams. He fumbled for the wall, found the hand towel, and buried his face in the thick terry cloth as the sobs rose up. A howl wasn't too far off.

The door swung open again, and she was back, the curtain of her hair swinging against his cheek and neck as her sturdy arm wrapped around his waist. "Emmett, let me help you. You've been through a lot, more than you realize, and it's socking it to you. Don't be so tough. Let

me get you undressed and in that shower. You'll feel better. Promise."

*Miss Sunshine again, probably has birds flitting
around her head.* Something inside of him snapped, made
him nasty. "I don't need any help! I'm sick and tired of
everyone coddling me, treating me like I'll break. I'm
blind, damn it, and today's little joy ride has taught me I
have to accept my limitations. It's pure luck that man is
all right, and I need a little time to process that, so how
about you get out of here and leave me alone?"

Emmett could feel her withdrawal even before Casey
stepped outside the door, like he'd slapped her—hard.
The pain welled up, forcing him to chew on it, swallow it,
and choke it down, forming a cold, hard lump in his
stomach. He wouldn't blame her if she kicked him out.
Emmett couldn't even stand himself. Why would anyone
else? *What are you doing, biting the hand that feeds you?
Big mistake.*

ⲉⲟⲉⲟ

Casey stood against the wall, swiping at the tears
running down her face, trying not to be hurt. He'd been
through a lot. It was completely understandable to lash
out. *Doesn't make it any easier.* She listened for movement inside, waiting for the heat in her face to die down.
There was a brief pause, the shower curtain rattled, and
the water began to splash.

Clearing her throat, she pushed off the wall, went to
her bedroom, grabbed Paul's clothes, and a pair of her
own pajamas. Grabbing hold of her courage, she stepped
back in the bathroom and pulled the curtain aside. Emmett had his head pressed against the wall, shoulders
bowed as the water beat down on him. That he didn't
even acknowledge her presence nearly did Casey in.

"Misery loves company, so here I am." One more step, the hardest one to take, and she was sharing the tiny space with him.

A sudden lunge and he swung around, pulling her into his arms, his lips sealing over hers as the water encased them in a warm, wet rush. "God, I'm sorry I bit your head off. I didn't mean any of it. I do need help, lots of help. Most of all, I really need you." His hands were roving over her body, playing her like a fine instrument and driving her in closer when Emmett froze and his lips curved upward. "Case, you're still wearing your clothes."

A fit of nervous giggling stole her breath away as she glanced down. "Yeah, I guess I am. Talk about being impulsive. Guess you're not the only one."

Her fingers started fighting with the buttons of her shirt when his hands closed around them, steady and sure.

"Let me. I've got this covered." Any sense of awkwardness was gone as he made a trail down the front of her, deliberately taking his time. Casey closed her eyes, wearing his shoes for the moment, allowing her senses to take over as the blouse dropped to the floor, followed by her bra, skirt, and underwear. The water, the steam swirling around them, his hands, his body, his lips—all of it was absolutely mind-blowing.

A collage of colors and patterns exploded across the dark canvas of her eyelids. Emmett hit the knob, turning off the shower, and they stumbled through the curtain, onto the floor, sprawling in a tangle of limbs. She had to get closer, would crawl under his skin if there was any way. "Casey." His voice slowly penetrated her brain, made her open her eyes to find herself plastered to his body. "Case, it's pretty cold down here. What do you say we take this to someplace more comfortable?"

They were in a puddle, and the water was running in rivulets down his face, droplets falling from her hair into

Emmett's golden eyes. Casey scrambled up off the tiles to grab a towel, and he had hold of her again, pulling her back down, wrapping them both in terry cloth. "What about someplace more comfortable?" She barely managed the words before he pressed her down on the floor, making sure the towel was under her body, his hands braced on either side of her head.

"In a minute. Can't wait here, not a second." Casey rose to the occasion, opening herself to him, showing him the way home, even though Emmett needed no assistance in that department. Definitely *not* a man who needed any help in all matters that counted—mind, body, and soul. His forehead pressed to hers, more water dripping on her face, so like his kisses that she had to press her lips to his. "I love you," he whispered as they broke apart, sending her off kilter, over the moon.

The surprises kept coming as he rose up from the floor, first to his knees, then to his feet. Seeing him stagger for a moment, Casey realized he had to be exhausted. She reached for him, meaning to give him support when his strong arms caught her up once more and carried her to the bedroom. Emmett laid her down with a sigh, his lips brushing her cheek, and she locked hers with his insistently.

"I love you too." An indescribable smile crossed his face at the sound of her words, a light making his golden eyes glow, and he slipped away into a heavy slumber.

Casey knew what it was to be in a combustible state, enduring such contrasts, from steaming water to the cold tile and now this cozy nest. She drew closer, like a spoon. He was like a furnace. Next to him, she'd never grow cold. Her hand rested on his chest, and she relished the even rhythm of his heart. Closing her eyes once more, she became lost in the sound of his breathing. Like the tide rolling into shore, his pull carried her with him, and she knew the words had not been idle. Casey loved him like no other.

♥♥♥

Waking up in the arms of a woman, after a night of making love. Nothing better. *Having my cake and eating it too.* Fuzzy headed, every joint in Emmett's body had gone loose. Good thing he wasn't made of bolts. One move and he'd fall apart.

*Coffee. Gotta have it. Now.* One coherent thought penetrated the rest of the muddle and made him poke a foot out of bed to test for the floor. The feel of Casey's arm lingered on his chest, skin on skin, her breath on his neck, bathing him in her scent. There was no inclination to ever move again.

Dredging up some will power, he finally managed to shed the covers and stand up. Every part of him screamed to crawl back in. Shivering, Emmett fished around on the floor for his T-shirt, tugged it over his head, and made his way to the door. "*Damn it all to hell!*"

Casey snorted from the vicinity of the covers. "What's wrong, love? Did that attack dresser jump you?" Laughter followed, muffled by covers or perhaps a pillow? His fingers itched to fling something at her, anything, but he held on to a modicum of control.

Emmett's knee throbbed as he stood with his hands on his hips, fighting back a torrent of curse words. "A night with you and you've got me so turned around, I forgot where I was. Stop laughing, why don't you? I'm dying here."

Footsteps came his way, an arm around his waist, and her lips skimmed his back, shoulder, neck, light and fast as a hummingbird's wings. "Let me look. I'm a doctor." Another kiss to the offended area had his fingers clamping down on her shoulders. "Why don't I show you the way? You're at my house. I know it best."

Emmett filled his hands with her, felt her warmth, her hair brushing his face, and he was moving back to the bed. "I can find my way just fine once I'm aware of my surroundings. I am very aware right now." Pressing her down on to the mattress, he tugged the blankets up to their shoulders and held her close, burying his face in the crook of her neck. "Good thing it's Saturday because I'm not fit for much."

Casey's laughter came to him again, a musical sound, her fingers dancing over his skin. "What *are* you fit for, Em?" Her hand stopped its wandering and took pause on his heart, sure to feel its wild beating while his body began to tremble.

His lips grazed her collarbone and his palm pressed against her chest, finding a strong rhythm to rival his own. "I'm fit for you. I do love you, Case, more than anything." She echoed his words and drew him in for another kiss. *Who needs coffee? This is better.* Lost in her arms, her body, no longer aware of where he left off and she began, sweet oblivion took him down for the count.

# CHAPTER 14

The day had been long, excruciatingly so. Nonstop in the clinic with severe cases of the flu, always scary because of how they could turn; nasty bouts of the stomach bug; and a patient with pneumonia that was troubling her. Casey would have to keep a close watch. She'd call Mrs. Jennings, check in on her in the morning.

Mr. Howard was still weighing on her mind. Recognizing classic signs of a heart attack—shortness of breath, a burning in his chest, and pain radiating along his left arm—she'd called for the ambulance. No if's, no and's, no but's. No arguments.

Her father had exhibited the signs, had argued too well, blowing it off as indigestion, and lost in the end. Not this time. Hindsight really was twenty-twenty. When the ambulance crew confirmed her fears en route—a full-blown cardiac arrest underway—her knees went weak. Thanks to her forethought and their fast action, Mr. Howard was still alive. She prayed he'd stay that way.

Her feet hurt and her head pounded. All she wanted to do was sleep after taking a long soak in luxuriously hot bubbles. Better yet would be a soak with Emmett, the one island of calm in her life. Yes, Casey would get presentable and go as soon as she dredged up the energy. Feet dragging up the steps, she nearly stumbled over a woman perched on a suitcase at her door. "Mom?"

ひかひ

"Why didn't you call?" Casey stood at the stove, waiting for the kettle to boil, resisting the strong urge to cry. All she wanted was a little peace and quiet, to get a dose of Emmett. Glancing over at her mother, ensconced at her kitchen table, the chances of her evening ending the way she preferred were heading south.

"Can't a mother surprise her daughter?" Elsie Mitchell raised her eyebrows and pursed her lips, adding a dramatic effect to her injured tone. She was dressed impeccably in a hunter-green wool suit, the smart jacket and pants flattering her figure. Casey didn't know why but it aggravated her to no end seeing her mother so put together, nails painted—*manicured no less*—her dark hair frosted. And where were her worry lines? *Must have been botoxed away.* Wasn't a grieving widow supposed to be falling apart?

"I would've liked to prepare for you, that's all." *Or run away, hid out at Em's.* The teapot whistled, providing a distraction. Casey tucked her hair behind her ear and let her breath out slowly. The chair scraped the floor behind her, and her mother joined her at the sink, wrapping an arm around her waist. The day caught up with her in that moment, and she welcomed the support that was offered, leaning in to her mother.

"Sweetheart, you're obviously bushed. Why don't you go sit down in the living room, and I'll bring these out." She spoke softly, wearing a smile that recalled her childhood, making surrender easy.

Giving her mother a nod and a quick hug, Casey took up camp on the sofa, wrapped in a throw blanket, reveling in the feel of the hot cup in her hands when her mother delivered it.

Elsie situated herself on the other end and took a sip of her own tea, letting out a sigh as she sat back. "I'm sorry, honey. I should've called. It's just been months since I've seen you and I missed you. How are things at your new job?"

Casey shifted so she could look at her visitor, dusting off a grin and some enthusiasm. This was her mother, after all! "The clinic is wonderful, really. Most of the time, it's slow as molasses, and I'm getting to know everyone around here. Today was hectic, but nothing close to the ER." Shuddering at the memory of her last assignment, she buried her nose in her teacup. "How are things for you?"

Her mother set down her cup and leaned forward to pat her leg, eyes sparkling, more animated than she'd been in a long time. "I love Florida! I've got a group of friends at the condo. We shop, go to the spa, meet for lunch. There's always something to do, and the weather is incredible. I walk the beach out front every day, sometimes twice! We've got a heated, indoor swimming pool, and I try and take a dip as often as possible. It's absolutely invigorating! You really ought to come down for a visit, get away from the snow and the cold."

A sinking feeling made Casey swallow hard, fighting the burning behind her eyes and the unintended sting of her mother's words. She had obviously moved on with her life. Attempting to cover her emotions, Casey concentrated on the contents of her cup. "That sounds wonderful, Mom. I wish I could go, but I've only just started at the clinic. It's too soon for vacation time."

Elsie must have experienced some mother's intuition because she set down her cup and scooted down, wrapping an arm around her daughter. "Honey, if there's one thing I've learned, life is too short. Don't put everything off like your father and I did."

There it was, the sadness Casey expected. Looking into her mother's dark eyes, she saw the pain and sheen of tears, threatening to fall. "It took me some time to pick myself up after Charlie died. That's part of the reason I left. I didn't want you to see me that way, to worry, and I couldn't stand the memories. Thirty-five years in that house! To be there without seeing that face—I might as well have climbed into that coffin with him."

Her eyes closed tightly for a moment, her throat working as one drop slid down her cheek. Setting her shoulders, she opened her eyes and found her smile. "Once I realized that wasn't going to happen, I figured out that I was still alive and had better start acting that way. Your father wouldn't want it any other way. He'd want us to go on, to be happy. That's all we can do to honor his memory. Are you happy, sweetheart?"

Nodding insistently, Casey buried her face against her mother's chest, smelled her familiar perfume, discovered it was still a soft place to fall. "Yes, I truly am, Mom. I love this town and my work. Most of all, I've found someone, a man named Emmett Henry who lives outside of town. We've been spending a lot of time together. I've rejoined the land of the living, too, Mom."

Her mother's hand trembled as she began to stroke her daughter's hair, and her voice was no longer steady, emotional tides running high for both women.

"I'm so happy for you, honey. Tell me all about him." Casey closed her eyes, her heart starting to flutter as Emmett filled her mind. Taking great care, she began to paint a picture of the man who had become her everything.

෴

White lights glittered on the shrubs, like fairy lights or fireflies. When and how had Emmett managed? Casey had no doubt he'd done so on his own. The results wouldn't be nearly as satisfying if the man didn't feed his independent streak. A wreath of twigs hung on the door with cardinals, blue jays, and chickadees nesting in the branches, another seasonal addition. That he would spruce up the place for her mother's visit made Casey's eyes sting and her heart fill to overflowing.

One solid rap on the thick panel of oak and it swung open, an amazing smell and warmth pouring out to greet them.

Emmett looked good enough to eat, ruggedly handsome in the chocolate sweater that favored him and jeans that hung just the right way on his tall, lean frame. His dark hair was brushed until it shone, fashionably tousled, if purely accidental, and his honey eyes glowed as he turned toward the sound of their voices and opened his arms to draw Casey in.

"Hey, it's about time you got here." She stepped into the solid wall of his body, and his arms closed around her, steady and secure, his lips grazing her cheek. "I missed you," he told Casey softly, pulling her inside. She stepped away, and Emmett offered his hand, along with a welcoming smile. "Mrs. Mitchell, I'm Emmett Henry. Pleased to meet you."

Her mother's reaction was appalling, eyes widening and jaw falling open as her body went rigid. She accepted his hand briefly, stiff in her response. "Call me Elsie. Thank you for inviting us to your home."

She stepped back as if bitten, her eyes flashing in an angry glare directed at her daughter. *Thank God, he can't see her! Talk about a slap in the face.* A rush of heat flooded Casey's cheeks, filling her with shame at her mother's reaction.

Emmett, God love him, didn't miss a beat, gesturing to the living room with a little bow. "There's coffee, tea, and some appetizers in the next room. Won't you come sit down?"

He turned in Casey's direction, effectively blocking her with one hand latching onto her waist, the other resting on her neck, his sharp whisper meant for her ears only. "You didn't tell her, did you?"

"I don't think of you as a blind person, Em. I think of you as mine. Besides, I didn't want her to prejudge you." Her arms wound around him, and she pressed her head against his chest, listening to the steady rhythm of his heart.

A low rumble of a chuckle vibrated in her ear, and a reluctant smile tugged at his mouth. "I think she's done that already. Better dust off my tap shoes, get ready for my song and dance. Come on, sweetheart. It's show time." His lips burned a trail across her neck, jaw, and finally landed on her mouth proved she had been forgiven.

They settled on the sofa before the fire. Casey couldn't help but eye the recliners with regret. She'd much rather cozy up in Emmett's favorite chair with him. Her mother had already helped herself to a cup of coffee and a plate of stuffed mushrooms. Marveling at the fine china and teapot to match, she opted for tea, watching their host with pride as he carefully prepared his own cup of coffee without mishap.

Emmett raised the cup to his lips, and she could swear he tossed a wink her way as his arm found her waist and pulled her a little closer. *Never knew he could be such a charmer! Pulling out all the stops here. What other surprises are up his sleeve?* "So, Elsie, did you have a good flight up from Florida?" His tone was pleasant, his smile genuine, the picture of relaxed. Casey knew better, feeling the undercurrent of tension in his touch.

Her mother set her empty plate down and dusted crumbs from her lap. "Your mushrooms were wonderful. As for my flight, it went very well, thank you. I'm hoping for the same when I go back. I'm missing the warmer weather already."

Her coffee eyes roved around the room, focusing in on the mantel and Emmett's photos, causing her to stare in speculation. "Emmett, I hope you won't find me too forward. How long have you been—that is to say, how did you become—"

*Nothing like forgetting small talk. No beating around the bush for my mother.*

"Blind? No, you don't offend me." His hold on Casey's waist tightened, reassuring her. He really was okay with this. "After all, curiosity makes people wonder, and it is rather obvious. I had an incident in a barroom about a year ago."

Casey jumped in before her mother could jump to more conclusions. "He and his brother are horse farmers. They'd stopped in for a beer at the end of the day when Em tried to help a girl in trouble."

He raised his hand, giving a little shake of the head. This was Emmett's tale to tell. "A guy was threatening the preacher's daughter—sweet, little thing. I can't stomach a man hurting a woman. I stepped in, asked him to leave her alone. The guy hit me over the head with a chair. I've been blind ever since."

For the first time since their arrival, Casey saw a crack in her mother's hardened exterior as her gaze softened, and she actually leaned forward to take his hand. "What a terrible thing to happen to you. How *do* you manage to make ends meet?"

"*Mother!* That is none of your business. He's not a gold digger, for God's sake." Once more, his hold tightened while his free hand began to tap on the arm of the couch, keeping time with the pulse fluttering at the base of his throat. His jaw clenched for an instant, and there was a dangerous flash in those golden eyes before his smile turned them to sweet honey.

"That's all right, Case. She's your mother, looking out for you. You'd better believe that I'll want everything on the table should I be blessed with a daughter and she's dating some guy." Emmett paused, collecting his thoughts. *Steady as she goes.* "My parents—they're both gone now—set aside some money for me, and I've always been pretty wise managing my affairs. Add the settlements I was awarded for this—" He gestured to his eyes with a rueful grin. "—and I've actually got more money than I could spend in a lifetime. So, to make it clear, I am not after your daughter for her money. On that note, I need to check on dinner. You two do girl talk or whatever it is mothers and daughters do."

His tone was light, his steps sure as Emmett walked out of the room, but Casey knew when he was putting on a show. The man was hurting.

*Scratch that. He's angry,* she amended, listening to the rattling in the kitchen punctuated by the slamming of a cabinet door. Good, because Casey was fit to explode. "Mom, what is the matter with you?" she hissed, wishing there was something to throw at the woman on the other end of the couch. Too bad her teacup was empty. "Emmett is a great guy!"

"Well, he's certainly easy on the eyes and does seem like a good man." Elsie Mitchell set her cup down slowly and deliberately, sliding down the couch to take her daughter's hand, vying for her complete attention. "But, sweetheart, do you really see yourself getting serious with someone with his…limitations? Think about all you'll have to do for him, probably do already."

"Pardon me, Mrs. Mitchell. Sorry, Elsie. My parents taught me to be respectful. I'm going to try my best while I call you on what you just said, and no, I wasn't eavesdropping. My ears are better than most."

Casey felt a lump in the pit of her stomach as Emmett took them both by surprise, stepping up behind the couch without notice. His cheeks were streaked with crimson, his eyes glittering brightly, yet his hands were gentle when they settled on her shoulders, smoothing away some of her fears.

"I keep my own house. No hired help, no fairies, and definitely not Casey, although she tried one day, and I bit her head off for that." His tone was apologetic on the last, a crooked grin directed her way. "I clean, do laundry, cook. I'll admit, much as I hate it, a teenage boy does my mowing and plowing. I hear plenty of able-bodied people prefer such an option. I *do* clear my own porch and walk."

His jaw came up at that one, feet planted, standing tall. "I manage most of my affairs online, it really is a wonder these days, and keep my errands to once a month for banking and groceries. I could hire a health aide or something for that, but it's not necessary, thanks to my stubborn brother. Seems to be a family trait people tell me—his name is Wyatt. He's loyal as all get out and insists on taking me out, would do anything for me and it goes both ways."

His voice cracked on the last, emotions running high, but Emmett kept himself under control. "If not Wyatt, then it's his wife, Sammie. They live just a piece up the road. They have a beautiful little man, Jackson, named after my father. As a matter of fact, the night Casey and I met, when she got stranded in a snowstorm, your amazing daughter delivered my nephew. You'll have to ask her about that sometime. Right now, I hope the two of you will come join me for dinner before the food gets cold."

*Emmett-one hundred. Mother-zero.* Impressive, the way he made his strong, family values clear before effectively steering the conversation away from himself. Her mother was rendered speechless. Put in her place without a doubt, she excused herself to the bathroom, stuttering along the way.

Casey looked up to see Emmett with his head bowed, his eyes closed, chest rising and falling as if he'd been in a battle. Fitting, after such a duel with words. "Em, I am so sorry. I don't know what's wrong with her."

He straightened and moved around the couch, offering her his hand. She accepted, allowing him to draw her close and press a kiss to her cheek. "It's all right, really. I get it. I'm not every mother's idea of a good catch."

Casey ground to a halt on the way to the dining room and rammed her palms against his chest. "You listen up right now. As far as I'm concerned, you're the only fish in the sea for me and don't you forget it." Her voice was rising in volume, and she didn't care if her mother heard every word.

Emmett's hands skimmed up her arms, to her cheeks, a smile coming into full bloom along the way and he pressed his lips to hers, making her body go loose. "Okay, okay. You've set me straight. Is it because I'm easy on the eyes?" *He did hear what Mother said!*

A fit of giggles threatening to rise, she did the only thing to stop them, pressing her mouth to his until they both couldn't breathe. "No, it's because you really know how to kiss."

Her mother's heels came clicking their way. Stealing more kisses would have to wait until later. Emmett squeezed Casey's hand and brought her to the dining room off the kitchen, one he had not used on her other visits. They had taken all their meals in the cozy, casual atmosphere of the kitchen.

Setting foot inside the room, she had to gasp, and the tears were stinging her eyes once more. "Oh, Em! This is beautiful!" Candles were lit, and the fancy china laid, while steaming dishes of food awaited them. How long had it taken him to make everything look just so? If there was one thing Casey was sure of, this table had been prepared by his hands alone. He pulled out a chair for her, slid her in, and moved to the next, waiting expectantly.

Flustered once more, her mother slipped in to her seat. "Why thank you, Emmett. It's been a long time since I've been spoiled by a man." She smiled up at him, forgetting herself, as everyone did the more time they spent with this incredible man, falling under his spell.

His fingers skimmed up her arm, and he set a hand on her shoulder, giving back a genuine smile of his own. "My grandfather, father, and brother have taught me well. Women are to be treasured, more precious than anything else on this earth. Now please, help yourselves. I hope nothing's gone cold in all of the hullabaloo."

The dishes began to make their rounds at the table. Asparagus in hollandaise sauce. Twice baked potatoes topped with real bits of bacon, chopped in fine pieces. Steaks with shaved cheese and onion curls on top. Fresh-baked rolls kept warm under a towel. A bottle of wine should they empty the glasses that had already been filled. Chocolates for a taste of sweetness.

Emmett waited for his guests to serve themselves first, taking great care to fill his own plate, taking small helpings in an effort to keep everything in its place. Casey resisted the urge to help him when his steak almost slipped off the fork, but he made the save. The sound of silverware scraping on plates was the only noise as everyone became engrossed in their meal.

"Emmett, you have outdone yourself. I'm going to need to take cooking lessons from you, Casey too, I bet. It never was my strong point was it, sweetheart? Your father made the best meals we ever had." There, again, was the mother she remembered from before, not the cold, distant woman from the funeral or the polished and poised stranger that awaited her yesterday. Or the rude, contemptuous shrew that walked into this house.

Casey answered warily. "As long as he could fire up the grill. Daddy had that baby running all year round. It's probably part of what killed him. Please excuse me." She took her dish and fled to the kitchen, the sob rising and the tears finally breaking the dam. Scanning the room for anything, she saw a dish towel and made do, cramming it over her mouth. Her shoulders began to shake as her emotions finally took over.

Firm, strong hands were on her shoulders, turning her into the wall of Emmett's chest. Thank God, it was him. She couldn't deal with her mother right now. "Hey—hey. It's all right. You're all right. Let it out, baby. You've been holding this in all night, haven't you? Maybe longer than that. Let go. I've got you."

His voice was low and deep, a gentle balm for all the raw spots inside of her. He began to rock her gently, side to side, his hand cupping the back of her head, making her feel the total security of childhood, once more, when all was right in her world.

*Don't forget about his world going topsy-turvy.* To-night must have been rough on him too. She let out a lingering breath and pulled away, flitting over his lips with a butterfly kiss. "I'm good now. Thank you, really. Why don't I start the dishes and—"

The flash of warning in his eyes stopped her as his jaw visibly clenched, unclenching with an effort. "I'll wash," he said. "If you want to bring things out to me, that's fine. I don't want to take you away from your mother. You're my guests. Please go back to your mom, Case. She's worried about you. Remember that losing your dad hasn't been easy on her either. Looks can be deceiving. I know all about that."

His hands reached out, found her, and drew her in for a quick hug and kiss. "Go on now," he whispered in her ear before turning to the sink. She could hear the water running and dishes clinking already when she stepped into the dining room.

"Casey, honey. Please come sit. We need to talk." Her mother patted the chair beside her before dabbing at red-rimmed eyes. Some of the ice in Casey's stomach melted. She obliged, turning to her mother and examining her more closely, thinking about Emmett's words.

Lines of exhaustion had appeared around her eyes, her forehead was creased, and there was a dullness in her gaze. All the wind seemed to have gone out of her, and she was drooping. Further inspection proved dressing with flair, makeup, and a new hair-do couldn't hide the pain lurking in the shadows.

Her mother's hand reached out, and Casey grabbed hold, through the hurt. "Mother, what you did tonight was awful, absolutely awful. Em has made me the happiest I've been in a long time, even before Daddy died. All those years, sacrificing, working my butt off, a part of me felt like Cinderella at the ball, waiting to get picked to dance. I started to doubt it would ever happen, and then I stumbled into Emmett. Trust me, he was a reluctant prince at first. His confidence was shaken pretty badly, and you just added a few more dents to his armor, but I think I make him happy too."

She could barely keep her emotions in check but managed to push on. *Had* to push on. Casey owed Emmett that much. "I love him, Mom. You should understand that. You might be too jaded by Daddy's death that you're not willing to take a leap of faith, but I'm not. It's scary, and I don't know if we'll catch each other, but I've got to try. Can't you accept that?" Her voice broke on the last and she had to look down at her lap, or the waterworks would start running again.

A smothered sob broke from the woman beside her, and Casey found herself pulled into her mother's arms, Elsie stroking her hair the way she always had when a little girl needed comforting. "Yes, yes, honey, I can accept that. I'm so sorry for how I've behaved, and I'll apologize to Emmett too, I promise. I see how you glow, and now I know that he's lit the candle. I see it burning in him too. *Anyone* would have to be blind if they couldn't see how that man worships you." Elsie took a shuddering breath and broke away, standing up. "If you excuse me, I have someone I must make amends to immediately."

Shaking her head, Casey picked up her wine glass and drank the last drop, eying the bottle, wondering if anyone would notice if she drank the whole thing. Glancing at Emmett's spot, she noticed that his glass had been untouched. That settled it. He needed fortification more than her. Time to bring in the cavalry if necessary.

Grabbing the bottle and her empty glass in one hand, his glass in the other, she walked in to the kitchen just in time to see her mother giving Emmett a hug. *White flag offered and accepted!* Holding up the bottle, she called out brightly. "I think this moment calls for a celebration! How about some wine?"

Emmett accepted his gratefully, his throat undulating in slow waves as he drained the glass in about two swallows. Her mother wasn't far behind.

*What the hell?* Casey's second helping went down smoother then the last, making everything a little softer around the edges and dishes became a team effort. Her mother insisted, and Emmett actually surrendered. *White flag again!*

⌒⌒⌒

"Emmett, thank you for a wonderful evening. You've proven yourself to be a true gentleman. Most would've thrown me out in the snow." Elsie stepped forward and gave him a quick hug, her hand lingering on his when she stepped back. "Your parents would've been very proud of the man you've become, as I am of my daughter."

She turned to Casey next, pulling her into a fierce embrace. "Please forgive me, both of you, and blame it on an overprotective mother. I'm going to go back to the apartment now and leave you two alone as a peace offering. I'll come get you tomorrow, Case, and we'll go shopping, do lunch, my treat." A hasty kiss on the cheek and she stepped outside, but not before Casey could see the tears about to fall.

As soon as the engine cranked and retreated into the distance, Emmett had Casey pressed against the door, his hands roaming from her hips, up her sides. She had the impression that he was cataloguing each rib, continuing onward, lodging his fingers in her hair. His lips devoured hers, burning at their touch.

"Do you know what you did to me tonight? Coming in here, covered in that amazing scent, something out of this world and unfamiliar, and all I wanted to do was inhale more of you? Tormenting me when I had to behave! Couldn't give your mother *more* of a reason to hate me."

"She doesn't hate you—not anymore," Casey murmured, answering to his touch, like a fine instrument being tuned by his talented hands. Her back bowed, and her leg bent, sliding up the side of his body until his hand hooked her knee and her fingers dug into the nape of his neck. "You're pretty irresistible yourself. I couldn't drink any more wine, or I'd lose all control."

"And what were you thinking, wearing a dress? Listening to it swish, feeling that material glide against my skin, and nylons? Good Lord, woman, I want to rip everything off you and take you. Right here. Right now." His breathing was becoming labored, his voice getting raspier by the word. When her palm slowly trailed down the side of his cheek, to the hollow where his collarbone met his neck, halting at his chest, his heart was skipping.

For Emmett, everything was all about sensation, and she wanted to give him what he craved. Casey closed her eyes and savored the taste of his mouth, the warmth of his breath, and the scratchy texture of his sweater grazing her skin. Spinning the kiss out until time seemed to stop, she went loose in his arms. "What are you waiting for?" She asked in a faint whisper, on the brink of losing all capacity to speak or think.

Without hesitation, Em brought them down to the floor, his body shielding her from the hard, unforgiving tile and the cold draft sneaking in from a fine crack beneath the door. Hardly sated, he scooped her up after a breather and carried her to the living room, leaving a puddle of clothes behind, laying her out on the rug before the fireplace, reveling in the contrasting heat on his skin.

Casey loved to watch the dancing shadows of flickering flames flitting over his body, setting his eyes alight. This go around, they took their time, dozing off, wrapped in nothing more than each other. Sometime, in the wee hours of the night, Emmett roused her and tucked her under his arm, bringing her to his room. When morning stretched its first fingers of light across the bed, Casey awoke snug against his side, pleasantly sore, disinclined to move.

Shopping with Mom could start late. This girl was sleeping in.

# CHAPTER 15

*C*asey's coming. The words kept playing, a track on repeat, like a drumbeat thrumming through his blood and his head. Funny. She'd only been a part of Emmett's life for about six weeks, yet he felt like there'd be no making it through six minutes without her. Make that six seconds.

Like an addict needing a fix, playing the waiting game made him restless. *Getting so sick and tired of being cooped up in this house!* Stuck in a rut of the tried and true. *She deserves better, to see and do it all.* The voice in his head sneered, nagging at him, making him pace through room after room, wandering the halls, going from floor to floor, attic all the way down to the basement.

She'd been dropping by more and more often like a cool, tall drink after a long, desperate walk across a blazing desert. Sometimes, Wyatt would drop Emmett at her place, but her surprise visits were the best, out of the blue. Casey seemed content with the way things were, but this was Valentine's Day. Emmett should be taking her out, plying her with wine, good food, dressing her with jewels, dancing her around a fancy hotel room. Yet she was coming here and selfish fool that he was, Emmett was going to let her.

Movie night. Casey was bringing the flick. He'd take care of the ice cream sodas and popcorn. She wanted to spend time with him. *Lord knows why, but I'll take it, take whatever I can get.*

The movie was for a sense of normalcy, for her sake, because it's what you do with a date. Emmett figured he could occupy himself with breathing in the scent of her, soaking in her warmth, running his fingers over her. While she did the same, he could read the map that was Casey Mitchell, use his lips as a compass.

*The hell with this.* Out of sorts from waking up early, knowing he fell short and dwelling on it, Emmett couldn't stand the confines of his house or brain any longer. Field trip time. He'd cross over to his brother's place, pester Wyatt. He pulled on his boots, coat, hat and gloves, Trusty McGee in his pocket. Em wanted to go solo and rely on himself.

The air was cold, but not bitter, sun beating down and warming the top of his head. This journey was much tamer than the road trip to the clinic. Trudging through the snow, some three feet deep, was tough going. Emmett fell a few times, down on his hands and knees, having a hard time catching his breath. *It's like Catch-Twenty-Two, two steps forward, three steps back. Still have to ask Wyatt or Jimmy to clear the trail between the two houses.*

A little farther and he became disoriented, falling on his hands and knees, not sure about the right direction. Unsure of himself, hyperventilating, heart hammering, Emmett picked himself up and kept on going anyway.

*Add bullheaded to the checklist, another Henry family trait. Damned if I'm turning back.* The image of his father floated in his mind, so strong and clear, it was like looking at a photograph, and a voice rang out in his head, deep and familiar, striking a cord that vibrated to his soul. *'Get moving, son. Almost there.'*

ભ્રજ્ય

Sammie glanced out the kitchen window, enjoying the sight of the birds flitting through the trees. Several took flight, as if startled, as one of the smaller saplings shook, losing its coating of snow and a cloud of steam rose up in the air, followed by a flash of red, like a cardinal. *He wouldn't—yes he would, that son of a gun.*

Emmett was heading out of the woods, the scarlet cap she made him for Christmas like a banner. His footsteps were faltering. When he fell, she covered her mouth, holding back a cry at the unfamiliar sight of fear flashing across her brother-in-law's face. An instant later, grim determination took over. He gained his feet and kept moving toward the house.

Emmett came with his feet, hands, heart, and mind that God gave him. No phone. No cane. Nothing but guts, pure grit. Sammie's eyes started to sting. "Wyatt, your brother, the stubborn mule, is coming. Don't go out just yet, let him try and make it on his own, but be ready if he needs you."

ભ્રજ્ય

Emmett gripped his coffee cup with both hands, inhaled its reassuring scent, looking forward to gulping it down. Giving himself a mental shake, he cracked a smile and opened his arms. "Okay, hand over the little man. That cooing is driving me crazy. I've got to have him."

Sammy set the warm, squirming bundle in his hands, and he tucked him under his chin. The smell of baby powder. The touch of that amazingly soft skin. His heat. Listening to those sweet little nonsense noises filled Emmett with a sense of satisfaction. Mission accomplished.

Wyatt nudged him in the ribs, a little harder than was

necessary. "So, little brother, I heard about your excursion the other day. Word gets around these parts." There was a pause, and a work-hardened hand settled on Emmett's shoulder, clamping down firmly. "What the hell were you thinking, Em, then and today? You know, I'm getting tired of asking you that question."

Emmett took his time answering, snuggling with the baby, whispering some silliness. He brushed Jackson's downy head with his lips, his heart squeezing as Sammie collected him once more to allow Em to drink his coffee. He reached out cautiously to locate the cream and sugar. Sammie left the fixings to him. She knew how touchy he could be about doing for himself.

He took a sip, and another, listening to the insistent tapping of his brother's foot, demanding an answer. "Thought I'd get out. *You* wanted me to get out. So did Casey. So I got out. End of story."

Hiding a grin, he drank some more coffee, down to the bottom of the cup. The vivid picture his brother's smoky glare, scraping his hand over his face, as evidenced by the sound of skin rubbing against the beginnings of a beard, nearly made him laugh. *Pretty ironic, Em. You're starting to see better than you ever did with eyes.*

Wyatt's voice was soft when he spoke. "Please, Em, use some more common sense before you plan these escapades, all right? You've got plenty of people who will be glad to get out with you. Heck, Sammie would love to get out of this place now and then, take a walk, take a breather, okay? You don't have to be the Lone Ranger all the time. Even he had Tonto, remember? At least tell us what you're up to if you insist on doing these things, so we can send out the dogs if you don't show up. Understood?"

"Understood." Emmett extended his hand. His brother took it and pulled him in for a hug. Some back pounding, throat clearing, and rubbing at their eyes for imaginary dirt followed on both parts. "A big brother's job is never done, is it? Just like being a daddy." Emmett's voice was gruff as he turned his head toward the sound of his brother's breathing and a little hiccup. Jackson had relocated to Wyatt's waiting hands.

"I'd rather you took my arms and legs, my sight and sound before anyone took those jobs from me." Another slap on the back and Wyatt left the table. Emmett's sister-in-law poured him another cup of coffee, brushing his cheek with a kiss before she excused herself. They granted him the time and space to find his center, here where he belonged. In the hearts of his family.

୧୬୧୬

The truck idled in Emmett's driveway as he opened the door. "Thanks for the ride, Wyatt. Casey ought to be here soon. I'd best make myself presentable. I'm probably quite a sight." He could never be sure. Mirrors weren't objects of importance in his life before, just something taken for granted when it came to combing his hair or choosing clothes that didn't clash.

"Hell, Em, you'll be fine. The girls have always been in love with you, whether you were covered in mud after falling off a horse, sweating your butt off at the end of the football game, or just rolling out of bed. Remember that time you showed up at church in your pajamas? Dad just about skinned you."

A wave of laughter rose up between them, and Wyatt's hand gripped Emmett's arm. Touch was really important now, filling in the gaps. "Wouldn't mind seeing you in church sometime. Tell Casey we'd like to have her to dinner one of these Sundays to say thank you. I guess

you can come too. Try and behave yourself, little brother."

Emmett let his hand find the way and gave his brother a punch on the arm. It's what brothers did.

❧❧❧

He was standing on the porch, in his stocking feet,
flannel, and jeans, when a car rumbled down his driveway. The wind teased his hair, making him shiver. *Guess
you didn't need to comb your hair after all.* A bouquet of
roses and a box of chocolates waited behind his back.
Traditional gifts from a traditional man. *Except for the
eyes.* Emmett pushed the bitterness, nasty beast that it
was, away and pulled out a smile for her.

A clicking of footsteps sounded on the walk. *Heels?
In this weather?* The breeze carried the scent of her to
him next, that new perfume again, and Casey's arms were
around him, her mouth pressed against his. Her hair
whipped around his face as Emmett's free hand skimmed
up her sides.

*Lord, have mercy. Another dress.* "Are you crazy?
You'll freeze to death. Get in here!" He pulled her inside
the house, and this time Emmett was the one rammed up
against the door with considerable force from a relatively
small package.

"You make me crazy. Happy Valentine's Day, Emmett." Her voice was breathy, and he could hear the smile
in it. She took her time with the next kiss, lighting the
banked coals down in his belly, sending the fire flicking
through his veins. The flowers and candy fell to the floor
as he let his fingers do the walking. Buttons ran up the
center of the dress, making him grin. *Gotta love a challenge.* "Go ahead. Unwrap your present." She sounded
delicious.

Emmett cupped her face with his hands and set his mouth on hers, making her go still. "Don't mind if I do." Demonstrating remarkable patience and strength of will, he swept her into his arms and carried her to the living room. A thick blanket was already spread out on the floor, wine chilling in a bucket, a plate of chocolate-covered strawberries beside it.

Feeling his way with his toes, finding where floor ended and the quilt began, he laid her down and started working his way from the bottom button to the top. When he finally parted her dress with fingers that trembled, lace was waiting for him underneath. *Sweet heaven. Take me now, and I will go a happy man.*

☙❧❧

"Emmett, I look like the Staypuff Marshmallow Man! I can hardly move!"

Casey stood beside him in the field out back. She wanted to build a snowman, they'd build a snowman. First things first, he rounded up long johns, more flannel, heavy socks, coveralls and a spare coat, plus a pair of farm boots. It was hard to tell where the woman was beneath the layers.

He hooked an arm around her waist and drew her in, laughing as her scarf got in the way. Emmett tugged the wool down and planted his mouth on hers. "Can't have you getting sick now, can we? Who would take care of the doc? Let's get going. It's pretty cold out here, and I'm looking forward to getting you out of all of those clothes later on."

She returned the favor of a kiss, effectively turning up the heat, and he was beginning to wonder if they'd be capable of building anything. "I can't wait to do the same to you." Casey lingered a moment longer and broke away. An instant later and a puff of snow hit him, smack in the center of his chest.

"Hey, I went over this with Wyatt. Snowballs are no fair!" Emmett focused on the thud of her boots and source of giggling, picking up his own missile and letting fly. More came his way and there was only one way to end this dispute. An all-out charge and impact. *Whoosh!* They went down in a tangle of limbs, unable to feel a thing what with the barrier of winter gear. "Say Uncle Sam!"

Wheezy laughter was his answer. "What's he got to do with this?" Casey finally managed to squeak out. Emmett leaned in and skimmed her cheeks, nose, and mouth with his lips, tasting snow. *What did we come out here for?*

"It's what Dad always said when he wrestled us or got us with a tickle attack. It meant surrender. How about it?" Her answer wasn't what he expected.

Her fingers, encased in mittens, found their way under his collar and her lips settled on his neck, making him swallow hard. Hardly finished, she moved to his ear and caught the tender skin between her teeth, making him groan. An answering purr came next and then she blazed a trail across his cheek, jaw, finally coming to rest on his mouth. For an instant, Emmett forgot who he was and where he was. There was only this incredible woman.

"Well? Are *you* going to say Uncle Sam, or do I need to torture you some more?" The prospect of torture at her hands almost won, a near thing. Choking out the words, he reluctantly managed to get on his feet, taking her with him. "Still sure about that snowman? We can go in if you want, do something else," Casey teased playfully.

Emmett let out a deep breath he didn't realize had been on hold and squeezed her hand. "Oh, we will, later. Let's do what we set out to do in the first place."

Casey obliged, and they got a system going. She started the snowball, he was the muscle, rolling, packing, stacking. By the time they were done, the finished product was taller than they were. Casey stuck two sticks in the middle, wrapped her scarf around its neck, and added her knit cap.

Em fished in his pocket and pressed the contents into her gloved hands. "There. I raided my mother's button box and the crisper. That ought to do for a face."

Casey brushed his cheek with a kiss, the cold on her skin answering the chill that had set into his bones, but the heat of her breath made it worthwhile. A quick flurry of movement and she took his hand. "Take a look." Emmett pulled his gloves off with his teeth and let them fall to the snow, using his fingers as eyes to see their handiwork as arms came up around his waist and he felt her face pressed against his back.

"He's great, really. I forgot how much fun it was to build a snowman. Of course, frosty kisses, rubbing noses, and the warmth of your breath on my skin are additional perks I never had building them with Wyatt." Slowly, he turned around and opened his arms. Casey stepped in, fitting neatly beneath his chin. "The past few years have made me forget how fun goes until you came along. Happy Valentine's Day, Case."

She shifted, her hands migrating north, pushing his hat from his head, allowing her fingers to thread through his hair. "Same goes for me, Em. All I know is you give me something to look forward to every day." Her lips brushed his once more, finishing with an Eskimo kiss that made them both laugh. "How about we head in for some hot cocoa? I'm freezing my butt off."

Laughing, Emmett somehow finagled hiking her on his back. "No problem. I've got all kinds of ways that I can warm up that pretty behind." He turned toward the house, counting on his intrinsic navigational skills and her guidance.

"Wait a minute. Your hat! Didn't Sammie make it for you?" Casey leaned down, and that was all it took to send his balance off kilter, making them both keel over in the snow. They were on their hands and knees, fighting for breath.

The object in question found its way to his head, snow sliding down his neck. Emmett's cursing only caused more sputtering. He took matters into his own hands, effectively shushing Casey by pinning her beneath him and covering her with kisses.

"Warm yet? No. Let's try this again." No more mishaps befell them on the way in. Peeling out of their layers was an oh-so-enjoyable finish to their adventure. The cocoa was placed on hold while Emmett settled Casey on his lap in the recliner by the fire. He slowly stripped her feet of wet socks, plying her toes with kisses and making her shriek. She wouldn't be quiet until his turn came next. By that point, cocoa was the last thing on their minds. An avalanche would make for a welcome cool-down.

* презрителем*

The movie was over. Emmett was vaguely aware of that fact because the talking had stopped some time ago and mellow music was playing. Casey had chosen some chick flick. He'd tried to pay attention to the story line, really, but she was just too darn distracting. Stuffed with popcorn and chocolate malts, moving was not an option, and he didn't mind.

She let out a sigh while his fingers played through her hair. "Mmm. That feels so good, someone else touching my hair, especially when you do it. You'll have to wash it some time. I love when they do that at the salon.

Of course, if you do, I won't be able to control myself."

She flipped over and rested her chin on his chest. "That was a really good movie. I'd love to travel like that, go to Italy, all over the world. I've never gone anywhere. I always had my nose in a book while everyone else went on break."

Emmett felt his stomach start to twist. She wanted the world, but he couldn't give that to her. *What—with me and be my seeing-eye dog? No thank you.* "Home is mostly all I've ever known. We went to a few horse-shows in neighboring states. I've never even been to Disneyland. Dad was always working too hard to keep the farm going. He always wanted to go, but growing up came too fast, and it never happened. Not much point now."

The fireplace popped as a log shifted and Casey rose up on her knees, covering his face in feather kisses.

His words trailed off. "Oh, Em. You can still go places and do things. Think how strong all the rest of your senses are now. I could tell you everything, let you see them through me. I mean, really, think how amazing sleeping with me is without sight. I've kept my eyes closed a few times. Words can't do it justice, and seeing wouldn't either."

Emmett pressed his hand to the back of her head, bringing her in for a close-up. "You might be right. Why don't we go upstairs and try it again, see if you can paint me a clearer picture with that scrumptious body of yours?"

She didn't say a word and didn't need to either. The hum in her touch proved how eager Casey was to take him places.

Letting her lead the way, Em knew, he'd go anywhere she wanted. *To the ends of the earth, baby...and back again.*

❧❧❧

Nestled in the covers, her body warm against his side, the sound of her soft breathing reminded him what it was to no longer be alone. Emmett wanted this to never end, more than anything in the world. He kissed the top of her head, and she sighed quietly, snuggling closer.

His heart began to pound. Terrified. This girl deserved to see it all, much more than his little patch on earth. What he had to give wasn't enough. Wide-eyed, enveloped in darkness, fear chased Emmett's sleep away.

Morning shook him awake too soon. Emmett came up out of a disturbing dream that scattered with the sounds of cooking downstairs. Scraping his hands over his face and through his hair, he gave it a tug and climbed out of bed. Venturing downstairs, he was out of sorts, grumbling like a bear. "'Morning." He said gruffly and slid into his customary chair at the table. A steaming cup of coffee was already waiting. *Must have heard me coming. Probably sound like an elephant.*

A whiff of perfume drifted his way, and Casey was behind him, hooking an arm around his neck and giving him a kiss on the cheek. "Good morning. You slept late. That's not like you." Despite his inner tug of war, Em couldn't help himself. He turned around and buried his head in her middle, his arms wrapping around her.

"I didn't sleep well. Too many distractions." His hands scoped out the territory and nearly sent him swooning. She was wearing his button down, her sleeves rolled up, hair in a top knot. His fingers played with her hair tie and set the heavy curtain loose, allowing him to revel in its sway around his face. He liked her hair down. Playing with the smooth, weighted length of it, Emmett almost forgot why he was upset and what had robbed him of his sleep.

Casey looped her hands around his neck and kissed the top of his head, moving down to his mouth. "Well, I'll fill your belly with breakfast, see if I can wear you out, and put you back to bed for a nap…only if I get to take one with you."

With that, she was flitting away like a butterfly dancing around his kitchen. Emmett listened to her light footsteps making the rounds and rested his head on his hand. His temples were starting to throb. He really ought to go back to bed now, before saying or doing something regrettable.

Platters made contact with the table, and the scent of good cooking floated around his head. Casey slid onto his lap, taking him by surprise and started feeding him tidbits. That just aggravated, something he couldn't do in return, not without looking hopeless. "So, I was thinking. How about we go somewhere today? We could go to a museum or the movies, head to a mall, and I'll tell you what's good for window shopping."

She pushed a strand of hair behind Emmett's ear, and everything came to a head. He pushed her away, came up fast, and started pacing, mentally counting the steps in his kitchen so there'd be no crash landing or some other such embarrassment.

"No going out. It's no good. I can't. I've tried. Everyone just thinks I'm pitiful. If I can't see anything anymore, there's no sense in traveling. I don't want to feel like I need an interpreter to understand what's going on around me. We'll have to make the best of it right here."

Casey's bare feet padded across the floor, and tears were in her voice when she touched him. God, he hated when a woman cried. It ripped his insides up. "If you can't get out of this house, can't face up to the outside world again, then I can't do this, Emmett…"

Her last words trailed off on the tail end of a sob, and

she rushed out of the room, her footsteps pounding up-stairs. A mere few minutes later, the front door slammed as she ran outside.

The panic rose up inside of him, and Emmett raced out the door, barefoot, in a T-shirt and pajama bottoms. He stubbed his toe in his haste, falling down the steps, floundering on his hands and knees in the snow. "Casey? Casey!" The desperation in his voice sounded in his ears. *You could lose her, you idiot! Not many opportunities to meet people out here.*

Heavy boots thumped his way. *She took your boots.* That thought rocked his world. Her breathing was ragged, warming his neck as she came down in the snow to join him, on her knees. Casey's hands took his, clinging to him as if for life. She was trembling almost as hard as he was.

Emmett's face threatened to crumple as he fought to keep it together. "I don't want to lose you, but I think you'll regret staying with me. You deserve the universe. What do I have to offer you?"

Casey pressed her hand to his chest. "This big heart." Her fingers ran through his hair next. "This beautiful, sharp mind." Her arms wrapped around his chest next. "This soul, your memories, your strong body and back, and these hands that can do magic. You offer everything you've got, give it your all. Best of all, you see me better than anyone else, even better than I do because you're not hung up on the outside. You only care about what counts—the inside."

Emmett broke, head bowed, shoulders shaking, and Casey wouldn't let go of him. "But *my* insides—they're such a mess."

Laughing and crying at the same time, Casey kissed him, cupping his face in her hands. "But what a beautiful mess, and we'll find our way through it together."

# CHAPTER 16

E m, I can't come over today. I'm sick as a dog."
Holding her nose, Casey did her best to sound pitiful and make her throat sound scratchy. She had
been practicing all morning. *You should win an Oscar.*

"I'll call Wyatt and get there as soon as I can. Heck,
I'll walk if I have to." Not even an instant of hesitation.
She sat down at the kitchen table and buried her mouth in
a towel. Otherwise, a laugh attack would give it all away.

"You don't have to do that, really. I don't want you
getting sick, too. No, stay home, Emmett. I'll call when
you can't be contaminated. I think it's the flu. I'm aching
all over, I've got a fever, chills, and I look like a disaster."

His laughter reached out to her over the line, a warm
blanket wrapping tightly around her. "Casey, I couldn't
care less how you look. You could be bald or wear a mop
on your head. Being sick definitely doesn't make a lick of
difference. You get under those covers, drink plenty of
fluids, and I'll be there as soon as I can."

The phone line disconnected before she could put up
any more arguments. *Got him, hook, line, and sinker!* She
couldn't believe how easy it had been. Springing up from
her bed, Casey started dashing around her apartment like
a crazy woman. Time to initiate phase two of her plan.

Making a few last-minute preparations, the shower was the next order of business. She'd been scrambling since daybreak, in hopes that her ruse would work. *Better get washed up and presentable. Knowing Em, he'll be here in an hour.*

Make that a half hour when the key rattled in her door. Casey had insisted on giving him a spare, and he'd done the same for his house. A just in case measure. One never knew when they might need an emergency dose of each other.

"Case, I don't want you to get up. Stay in bed. I'm just fighting with the lock." She had to cover her mouth to hold back the giggles as a blistering string of curses let loose on her doorstep. An instant later and Emmett pushed his way in, juggling a bag of groceries, a veritable gold mine of all things known to man to cure the common cold. "Case, I'm in," he called out only to mutter under his breath. "Smooth. You probably woke her up."

"Oh, I'm awake." She stepped forward and looped her arms around his neck, planting a kiss on his lips and stealing his breath away. His hair was dusted with snow, his cheeks flushed from the walk up the steps, wearing the cold as an extra layer on his coat. He made Casey begin to shiver as his hands skimmed over her body, a reaction that had nothing to do with the chill.

Emmett's eyebrows shot up to his hairline, and his mouth turned up in a grin. "This does not feel like the body of someone who's sick. Are you—you are, you're wearing a bikini." He inhaled deeply, and she couldn't miss the mischief sparking in his honey eyes before they drifted closed.

"You smell heavenly, like coconuts. Did I fall and hit my head or something? I hear Beach Boys' music playing and it is hotter than July in here. Maybe I'm still asleep."

He gave his arm a pinch, wincing and making her laugh. "Nope, not sleeping. Okay, spill it, Doc."

Casey kissed his cheek, then his neck, moving behind him and sliding his coat off broad shoulders. She ran her hands down the reassuring layer of flannel and pressed her cheek to the middle of his back. "I decided to get you out a little at a time, baby steps, you know? This is a test run of a day at the beach so we'll be ready for the real thing because I *love* the beach."

She hung the coat up on the rack by the door, passing in front of him to kneel down and start working on his laces. Emmett set the grocery bag on the floor and rested a hand on top of her head, his fingers playing with her hair. She'd left it loose, knowing how much he loved that fall around her face. Nudging his calf, she eased off one boot as his foot lifted into the air, alternating with the other.

Rather than help Casey to her feet, he came down on his knees, his hands skimming over her arms and becoming still at her waist. Giving her a tug, she fell into him and inhaled the spicy scent of his cologne. "This is one field trip I can handle. Beach baby, take it away." A little more snuggling and kissing ensued until she jumped up and grabbed his hand.

"Come with me. Oh, by the way, I owe you." She spun around, hooked her hands on his ears, and pulled him in for a close-up kiss that stretched out, making them both get a little wobbly. "That's for being the cavalry so quickly when you thought I was sick."

She turned back around, and his hands were on her hips, making her laugh as Emmett tailed her into the bedroom. "There's a swimsuit on the bed. You'll need it. I'll be waiting in the living room." One more peck on the cheek because he was simply so kissable, and Casey flitted out to the next room.

She turned up the stereo, filling the room with the rush of waves rolling into shore, and carefully arranged herself to wait. Her nails were freshly painted, her legs shaved and made smooth with moisturizer, her hair brushed to a high gloss. Strange, really. She'd spent more time preparing for this date than with anyone before who could actually see her. Placing a hand on her stomach to calm its fluttering, Casey pushed out a deep breath, sucking in sharply at the sight of the fine specimen that stepped out of her bedroom.

The suit fit Em perfectly, hugging firm thighs and cutting off at the knees. The material depicted a sunset on the ocean. Casey had chosen his bathing suit because the sky matched the color of his eyes perfectly when his gaze was illuminated by the crackling of his fireplace at home.

He listened for the sound of her breathing and cautiously eased his way across the room, stopping short when a barrier blocked him. His hands settled on his hips and Emmett started to laugh, a deep, rich sound rolling up from his belly, a sound she'd rarely heard. "Casey, do my senses deceive me or is there a kiddie pool sitting here on your living room floor?"

"What can I say? I'm ready to play." She dipped her fingers in and flicked a few drops his way, making him laugh even harder. "Come in here, Em. The water's fine. It's a tropical beach, baby. No goose bumps to be found." Her hands swished in the water, providing a navigational beacon.

Shrugging in surrender, Emmett picked up his foot and stepped in, sighing as he sat down beside her and stretched out in the pleasantly warm water. Casey reached out to the coffee table and set a glass in his waiting hand. "Have a piña colada. Watch the umbrella!" *Watch—bite your tongue!* How many times did they all use words referring to sight? How they all took it for granted.

Emmett's mouth found the straw and her toes started to curl. He leaned back, his arm resting on her shoulders, and took a long draw on the frosty drink, shaking his head in disbelief. "This is amazing. You've thought of everything. Do you need some sunblock? I wouldn't want you to burn, and I'd really like to get my hands on you."

Casey took the drink from his fingers and moved to his lap. "I've got some skin cream you can liberally apply all over from head to toe when we get out. Right now, I can think of some other ways to keep ourselves occupied." Emmett let loose a little growl, and his head dipped to hers. Yes, hands down, this was the best trip ever.

ೞೞೞ

Her head was pleasantly fuzzy from the drinks, her body toasty, heated by the furnace next to her and the thick comforter covering them as they took up residence on the couch. She ran her fingers through Emmett's hair, delighting in the way his lips curved upwards at her touch. Moving closer, she whispered, "Before...if you could go anywhere, where would you choose?"

He opened his eyes and tilted his head her way, creating the illusion that she truly filled his gaze. The sunlight made the gold blaze so brightly, it hurt Casey to watch, yet Emmett didn't even blink. "Oh, I always wanted to go out west to see the last of the wild horses, do the cowboy thing—and Alaska, now that would be amazing. Wyatt and I planned on cruising Route Sixty-Six..." His words trailed off, and sadness crept in. "We thought there'd be plenty of time, but life got in the way." A hard swallow and his attention turned to her, a grin dispersing the temporary bout of darkness. "What about you?"

Casey's hand rested on the side of his face, her fingers beginning to stroke his temple, making his eyes drift closed and his body loosen. If nothing else, she had the power to transport him to a happy place. "Well, I went to Disneyland once when I was little. Daddy said every princess should go see the castle at least once in a lifetime. I loved the park, but one trip to the beach, and I was hooked."

Emmett shifted to his side and pressed his forehead to hers, his voice dropping down soft and low. "I've never been to the ocean, only lakes. Show me." His hand brushed along her body and settled on her hip, applying pressure, waiting for an answer.

Casey closed her eyes to sift through snapshots and postcards in her memory. "Oh, the beach was incredible. I could've stayed there all day, feeling the white, hot sand running through my toes, scampering along the shore and watching the tide wash my footprints away. Mom and Daddy would grab my hands and swing me, launching me up in the air and out in the water that was the same color as a blue sky on a cloudless day and as warm as my bathtub."

She was silent for a moment, visualizing that endless, sapphire banner that spun out over her head. "In the evening, the sunset was like tie-dye, pink, purple and red or gold and orange, dripping down to the horizon. The sound of the waves rolling in and out was my lullaby each night in our cottage by the water, and I could still taste salt on my lips from my swim. My skin was hot from sunburn. I cried when it was time to go home."

Letting go of a sigh, she propped herself on an elbow to look down at Emmett. His eyes were open, and there was a dreamy expression on his face. "Thank you for taking me with you to the beach, earlier and right now. You make me want to do it for real."

He reached up, entwined his fingers in her hair and met her lips with his. "I can almost taste the sea salt and hear the surf. I can picture lying in the sand, letting the tide wash over us." He closed his eyes, a crease of concentration appearing between his eyes until his head nodded. "Mmm, I feel the heat too—oh, wait a minute, that's you." He smiled and kissed her neck. "So, it was your father's idea. Sounds like someone I wish I knew. Tell me about him."

Casey sat up then, wrapping her arms around her knees, the pain poking at her and making her suck in hard. Emmett came with her, his arm around her shoulders, his breath tickling her ear, loosening the knots in her stomach. It was still so fresh and raw inside, making her skirt away from thoughts of one of the greatest men she'd ever known.

*Come on, Case. Talk about him. Bring him back for a little while and leave the hurting behind.* "Daddy was a dreamer, and he taught me to dream big, while Mom was the practical one. He was a high school English teacher and looked the part, wearing tweed jackets with his jeans to school, his glasses on the top of his head, forgetting where he left them, hair always disheveled, running his hand through it during grading or lecture. Daddy read me bedtime stories every night, everything from fairytales to classics. He took me to the movies, the theater, museums, and exhibits. That man loved to expose me to everything that could broaden my horizons."

She had to swallow hard. Emmett squeezed her hand, encouraging her to go on. "One of the greatest gifts was the year I took his American Literature class. Seeing him in his element, doing his job, filled me with awe. I saw how the kids responded to him, how much he loved it, how it fit. My friends wondered, even my mother, how I could sign up for one of his classes. I'm so glad I did. Seeing the way he reached out to kids that year taught me to find my passion and give myself to it completely. My father, the teacher, was my best teacher ever."

Emmett nodded. When he spoke, his voice was thick with emotion. "There's something about fathers. My dad was a tower of a man. Watching him with the horses, I thought he was the biggest man on Earth. He taught me everything I know about them and a love for them, but not only horses, about everything that counted in life. Manners. Respect. A hard work ethic. Accepting the hand life deals you. To love with all you are. Seeing how he handled my mother's death, never letting it bring him down, I've tried to do the same."

His face twisted for a moment, a ripple there and gone. "I know I haven't been as good at it as he was." Emmett kissed the top of her head. "So, if your father was reading our bedtime story, would it be a fairy tale or classic tragedy?"

Casey faced him, head on, to watch the sunlight streaming in, casting him in its glow. Her lips grazed his forehead and then both of his eyelids. "You are definitely my fairy tale prince, and I'm the princess who has come to the rescue to break your spell."

Emmett held her close, pressing her head to his chest. "You have broken the spell I've been in. You made me stop feeling sorry for myself, pried me out of that house, brought me to the beach."

He started chuckling softly, his fingers mesmerizing as they danced through her hair, down her back, and began to draw circles, maybe a heart? Her heart began to flutter, ready to take flight. "As a matter of fact, I enjoyed the test run so much, I'd go for the real thing as long as you're with me." She soared, and Emmett went with her.

ℰ𝒟ℰ𝒟

Waking up with the dawn chasing away the night, darkness fading to gray and color bleeding into the room once more. On a *Sunday*. Not minding one whit for once as the dawn tiptoed in because Casey could take her fill of Emmett while he slept. The crease between his eyes, from concentrating on navigation, his surroundings, and the inundation of information from his senses, was gone. The lines of tension around his mouth were wiped clean.

In sleep, the evidence of the struggle—to keep it together, to hold back the anger before the dam broke, to beat self-pity into submission—disappeared. The hands on the clock of time turned backward to days gone by. A younger, carefree Emmett lay beside her, brimming with possibilities. A smile began to bloom across his face, brighter than the sunrise, and Casey held her breath.

"Haven't you heard it isn't polite to stare?" The words spilled off his tongue, slow and lazy. He rolled onto his side, and his hand caressed her body until it rested on the groove between her ribs and her hip. His gaze turned her way, illuminated by the first morning rays, becoming a shimmering torch, and Casey was a moth, tempted and tantalized by the light in his eyes.

She drew herself closer, her fingers finding their way to the nape of his neck, her head pressing against his chest. She could feel the racing of his heartbeat, a bird's mad fluttering to be set free from its cage. "How did you know?"

Emmett laughed softly. "Because I could hear the change in your breathing, the shift from sleep to awake, feel your body start to hum. And your heart…"His hand drifted until it settled on her chest, and he nodded in confirmation. "Kicking it up."

He took her hand and pressed her palm to his chest.

"Like mine." The smile stretched wider, and his mouth skimmed her shoulder, collarbone, and jaw before touching down on her mouth. "Good morning, beautiful. What are you doing up at such an hour?"

Casey returned the greeting, drawing it out, ensuring both were wide awake. "Getting as much of you as possible. Early isn't so bad when you're around." Her chin tilted upward as his mouth brushed the tender skin of her neck and his breath tickled her ear. *That bird with the worm had the right idea. I'd get up at the crack of dawn all the time if every day started like this.*

"I don't mind early. I like getting out of bed, stepping out on my porch with my first cup of coffee, feeling the sun on my face and listening to the birds chatter as the world wakes up. Makes me feel like the day might have some potential." His hands roamed over her body, then her lips. "Mmm. There's definitely some potential here. Early's best with you."

Casey felt as if she was melting down. Disentangling herself, she set her feet on the floor and gave his hand a tug. "I've got a really good way to wake up. How about another shower together? Going alone is a real disappointment."

Emmett hooked his hands on her waist and let her do the honors, starting the shower, and pulling him under the rush of warm water. Casey's arms looped around his neck, her lips on his skin, and the water rained down while the dance they knew so well resumed.

"Wait. Just wait." Emmett sounded like a marathon runner, fighting for breath as he gave her the fantasy she asked for. He picked up the shampoo and washed her hair, then conditioned it, taking his time, massaging her head, turning her whole body to Jell-O. Casey could barely stay on her feet.

"Good God, Emmett. I know I mentioned having my

hair washed at the salon. It was never like this at the hair-dresser's."

His laughter bubbled up, and he planted a kiss on her lips.

"Not finished here yet." His hands fumbled along the wall, felt the shower head, and removed it from the cra-dle. With a touch that was gentle but firm on the nape of her neck, he bent her over, running water all over her head and the rest of her body.

By the time the shower head was back where it belonged, Casey was grabbing hold of him for support. "Do you have one of those scrubby things, some body wash?" His voice was strained, Emmett's jaw clenched. This wasn't easy on him either.

She nodded her head against his chest, kissed his shoulder, gave it a little nip, and put the requested items in his hands. The scent of coconut rose around them, floating on the cloud of steam, as he lathered up and started rubbing the bath sponge over her body, from her neck down to her toes.

Casey, with what scraps of cognitive ability she had left, took over next, giving him the same treatment. Em-mett's face twisted into a mask of pleasure that was bor-dering on crossing over to pain. The sponge slipped from her fingers, and she stepped into his arms. He was shak-ing, eventually choking out the words. "You shatter me."

Her lips latched on to his once more and her hands were on his neck, hanging on. "Good thing I can pick up the pieces." They stepped into each other. If they were clothes, they'd be wearing each other. Eruption was inev-itable.

When all was said and done, the water turned off, and they sat in a tangle of towels and bathrobes on the floor, Emmett twisted a lock of her hair around his finger, round and round. "Since you've got me feeling so adventuresome, do you want to go to the diner for breakfast? I think Wyatt wants us for dinner too. They want to say thank you."

Casey grinned and kissed him one more time. "Sounds great, although I should thank *them* for bringing us together." Emmett's eyes closed and he winced. "What is it?" she asked. "What's wrong?"

A shake of his head and his smile was back, if somewhat forced. "There's one more thing. Do you mind going to church with me? Wyatt and Sammie go all the time. They want to save my soul or something. Maybe they think a miracle will happen. You know—the lame will walk, and the blind will see, and all that—"

She stopped his words with a kiss and held on tight. "Em, I'll go anywhere with you. As for miracles, don't discount them. I'm a doctor, and I've seen the unexplained happen many times in the ER. One might creep up and take you by surprise."

Casey laid her head on his chest and listened to the steady thumping of his heart. His fingers were still wandering through her hair. She'd noticed that his hands were often in motion, even when the rest of him was still, evidence of the constant current of impatience running through him. Emmett let out a long breath, as if he'd been holding it, chewing on a thought, and his lips skimmed her forehead. "One already did. God gave me you."

# CHAPTER 17

W hat color is that dress you're wearing?"
They were seated in the Henry family pew,
one they'd laid claim to generations ago. If
Emmett ran his hand beneath the bench, he'd find the
spot where he and Wyatt had carved their names with
pocket knives. Casey shifted beside him, the material of
her dress making a slight rustling noise, and her leg
brushed against his, nearly stopping his heart.

"Red. It's my Valentine's dress." Her hand took hold
of his, and the familiar heat that was theirs ran through
his body, making his pulse skitter and his face flush.

Emmett's eyes closed and his hand tightened its grip
on hers. "What are you trying to do to me?" Even though
the words were pitched in a whisper, he could hear Wyatt's chuckle beside him, Jackson's cooing in Samantha's
arms, and the murmuring of those around them in a rolling wave of sound. A hard swallow and he whispered in
her ear. "You are making me think unholy thoughts."

"Emmett!" A little shock, tainted with laughter, vibrated in Casey's voice and her high-heeled shoe slid
against his pant leg. Reaching down, he skimmed her nylons at her ankle, and the heat rushed to his face, nearly
had him gasping.

*Water! Need water now!* Good thing the Henry family pew wasn't at the front. Church was going to be tough today. A penance.

The music swelled, and there was the general commotion of people rising to their feet. The preacher must have made his appearance. They launched into the first hymn, words stamped on Emmett's brain since childhood. They'd gone to church with Mama at their side. When she died, his father kept with tradition, a comfort perhaps, one that continued into adulthood and carried them through the pain of losing him.

After Emmett's accident, he stopped going, a sore spot between him and Wyatt. His brother walked the straight and narrow. He voted Republican. He drank Jack Daniels. Things were black and white. People went to church on Sundays.

Emmett had agreed until robbed of his sight. Prayers hadn't helped him, although he'd never prayed harder in his life. *You are alive, aren't you?* There was that nagging voice again, reminding him to have a little more gratitude. Church was supposed to give a person peace. It only gave him more questions and time for doubt to brew while he sat there stewing and started questioning *everything*.

Still, Casey was beside him, and that helped. He fidgeted. Fiddling with his shirt. Tugging at his collar. Finger combing his hair. Running a hand over his face. Probably looked decent. Her hand tightened its hold on his, calming him. He could do this.

Her hair brushed his cheek as she leaned across him to pick up the bible, smelling of some floral and citrus blend, absolutely intoxicating. Feeling a little dizzy, he closed his eyes and tried to concentrate on the words of the sermon. When that didn't work, Emmett counted the beats of his heart and pictured the fluttering of Casey's pulse. If he skimmed his thumb over her wrist, there it was, soft as a humming bird's wings. The music rose once more, bearing them up to their feet. A good thing because behaving was getting harder by the minute.

❧❧❧

"About time we saw you, Emmett. That Henry pew doesn't look right without you in it. Every time I give the sermon, I find myself looking for you." The pastor took his hand in a firm grip and pulled his lost sheep in for a hearty embrace, thumping him on the back.

Emmett couldn't help but smile. John Luke Matthews was a good man and well-suited for his calling. He often joked that his path in life was a given, thanks to his name. Although he was young, about Wyatt's age, the congregation had grown to love him in the decade that he'd called their church home.

Small wonder. He looked more like a farmer, broad shouldered, tall, and always smiling, more than capable of bearing the burdens of his flock with his easy-going manner and big heart. Em could picture the twinkle in his chocolate eyes and the way his dark hair was always falling into his face, no matter how the man tried to tame it.

Feeling Casey's hand on his back, Emmett stepped back and took her hand. "Pastor Matthews, I'd like you to meet my girlfriend, Casey Mitchell. Casey, this is John Luke Matthews. He's a whipper-snapper, but we figure we'll keep him."

"It's nice to meet you, Casey. I've heard many good things about you at the clinic. I've been putting off my annual exam, but maybe I'll go. After all, you got our friend Emmett back in the fold. I've been trying for about a year. Now, go enjoy this beautiful day that God has given you. I do believe there's a hint of spring in the air."

"Don't get complacent, John Luke. You know that

March might come in like a lamb, but there's a good chance he'll be a lion and bite you in the butt when it's time to leave. Good to see you again."

Emmett pumped the pastor's hand, and Casey took over, guiding their way out of the church. There were more handshakes, pats on the back, and hugs from other members of the community before they finally made it to Casey's car. Emmett leaned up against the door and let out a sigh. "Whew. That was exhausting."

Hands were on his waist, running up his sides, coming to rest on his shoulders. "People are happy to see you, but don't worry. I might be able to revive you." Her lips grazed his, and his arms took hold of her. One more kiss and they were both beginning to wilt.

Casey stepped back and cleared her throat. They were in a public place after all. A display wouldn't do. "I really enjoyed it today. It made me think of all those years Daddy made us go. He said church was a good time to take a time out, to be still, and sort through all the muddle in your brain. Pastor Matthews is really good, too."

"Yeah, yeah he is. Hey listen, would you mind walking over to the cemetery beside the church? It's my parents' anniversary. I want to give them those flowers." He'd handed a bouquet to Casey when she'd arrived, grabbing another off the table on the way out. She hadn't questioned him. Probably thought they were for Sammie.

The car door opened and closed. Casey's hand took his, setting the tissue-wrapped bundle in his fingers, and they began the short trek across the lot, down a slate path, through the gate of the white-picket fence, and over the meandering path.

"They're under that oak in the back. Mama loved trees. She used to climb them with us and have picnics." A few more steps and they came to a stop. Emmett eased down on his knees, onto the snow-covered ground, heedless of the cold and wet seeping through his clothes. Casey's hand guided him to the stone and the letters, tracing them with him. The sun was warm on his back, and the wind had a milder quality to it, offering the promise of the season to come. If only those he'd come to visit could be here to share the moment.

"It would be thirty-five years today. Can you imagine thirty-five years with one person?" Her words were hushed, as if afraid of disturbing those who slept around them. "My mother and father made it to twenty-eight."

Said in a whisper, Emmett almost missed the last, but his fingers felt their way across the snow and found Casey's hand. They leaned against each other for an instant, finding strength and a little peace. He laid the flowers down and pressed a kiss to his fingers, then to the stone, repeating it again, one for each name.

"Mom, Dad, I know you're not here, but if you're tuned in, this is Casey. We wanted to wish you a happy anniversary. Love you both." He rested his palm on the hard, unforgiving granite and shivered from its chill. One tear slid down his cheek, and then he was pulling himself to his feet, pushing past the pain, taking a deep breath. "Enough of this. Come on, Case. The land of the living is waiting for us."

*⁓ঌ⁓*

The girls were in the kitchen, bustling around, chatting, laughing. The baby was sleeping in his bassinet, next to his father. Wyatt yelled at the drivers on the screen a few times while Emmett nursed a beer. Following racing on television had really lost its thrill since he'd lost his sight.

Radio broadcasts were better, filling in more of the

gaps, but sports as a whole really didn't do it for him anymore.

A strong odor drifted his way, making him wrinkle his nose. "Wyatt, either you need to change your shorts or little man needs some attention." Soft snoring was his response, another hazard of televised sports. Shaking his head, Emmett pushed up off the couch and worked his way across the room. While his level of comfort wasn't as good as at home, he could navigate pretty well in his grandparents' old place. His fingers found the warm, squirming bundle and he scooped Jackson up against his chest. *Time to put being an uncle to the test.*

Footsteps tailed him into the nursery, their cadence and the scent of perfume announcing their owner. Casey. Emmett tossed his words over his shoulder. "I need to do this on my own, prove that I can. You can inspect, okay?"

Letting out a long, slow breath, he juggled the baby in one hand, feeling for the changing table with the other. He shook his head, letting the on-going dialogue in his head slip out. "No, can't do it up here. Makes me too nervous. Down on the floor, that will be best."

A search of the area turned up a soft towel, the perfect cushion. Emmett laid Jackson down, turning back to the table to round up wipes, powder, and a diaper. He laid everything out and went down on his knees, rubbing slick hands on his jeans. "For God's sake, I'm having a panic attack here. Not like I'm doing surgery."

Casey didn't say a word, simply rested a hand on his shoulder and gave a little pressure. It was enough to help him center himself and bumble his way through. The new diaper was in place, the old one in the genie, and Emmett's palms were pressed to his thighs, his head bowed.

"You did it," she whispered and planted a kiss on his cheek in recognition of one more, small accomplishment, something most took for granted. Neither was aware that

Sammie and Wyatt were peeking in from the hallway.

Emmett returned to the living room, Casey's arm around his waist, little Jackson snug in his arms. Wyatt's voice rang out, light with teasing. "You're looking pretty white there, and is that sweat on your forehead? I know some of Jackson's surprises can be pretty toxic. Gotta be able to handle those diapers to babysit."

Emmett grimaced, transferring the baby into Casey's waiting arms. "Oh, don't you worry. I can handle it until Little Man walks." The resentment left a sour taste, twisting his features and pushing him outdoors for fresh air.

Casey followed him to the railing and rested her hand on his tightened fist. "Emmett, he was just fooling with you. You did a fine job. Come back in. Dinner will be ready any minute." A kiss on his neck and clenched jaw helped to loosen things up a bit. She had a way of softening any blow, always knowing what to say. Emmett let her lead him back inside.

Wyatt was waiting for him and pulled him aside with a firm grip on the nape of his neck. "I'd trust you with my life and absolutely, hands down, with my son. Eyes or no eyes. We'll figure out a way, make it work, get one of those leashes for kids. You *will* babysit our boy. You'll be the first person we call." Somehow, they wound up in a hug, breaking away, teasing each other gruffly, ending up in the living room once more until they were called to dinner.

The meal was a welcome, but a short respite to the never-ending race. Settling in on the couch, listening to dishes rattle in the kitchen, fighting back the sensation of déjà vu. Thinking on most of his days feeling like he'd been there, done that, Emmett grew sullen.

Victory Lane time arrived, his favorite driver, and it really stuck in his craw, one more thing taken away— missing that moment of triumph, hands in the air, face-splitting grins, and bottles of soda, champagne and what not spraying all over the place. "Did he tear up the infield? What about flipping off the top of the car like he used to? Yo, Wyatt, come on. You're slipping as my interpreter. Oh, forget it!" he said, ready to jump out of his skin. *Won't matter. You can't jump high enough or far enough to get out of your head.*

Moving to get up, Casey provided a distraction, settling on Emmett's lap and looping her arms around his neck. His hands trailed over her nylons and the slippery material of the dress, calling to mind Valentine's. He let his lips do the walking until she broke away.

"Em, there are others here…"

A low chuckle bubbled up, and he waved off her objections. "They've seen it all, know all about the birds and the bees. They have a baby. Unless you want to go someplace private…" She giggled and gave him a little of his own medicine until a hand clapped him on the back.

"Hey, love birds, the thaw is coming. Want to take a few turns around the pasture with Bonnie and Clyde? They've missed you, and they're mighty restless after the winter. Feeling neglected, I bet." Emmett set his jaw. The idea of riding wore on frayed nerves, especially since he couldn't go solo anymore, and his brother just had to keep pushing him.

"Come on, Em. You know Bonnie will follow Clyde, and with all the snow, they'll go easy. What do you say?" Casey's hand found his knee and gave it a squeeze, prompting him to act. He could feel the anticipation humming in her touch, hear Wyatt's eagerness to see him back in the saddle again.

Plowing on before he could bite his tongue or regret it, Emmett's reply was rather breathless. "Okay. Sounds good." *So why is my gut churning?*

Wyatt led them both upstairs, handing Casey a

change of Samantha's clothes in the bathroom, a set of his own for his brother. Emmett found himself breaking a sweat for the second time that day, kicking off his church clothes and swapping them out for what the Henry brothers knew best—jeans and flannel. His fingers kept fighting with the buttons when the door opened and closed with a click.

Casey tiptoed across the room, throwing herself at him until they tumbled back onto the bed. "That's for getting me started earlier on the couch." One mean tease of a kiss, his hands navigating to her perfect hips, and she slipped out again. Emmett's mouth went dry thinking about her, and his heart began to race. *Never underestimate the power of a woman.*

When they ventured on to the porch, outfitted to ride, Wyatt was waiting for them. Casey's fingers interlaced with Emmett's, and they walked across the drive, out to the barn. The door slid open, creaking on its hinges, and Emmett stepped forward, slipping free of Casey's grasp. He hadn't set foot out here since his horses had to be sent away.

The aroma of straw, oats, and the stately animals nearly swallowed him whole. He closed his eyes and breathed in deeply, straining to hear the ring of tack, harness, and stirrups, jingling his way. Warm breath lifted his hair, and velvety skin brushed his cheek. His arms came up around the strong column of a horse's neck, and he buried his hands in her mane. "Hey, Bonnie Bell. I missed you too, girl."

A hand clamped down on his shoulder, and there was a tremor in Wyatt's voice when he spoke. "Come on, Little Brother. She's waiting for you. Let's get you back where you began."

Some helpful guidance and Emmett's hand hooked onto the saddle horn. Wyatt placed his foot in the stirrup and gave him a pat on the back. A rush of air and Emmett was up, his leg swinging over, his body remembering the way. His brother came around and made sure his other foot was secure, his hand steadying Emmett's leg. "You all right up there?"

It seemed like he was higher than ever before on a precarious perch, one that a body could topple out of without notice. The saddle horn became an anchor as his heart began to skip. Bonnie whickered, reminding him that she was waiting. Reaching out, one hand found her mane and latched on.

Emmett closed his eyes and squared his shoulders. "I'm fine. Go help Casey. She hasn't done much riding." When his brother still didn't let go, Emmett grinned reassuringly and tossed out a wink. "Go on now, Wyatt. This girl is chomping at the bit. Can't you hear her?"

The mare was practically prancing, hooves shifting from side to side, head pulling at the reins. Heavy footsteps receded, and his brother's instructions were given in a quiet but authoritative tone. Casey's nervous laughter and a squeal rang out as she was boosted into the saddle.

Emmett leaned forward and rested his cheek on Bonnie's neck, pitching his voice low for only her ears. "Go easy, girl. Things are different now."

The clomping of hooves approached, and the breeze of Clyde's passing lifted Emmett's hair. "You're sure about this, Emmett?" Casey asked. "I've only been on a little pony and a short trail ride in the Adirondacks. I won't know what to do if he takes off on me." The words were said lightly, but the uneasiness was there underneath.

Hearing Casey trying to find her courage helped him to pluck up some of his own. *For Pete's sake, Em, you were practically born in the saddle. Remember—she's more anxious than you.* "You've got nothing to worry about. Going with Clyde is just a walk in the park. Any time a beginner wants to give it a go, we saddle him up, and Bonnie will stick with him for company. The only time Clyde will let loose is if Bonnie-girl gives him a run. We're not doing that today, right, Bonnie Bell?"

Bonnie took over, moving forward at a slow amble, positively moseying. The grin Emmett faked for Wyatt grew into a full-blown smile. Bonnie, usually one of the spunkiest, most spirited horses of the bunch, was set on taking good care of him. He likened it to a Sunday drive. She wouldn't let anything happen. Neither would Clyde.

The tension eased, and the knots in his body loosened, easing into the rhythm of the horse's movements. The roll of Bonnie's strong muscles and the heat of her flanks felt soothing and right. The sun was warm on Emmett's face and the top of his head, Casey's laughter and wonder warmer yet as the mild air filled his lungs with every breath. For the first time in months, he felt truly alive, invigorated.

The mare put him into a trance with the gentle sway of her body and the chime of halter, reins, and creaking of the leather saddle. He didn't even realize she had stopped moving until he heard Wyatt's voice and Casey's boots touching the ground. "Little sore are you, Doc? That will wear off soon enough, once you toughen up. Head on in for some coffee and dessert. I think Sammie made a fresh apple pie to soften the blow. I'll take care of Clyde and his sidekick."

A little groan came from Casey's direction, and Emmett could sympathize. A welcome ache burned in his thighs, butt, and back from muscles not accustomed to being used in such a way in a long time.

A hand brushed his leg and made him start. *Must have been dozing.* "Ready to get down before you fall down, Little Brother?" A deep breath in and Emmett gripped the saddle horn, swinging his leg over and easing his way to the ground.

His hands rested on Bonnie's flank, and he found her mane, burying his face in the familiar scent and warmth. "I'll rub her down, Em. You go on in with Casey." His brother remained close, at his side, a hand on his younger brother's shoulder.

"No—no, I want to do it, Wyatt. Would you get me a cloth and a brush? You can put her in the stall when I'm done. I just need a little time with her, okay?"

There was no response except a slap on the back and receding footsteps. A moment later, supplies were being pressed into his hands. "I'll be tending to Clyde. If you need me, give a holler."

Emmett nodded and set to work, reaching underneath to unhook Bonnie's saddle girth. One great heave and he hoisted the saddle up and over. The brush came next, running it over her broad body, smoothing her coat, listening to her sigh in obvious pleasure. He fell into a rhythm, moving over her back, to her hind quarters, then to her neck and mane. Emmett shifted to the cloth, working the soft material over her from front to back and down her sturdy legs. If she'd been a cat, the mare would be purring.

He saved her head for last, relishing the feel of her face resting on his shoulder. His heart felt ready to split open wide in that bittersweet moment, so happy to be with her once more, longing for things to go back to the way they were. Emmett held on and let out a ragged breath. "I really wish I could see you, girl."

There were hoofbeats and the click of a stall door. Footsteps crossed the barn once more and a strong arm wrapped around his shoulders. "She doesn't care if you can see her, Em. All that matters to this girl is that you're here. The same goes for the rest of us."

Wyatt's voice cracked, and he stepped away, taking hold of Bonnie's bridle to lead her to her stall. Emmett propped himself against another door and waited to do what the brothers had done many times over the years of working the horses. They called it a night, walking back to the house together.

# CHAPTER 18

Casey's heart was skipping almost as fast as her feet, anxious to get away before there was any chance of someone calling her back in. *Freedom tastes so sweet!* Her appointment load was miraculously light for a Friday, and her nurse practitioner had graciously volunteered to take care of whatever might come in. That meant the luxury of an entire weekend with Em and then some. If things went well, she might even stretch it until Monday. Her fingers tapped on the steering wheel while the butterflies took flight in the pit of her stomach. What a perfect way to ring in the first day of spring!

The car coasted to a stop in Emmett's driveway, tires rumbling on the gravel stretch. Surely his sensitive ears would tune in. Her high-heeled boots clicked on the walkway, another calling card, and she held her key at the ready, fitting it into the lock. Casey considered herself fortunate to be a member of a select few who had the privilege of owning a spare key to the original Henry Homestead. Wyatt and Sammie were the only others who belonged to the club.

She stepped inside and slammed the door in her enthusiasm, covering her mouth, heat spiking to her cheeks. *No surprising him now.* "Emmett?" Her voice rang out, echoing through a house that was quiet—too quiet. Casey half expected him to catch her on the way in. A quick in-spection didn't turn him up anywhere downstairs. She walked to the back window and glanced outside. There was no sign of him in the field. "Em? Where are you?"

"Up here." She found him in the bedroom at the end of the hall, one where the door was always closed. The room was spacious and masculine, rich in brown and hunter green tones, but her eyes were immediately drawn to a large wedding portrait hanging on the wall.

The bride was a small bird of a woman, tucked into the protective shelter of a broad chest, with hair that trapped the sunshine falling to her shoulders and eyes of a blue as bright as the hydrangeas that used to grow in Ca-sey's mother's garden. The groom looked like Emmett's twin, except the hair was clean-cut, not as unruly as his son's, his soft brown gaze locking with Casey's, and she was spell-bound. *That could be you and Em.*

"Case?" A rustling noise snapped her out of it to find Emmett, in the middle of an ample, antique bed built from a dark wood, dressed in his standard wear—flannel, jeans, and sock feet because he preferred to go without shoes to feel his way.

He was sifting through a box of buttons, letting them rain through his fingers, a line between his eyebrows carved deep in thought. The brush of her kiss on his cheek, and it was wiped clean, a smile creeping into his voice and lighting his eyes. "Hey, what are you doing here already? It's noon or something like that, right?"

His arms snagged her and gathered Casey in, giving his lips a chance to wander up her neck, along her jaw, and to her mouth. She almost forgot the question. "Oh, they sprang me early. My nurse practitioner said she has it covered. What are you up to?"

Emmett turned her way to bury his face in her hair and inhaled deeply in appreciation. "Oh, I've been bored, trapped in the land where time stops, waiting for you. I got up early and went for my walk, cleaned, listened to a book, listened to the radio, listened to the television. Sometimes my ears get really get tired of listening, especially when the scenery never changes, you know?"

He pulled back with a rueful grin and his head tipped against hers. "So, instead of rattling around anymore, I came up here to dust off some memories." The grin faded and the line returned between his eyes. "Mama's really tough to hold on to. I only have scraps of her since I was four when we lost her. Pictures used to bring her back."

Emmett fell silent, and his hand fumbled on the bed until he caught up a slip of material. "I found this handkerchief in her dresser drawer." He pressed it to his face and passed it on. "I think Dad must have kept buying her favorite sachets because it smells pretty strong, just like she was here yesterday. She used to sing to me, rock me in Gran's rocker, read to me. I remember powder. She loved to wear powder and always covered me and Wyatt head to toe at bath time."

Casey returned the hanky, resisting the temptation to use it, and he nodded, gesturing to a gold box resting between his legs. "This button box was in the drawer too. I used to play with it all the time. We'd count them, Mama and I, look at the colors, study each one. I thought it was a treasure box." He ran his fingers through the pile of buttons, picked one up, and flipped it in his hands, back and forth. "My father, he's easier to call to mind, but harder to handle. I imagine you can understand that, what with losing your dad a little while ago."

Casey set her hand on his and the button stilled. "I haven't taken out any of my photo albums since." She laid her head on his shoulder and Emmett began to stroke her hair, a ragged sigh letting loose as the button slipped from his fingers. "They only make me cry."

"That's just it. I don't need pictures to remember my father. I look over my shoulder with eyes that can't see, hear the echo of his boot steps and the rumble of his voice. Today, I stepped into the closet, to the back and the remains of my father's clothes. The smell of Old Spice hit me and nearly knocked me down. Feels like he's still here." Emmett choked up and couldn't say any more.

Casey kissed his cheek and whispered. "He *is* still here. In you, in Wyatt, and in Jackson. Henrys are built to last." Her eyes began to burn as they wandered to the wedding picture and the young couple staring down at them, filled with hope and promise.

Clearing her throat, she squeezed Emmett's hand tight. "All right, you've been digging up memories long enough for one day. We're getting out of here, my surprise. Pack a bag for two, maybe three nights and let's go."

Emmett's eyebrows crept up with a hint of a grin, and his hands gave her hips a squeeze, but he didn't argue, didn't even question her. Funny, the more time they spent together, the more Emmett was willing to push the envelope of his tolerance for the outside world. As for Casey, her universe had become much smaller, narrowing to what mattered most—the man in this room.

The button box and handkerchief were carefully returned to the dresser drawer because Emmett needed a place for everything and everything in its place. He headed off to the bedroom, Casey trailing behind, hanging back, marveling as he went about his task. No wasted steps or lost time handling the simple, day to day. Finding the suitcase tucked on the top shelf of the closet, snug against the door. Laying it out on the bed, open wide.

Back to the closet, fingering his shirts and sweaters, counting his way in, picking a few, folding them and layering them on the bottom. Switching to the dresser, pull-ing out jeans, t-shirts, pajama bottoms, underwear, and socks. Making sure everything was orderly, like his home. A pause, hands resting on the suitcase and he turned her way. "Well, are you going to stand back there all day and send me into withdrawal or get over here?"

Laughing softly, Casey stepped behind him and wrapped her arms around his waist, pressing her face against his broad back. He smelled like sunshine. "You want me to grab your comb and toothbrush or do you want to be Mr. Independent?"

Emmett turned and skimmed his fingers over her hair and took hold of her cheek to eventually land a kiss on her lips. "Hmm. Independence is overrated. I'd rather let you take care of me." Casey gave the kiss back and then some, grabbing his hand and tugging him along to the bathroom. The door closed, and he was captive, his body pinned by hers. "Case, we're not going to get far if we don't get going."

"Okay. We'll pick up where we left off later. I'm grabbing your comb, electric razor, and your toothbrush. Oh, can't forget your cologne because it smells so good even though you don't need any improvements. Am I missing anything?"

Emmett stepped away from the wall, his hands emp-tying hers, setting everything down on the counter. He simply had to have another taste of her.

"Nothing except the fact that you're driving me cra-zy." His voice was a whisper, his breath tickling her cheek.

For an instant, everything else went away except for the strong set of arms holding her and the kisses upon kisses. "Casey, we had best go now, or we'll never go."

∽∾∽

She drove for a long stretch and wouldn't say where. His hand tapped on the door along with the music, the other hand settled on her thigh, making her skin burn like a brand. The temperature was rising in the small, enclosed space. *Much hotter and I'm opening a window.*

Emmett must have felt the same. He peeled off his flannel shirt and tossed it in the back seat, revealing a spotless white T-shirt that molded to his chest perfectly. Casey glanced his way, saw his teasing grin, and shook her head. What the man did to her.

They rolled to a stop about two hours later and it took everything she had to get out of the car instead of throwing herself at his long, lean form. Emmett moved slowly, unfolding his tall frame at his own pace. "Okay, where are we?" He leaned on the top of the car, propping his chin on his arms.

Casey walked around to his side and hooked a finger in his belt loop. "We are at a bed and breakfast." A moment's pause and his cane flicked out of his left hand, snapping into place, tapping left to right in a small arc while she led the way across a walkway of slate.

"A bed and breakfast, eh? I can't think of a better way to finish and start my day than by lying in bed next to you, doesn't matter where. Maybe the breakfast can be in bed, too. Only one problem—it's a little early to be turning in, isn't it?"

His cane clunked on wood and Emmett took the steps one at a time, until he hit the hollow ring of the porch and planted his feet. "So where is this bed and breakfast anyway and what's it like? I need details, remember? Don't leave me hanging."

*How does Em always make me forget he can't see?* Casey took his hand, swallowing hard as they crossed a broad expanse to stop at a railing overlooking the yard. "You'd feel right at home, but I'm not telling you our exact location until tomorrow, only a description. We're at an old farm house, like yours, a big place that reaches out to you and pulls you in from a long, winding drive. They painted it the soft yellow of buttercups with white trim, like cupcakes with curlicues. The porch wraps around the front and one side, begging you to have a sit down in white rockers here and there. A white picket fence is in front of the house and probably has a garden in the spring filled with old fashioned flowers."

She gripped the railing tight and breathed deep. "Can you smell it? There's a stand of big, fat Christmas trees sheltering the house from the wind to the back and along the sides. We're on a hill with a long, rolling lawn that leads to a pond with a dock and a rowboat overturned on top. Off to the right of the house is an old carriage house for a garage, painted to match. Everything about it says come in and stay a while."

Emmett's hands tightened on the sturdy railing, and he turned his face toward the east, sunlight spilling into his eyes and taking Casey's breath away. "No, everything about you makes me want to stay a while, wherever we are." His smile was almost as bright as his golden gaze.

He let go of the railing to run his hands up her arms and thread his fingers in her hair. "In case I forget in all the excitement, thank you for every minute." His head tipped to hers, and their lips touched in a kiss that spun out and made her knees grow weak. Casey needn't have worried. Emmett was strong enough to catch her before the fall.

ℰ✺ℰ✺

The curtains were fluttering next to the sliding glass door left ajar, birdsong drifting in as first light announced daybreak. Casey shivered climbing out of bed and pulled on her robe and slippers. "Em? You all right?"

She stepped outside to find him standing on the balcony of their room, head tipped to the sky, eyes closed as a cool breeze made his hair flutter. The air had lost its bite and hinted at warmth to come. Hearing her footsteps, his hand reached out to her, and she caught it.

"Good morning, beautiful. I'm sorry I forgot to close the door. Did I wake you?" He tucked her in under his arm, the furnace that was his body doing a better job than any robe ever could. Casey buried her face in his chest and caught the scent of spring as he kissed the top of her head.

"It's all right. It's a beautiful day that shouldn't be wasted. Do you want to head down to breakfast or wait a while?" A low rumble of a chuckle had her tilting her head to look up at his broad smile. "What's got you smiling so big?"

He shook his head and gripped the nape of her neck, massaging the muscles and making everything go loose. "You just made me think of quite a few things we can do before breakfast. What do you say we go back to bed for a little while and discuss the possibilities?" Before she could even answer, his strong arms were sweeping her off her feet, and Emmett carried Casey inside like she weighed nothing more than a feather. In the end, they found plenty to do and didn't even have to say a word.

cↄeↄ

"How about some more bacon and eggs, Emmett? A fine man like yourself, we've got to keep you big and strong," their hostess, Mrs. O'Leary, said with the slightest lilt leftover from decades ago in Ireland.

Having experienced times when food was scarce, she didn't believe in skimping now. Her ample figure, covered in a blue and white checked dress with a snowy apron was a testament to indulging in her good cooking. Her white curls, rosy cheeks, and twinkling blue eyes called to mind grandmas everywhere, a perfect Mrs. Claus.

A platter of food waited in one hand while she poured from a carafe of coffee in the other. Casey raised her hand in a signal to stop before she ended up with a bad case of the jitters, already filled with anticipation for their day.

Their host slapped his paper down on the table and tossed his guests a wink. "Annie, the poor man is going to burst. You've already given him two heaping plates, he's still got his muffin, and that's his second cup of coffee. Next thing you know, he'll be sneaking food to Blackie under the table." The black lab's tail began to thump at the prospect.

Dennis O' Leary snuck a piece of bacon to the sweet pooch, a finger to his lips to keep mum. Hair of a faded red was thinning, and he wore wire-framed glasses that couldn't hide the mischief in eyes the color of shamrocks. Finishing off his plate, he stood and collected his dishes as well as some of the others on the table.

"Don't mind Annie. She always cooks for an army. If you'd like to join us for dinner tonight, you're more than welcome. We don't anticipate any others and enjoy having young people to liven up two old codgers like us. I hope you two will enjoy your visit to Frost's farm." He strode out of the room, whistling cheerfully, acquiring a shadow in the form of a dog hoping for choice tidbits.

Emmett set his fork down and reached for Casey's hand, linking their fingers. "You remembered." His voice was soft, wonder lighting his eyes. She took his other hand only to find herself relocated to his lap. "I've always wanted to go to his place, find out what inspired him to write the way he did. I'm glad I'm going to see it for the first time through your eyes."

"Me too." If only he could truly see it. Her fingers ran through Emmett's hair, pushing his bangs away from eyes that drifted closed. His face smoothed and he let out a sigh at her touch, completely under her power. Casey looped her arms around his neck, winding up for a good kiss when Mr. O'Leary returned to clear. He couldn't hide his grin.

"Oh, don't stop on my account. You remind me what it is young people do to stay young. Annie-girl, where are you? I'm thinking you need a thorough kissing. These kids out here know how it's done. Let's give it a go." Off he went, on a quest for the lady of the house. Peals of laughter suggested he found her.

Robert Frost's farm. His inspiration for a river of words that ran through generations and spilled from the tongues of young and old. A small, unassuming house set high on a hill, surrounded by a blanket of white, winter's hold not yet broken. A picket fence, a stone wall that called to mind "Mending Fences" and grounds to roam, a place where one could think.

Casey tried to do it justice, painting pictures in words, guiding Emmett's steps, fueling his imagination. They took their time, passing through each room, Emmett running his hands over everything, Casey describing each color, piece, and room setting.

It was the walk through the woods, making him kneel to feel yet another stone wall and cross a tiny, wooden bridge, that meant the most. The words of Frost's poems bubbled up and rushed out as she read from a book tucked in her pocket and Em took over from the heart.

"I read them all the time growing up. They're buried up here." He tapped his head. "Every now and then, I pull one out and try it on for size again. They always fit." The grin that he'd been wearing slipped away as his hands tightened on the railing. "Something there is that doesn't love a wall, that wants it down," he whispered. One hand balled into a fist and banged on the solid wood with a resounding thump. "God, I wish I could tear *this* wall down." Emmett waved at his eyes. "I want to see all of this. Most of all, I want to see you."

She took his hands in hers and pressed a kiss to both before taking hold of his lapels. "I know, and I want that too, but you have to remember something, Em. You have been given a gift in some ways. You can create a world that is more beautiful than anything out here, not to mention you see better with your heart than most of us do with our eyes."

His arms came up around her, and he buried his face in her hair, unable to answer. There was no need. The sun warmed their backs and heads, the wind made their clothes and hair flutter, and slowly, the hurting ebbed.

"I'm sorry. I didn't mean to ruin this. Sometimes, the bitterness floods in, and I have a hard time beating it down again. You really did a wonderful thing, bringing me here. I promise no more whining." Emmett gave her his smile, one of his greatest gifts, and skimmed the top of her head with his lips. Casey made sure to hold his cheeks and catch a kiss. "Ready to go back?"

"Anytime you are." She hooked her arm through his to go back the way they came, his steps sure, as if remembering where to go on their own. The sun was on its downward slope as they neared the house and heard the clip-clopping of horses' hooves. Emmett's head tilted to the side, listening intently, forehead creasing in thought. Casey couldn't help laughing. "No, you're not imagining things. There's a carriage waiting in the lane. They offer rides. I saw it in the flyer."

"Let's go." Visibly brightening at a chance to inter-act with horses in any way, Emmett gave her hand a tug and moved with confidence in the direction of what had to be music to his ears. A black carriage pulled by mighty Clydesdales came to a stop, the gentle giants pawing the ground and huffing through their noses as Em ran his hands over both, his smile growing wide. "You're like my Bonnie Bell and Clyde. I bet you're beauties."

An elderly man in a checkered cap like Elmer Fudd's, Carhartt coat and pants, sat perched on the driv-er's seat. He touched the brim of his hat and gave the couple a wink. "That they are. Care for a ride, folks? I'll be happy to give you the grand tour."

He was down in a flash, surprisingly agile for his age, holding the door open without even waiting for an answer. "The name's Hank." At Emmett's insistence, Ca-sey went first, accepting a hand up. She turned back for Em but needn't have worried. Hank had the younger man's elbow in a firm hold, guiding his step without fan-fare.

The driver climbed back up and called over his shoulder, "A chill is settling in now that the sun is on its way down. Take hold of that blanket down there and make yourselves cozy. There's a thermos of cocoa too and a couple of mugs in that basket down there, some other sweets, Lord knows what. Never know what my wife will get a hankering for." A pull on the reins, and they set off at an easy gait.

Emmett drew Casey snug against his side and cov-ered their laps, his arm wrapping around her waist. "I don't need a blanket to cozy up to you." His smile was infectious as was his mood, making her heart lift and her blood begin to sing. He grazed her jaw with his lips be-fore finding his way home, and the heat rushed to her face. No doubt about it, no need for blankets here.

"*Em!* There is a driver with us!" She pulled away to see the answering flush in his cheeks and the fire of sunset reflected in his eyes. The scenery around them faded away, no contest to the view beside her. Casey leaned her forehead on his and held on to the front of his coat, fighting to rein in the wild beating of her heart.

Hank chuckled above them, glancing back and giving a wink. "It's all right. Nice to see young people have a spark. I'll have to try it with my Ethel tonight, see if I can light any fires." He had them all laughing as the carriage rattled over the bumpy lane and his commentary carried them back in time.

# CHAPTER 19

"Em, come on! Let's walk the pasture. I want to get out!" Casey was lying on his lap on the chaise lounge, facing the back fields. They wore sweaters, jeans, and sock feet, a classic combination for soaking up good weather. April heralded sunny days, a breath of warm air, and letting go of the snow.

Emmett felt good, too good to move. "We are out. I've kind of got my hands full right now." His fingers were wandering, one entangled in her hair, the other tapping on her thigh to the rhythm of his heartbeat. "Why don't we hold down the fort?"

She rolled over and gripped his shoulders, applying pressure, adding a kiss for persuasion. "Please, Emmett! I've got cabin fever from being cooped up in that office at the clinic all week long. The buds are popping on the trees, the grass is turning green, and the world is waking up. We need to be out there!" He didn't have it in him to deny her.

"All right. Grab the barn boots in the entryway. We'll be mucking about out there what with the meltdown and the rain. Might need an ark." The image of the two of them rolling around in the mud filled his mind and made a smile bloom.

The pitter pat of feet came his way, and Casey

plopped down beside him while something thumped nearby.

"Go on now, slip them on and let's get going." Emmett barely pulled on his rubber boots, and she had his hand in hers. One hearty tug and he was up, moving across the porch, down the steps, to solid ground. A few paces, the click of the gate, and they were off. No cane. No fence to guide him. Only her hand. More than enough to take a leap of faith.

Carried by her conversation, laughter, and the occasional smile in her voice, the day passed quickly. Casey planned ahead, a lunch and thermos of sweet tea, brewed in the light of a hot sun the day before, packed in a sack on her back. Perched on the railing of the fence, they ate their fill, drank the jug dry, and walked farther than Emmett had ever gone on his own.

The closing of the day found the couple meandering their way home, Casey on Emmett's back, shouting directions, shrieking when they nearly fell. Not wanting to cook, they ate popcorn and drank wine until his head was fuzzy, telling stories until their tongues nearly wore out. In bed that night, he was tired, a good tired, reminiscent of days spent working sun up to sun down with the horses. Sleep wasn't long in coming, especially with the woman by his side as a lullaby.

The nightmare took him completely off guard, thrusting him back in that barroom, a place he hadn't been since Casey became a light in the darkness. It grabbed him in its teeth again, rattling him and shaking him awake. Emmett came up fast with his head fit to split wide open, the images still blasting through his mind. Taking care not to disturb Casey, he stumbled downstairs, weaving like a drunken man, holding on to his head with one hand, the wall with the other. His fingers trembled, trying to get to the pain pills over the sink, when his legs gave out. Emmett hit the hard, unyielding floor, and he was out.

He was shivering from the cold when he came to. His face hurt, one cheek scraped raw. "What the—" Disoriented, not knowing where he was, Emmett began to analyze. *You know you're on the floor, but which floor?*

The floor—it was smooth and hard, but not the tile of the bathroom or hardwood of his bedroom. Couldn't be the living room—that would be warm from the hearth, and there was a throw rug. His heart started to thump anxiously while his mind ran through the gamut. He reached out, his fingers skimming the surface, noting the texture, and his knuckles rapped on the cabinet, finally making the connection. *In the kitchen. You went to get pills, remember?*

"Emmett? Emmett! Are you all right? Your nose, your lip, they're bleeding!" Panic was creeping into Casey's voice, although she was fighting to keep her doctor cool, bare feet slapping on the floor. Warm, soft hands ran over his body, taking an initial assessment, pushing the hair off his face. She pressed a towel to his mouth, dabbing at his nose. "Can you sit up?" A sturdy arm and shoulder provided leverage to get him semi-vertical. "Easy. Go easy, Superman."

He wobbled, reaching out and her hand caught his, holding firm as an arm wrapped around his back. "Whoa. Vertigo is really bizarre when you can't see." Emmett's stomach pitched, and he swallowed hard, pressing his fingers to his forehead. "I—I don't know what happened to me. Too much wine before bed, I guess. My head hurt, so I came down for some aspirin and next thing I knew I was on the floor."

Casey left him for a moment, and there was the sound of running water. A cold, damp cloth covered his forehead, and a glass was placed in his hand. "Here.

Drink some water. Maybe you need to be hydrated."

He swallowed the whole thing in a gulp, unbelievably thirsty, and allowed her to help him to his feet. Her arm was around his waist, guiding him to the couch. "Okay, what's going on in that head of yours? What have you been keeping from me, little boy?" Her tone was teasing, but a serious undercurrent ran beneath it all.

"Oh, a few dizzy spells—getting off balance now and then—more headaches than usual. I figured it was par for the course. No reason to make a big deal about it. You get your head pounded, there's going to be some reminders, right?" The head in question felt too heavy for his shoulders. Emmett fell back against the couch and tipped his face to the ceiling, waiting for the dull throbbing to stop.

Casey's fingers settled on his thigh and dug in. "You're going in for tests. Tomorrow, to my clinic." *Brooks no arguments, stubborn woman.* "You can't mess around with this, Emmett." Her voice cracked, and she started to stroke his hair. It was the crack that nearly did him in and swallowed him whole.

Bleak, he rested his head on her shoulder, finding it too hard to hold up. "What's the point, Case? Can't get much worse, can it?"

She held him for a while, led him back to bed, tucked him in as if he were a child. Her body cupped his like a spoon, and the pain let go for a little while, only to come back in the morning.

Casey found him sitting on the side of the tub, his head in his hands, unable to trust standing up in the shower without falling down again. Even though Emmett couldn't see her face, he felt her reproach. "All right. I'll go."

ໜ

Emmett hated hospitals, lab work, and doctor's visits—hated them with a passion since being a good Samaritan kicked him in the seat of the pants. Call it an overdose of "restorative" care. Didn't have much to show for all that rehabilitation. *You're still here, ingrate.*

A day under the microscope was making the frustration build to no end, kicking up the anxiety level to the max. Listening to the hum and whir of the machines, the hushed litany of instructions, being moved this way and that, enduring scan after scan. *Sometimes* they remembered to talk him through it.

More prodding. Too much poking. Blood work—despised needles. They always jabbed him, made it sting. Why the hell did he need that if there was something going on in his brain? All the tests gave him time—too much time—alone in his head, the worry sharks circling, snapping their jaws.

What if something major was going on? He hadn't been honest with Casey. The…episodes…or whatever they were, the vertigo, the headaches, they were happening more often of late, getting in the way. Sitting in the clinic, getting a thorough going over, was making Emmett chew on his avoidance. He didn't savor the flavor.

The MRI. Now that was a trip. Probably not as bad for him as the experience was for those who could see, but still a tough one, enclosed in that tunnel, restrained. Being blind gave him an acute sense of claustrophobia. He needed space, to be able to reach out with all his senses, to compensate for what was lacking.

Emmett fought to steer clear of a complete panic attack. He took deep breaths, in and out, counting the beats of his heart pounding in his brain, doing his best not to shift in the slightest. *Don't budge and you won't feel the machine pressing in on you.*

He was close to the edge of his personal limits when

a familiar voice tossed him a lifeline. Casey chatted with the technician and sat next to his head, creating a steady hum of light conversation, something for him to latch on to, setting his blood to singing at her nearness. The heady scent of her, that blend of brown sugar and vanilla sweetness, drifted his way, riding over all else, giving him a whole, new set of desires and something else to think about. *Can't wait to get out of this contraption and put my hands on her.*

As soon as the test was over, she led him to her office to finish up his examination. Emmett was fully aware of the fact that he only wore a hospital gown. Of the sounds in the hall. People saying goodnight. Quitting time.

Casey's hair brushed against his face, her hand grazing his, leaving a burning in its wake. "Okay, I'm going to give you a few instructions. You follow them the best you can. Touch your nose with your right hand. Now your left. Do the same with your forehead. Touch your right hand to your left ear. Now again with your left hand. Touch your chin with alternating hands. Move your eyes side to side. Up and down. All right, I'm going to take a look in your eyes with my light."

All business and that turned him on even more. So competent. So sexy. Her hand took a firm grasp of his forehead, and she held his eyelids open, one by one, leaning in close, her breath kissing his skin.

"Hmm. People are heading out. The place is shutting down. Maybe I can get a chance to play doctor with a real doctor, try some of your instruments. I've fantasized about that since high school." Emmett grinned playfully and let his fingers do the walking. No malfunction there. His hands trailed up her lab coat, began undoing buttons, and caught her stethoscope before finding her face.

Concentration broken, impatience gave Casey's

voice an edge. "Em, I'm almost finished. *This is serious.*" She stepped back, leaving his hands empty. Only the sound of their breathing broke the silence.

His body went still, his wide-eyed stare aiming straight at her heart. "I know that, Case. Trying not to think about it here."

For the first time that day, Emmett let her see it—fear. There'd been plenty of aggravation, irritation, agitation. Now, uncertainty tightened his features, and his spine went rigid. He couldn't help but wonder—was the problem from lingering effects of his brain injury or was there a ticking time bomb about to erupt, like the aneurysm that killed Mama?

Casey took off her doctor's hat to become his girl-friend. She kissed his cheek and walked away, heels tapping across the floor, locking the door with an audible click. Picking up the phone, she punched in a number, making a quick call to Angie at the receptionist's desk. "I'm running late with Emmett and his results. You go ahead on out. I'll lock up."

The shoes clicked their way back to Emmett, her hands finding purchase in his hair. His fingers were grasping her arms, her coat, the dangling stethoscope, ripping away the flimsy gown to press it against his heart.

"Listen, Casey," he whispered, his voice raspy with need. "Can you hear it hammering? Do you know what you do to me?"

She swallowed hard, pressed his hand to her cheek, and nodded her assertion before pulling the stethoscope away to stick the cold metal against her chest. Emmett heard the answer in the hummingbird flutter of her heart.

His mouth found the way to hers, and she was climbing up on to the table, driving him down, finding it to be an extremely handy piece of furniture at that moment. Her heels dropped to the floor with a clatter, and he pinned her underneath. "I've got to tell you, Doc. You beat the fantasies, no contest. I always liked, 'I'm Hot for Teacher.' Better make that doctor." Her laughter bubbled up until Emmett quieted her with a kiss.

She broke away, breathing hard as if after a long run. "Do you want to see—I mean look at, I mean—know the results from today?" His finger touched her lip, the heat rushing to his face, his own breathing growing ragged.

Emmett shook his head emphatically. "No, it will keep until morning. Let's wrap up *our* exam. What do you need your patient to do, Doc? I am in your capable hands." *Playtime is over.*

 espe

SUNY Upstate Medical University Hospital. Going for the big guns. Out of her realm of expertise, Casey did her homework and found the best, a surgeon who specialized in all things cerebral. No guarantees, no promises, but he'd agreed to see Emmett based on the reports Casey sent his way. She was determined not to leave any stone unturned. Bulldog stubborn as they come, she talked her patient into going. Time to get in the ring for another round with doctors, hospitals, and potential torture.

Emmett sat in the waiting room, jaw clenched, arms crossed over his chest, staring straight ahead. Couldn't get Wyatt off his mind, the lie he'd told about a romantic getaway. They never lied to each other. Em might not be able to see his brother's face, but he'd heard the doubt and hurt in his voice. Wyatt had even grilled Doc, but they'd agreed—no sense in worrying him.

Emmett had done enough of making his brother fret in the past year. No need to give false hopes either. No way. No how.

Casey was off on some wild, goose chase, leaving

him stuck in his own head even more. *Can you be any more miserable?*

Heavy footsteps approached, there was a bit of rustling as someone sat beside him and a deep voice rolled his way in an easy, unhurried flow. "Name's Joe Ambrico. You here for Doc Woods or the other guy?"

The office was shared by two doctors in a collection of offices that formed one wing, only a small strand of the web that was University Hospital. Process of elimination made it simple for a conversation starter.

Emmett turned his head toward the source of sound, made an attempt at a level gaze, and extended his hand. He assumed it put people at ease, giving them a sense of normalcy, doing the expected. A strong calloused hand took hold of his in a firm grip. "Doc Woods. I'm Emmett Henry. Are you one of his patients?"

Sympathy ran strong for anyone else who had to endure the forced interference of doctors in their lives— they were a blessing and a curse, often hurting on the way to healing. *Except for Case. She's a Godsend.*

His companion let out great rush of air and his chair creaked as he settled in. "Oh, Doc Woods and I know each other very well. He's done quite the rooting around in my brain. The man's the reason I'm alive, a miracle worker I tell you. You'll be in good hands. You here for your eyes?"

Emmett nodded but waved himself aside, curiosity peaked by the stranger who was fast becoming an acquaintance through his open manner. "Do you mind my asking what happened to you?"

It bolstered Em's confidence, talking with someone who came through the other side with the surgeon. The guy sounded well enough, and Emmett took heart—he hadn't experienced a brush with death yet. Hopefully, that wasn't eminent.

"Mind if I show you?"

At Emmett's nod, Joe took his hand and set his fingers on the base of his skull, nearly making him pull away when he hit a nasty, raised bump and scar. Emmett cursed under his breath, eyes springing wide, hand tensing in recognition.

"Gunshot wound. I was a mess. Should've died. Would've without Dr. Woods." Joe's voice was low, and he broke off, working his way through the past. "I was in a coma then had terrible seizures. My memory was wiped clean. I didn't get it back for a year." There was another pause, and he pushed on in a rush. "I found out that I lost everything on the day I was shot. It took me a while to appreciate being alive, to be grateful for Dr. Woods's efforts. My new wife, Claire, really helped."

Lighter footsteps approached and a smile slid into Joe's voice. "She's expecting and God, I'm glad to be here for this go around. Woods is the reason and because I'm too thick-headed to die. I'm here for a checkup because my woman makes me behave. Claire, this is Emmett Henry. He's here for Doc Woods, too. Emmett, this is my Claire."

A cool, soft touch took his hand and held on a moment longer than the norm, making him feel like he mattered, that they might not know each other yet, but would soon. A unique scent, something that was a blend of floral and citrus drifted his way and material—a dress?—brushed his leg.

"It's a pleasure to meet you, Emmett. Jason Woods is the absolute best. I think I may have met your girlfriend in the bathroom. Dark-haired girl, green eyes." Nervous laughter and a pat on his arm. "I'm sorry. I mean a really sweet girl brimming with exuberance and determination."

Emmett really liked her. The girl could be Doc's sister. "Yeah, that's Casey. You can tell me what she looks like. I've already asked for a full description. The girl's a scrappy one, and a knockout, isn't she?"

Their enthusiastic agreement and Joe's slap on his back told him what he already knew. Claire left again, in search of something to eat. Emmett could practically hear Joe rolling his eyes, showing his good nature as he playfully teased his wife on the way out.

It was strange, being so comfortable with this stranger he couldn't see. They had a common bond, like war vets, telling their horror stories, sharing battle scars. A nurse interrupted their discussion, taking Emmett by the arm, ready to lead him to meet the doctor. *Or executioner.* The grim words flitted through his mind, wiped away when Joe pressed a piece of paper in his hand. "Here's my name and number if you want to talk or I can help you in any way."

Emmett took his cell phone out of his pocket with a rueful grin. "I have joined the modern age. My brother made me, but I can't program it. Do you know how?" Joe slipped the phone from his hand, pushed a few buttons, and set it back in his palm. "Thanks," Emmett said. "It was good meeting you, Joe. You were exactly what I needed today." Someone who had overcome worse could really change your perspective.

A strong grip applied pressure to his shoulder. "Nice to meet you too, buddy. Hang in. I'm number ten, speed dial. You need anything else, anything at all, you call."

Emmett raised his hand in a wave. He was led down a hallway when the scent of vanilla and brown sugar met him first, a warm set of arms wrapping him up next. Whatever happened later, Casey was his wings, parachute, and soft landing all in one.

# CHAPTER 20

Taking her turn in the waiting area, *holding tank*, tapping her foot, drumming her fingers on the arm of the chair, biting her nails—a habit that was supposedly broken in elementary school. Casey was jittery from way too much coffee, waiting for Emmett to get done with the next battery of tests. *Must feel like a guinea pig. Please, God. Don't let this be for nothing.*

"Dr. Mitchell, could you step into my office for a minute?"

Jason Woods stood with his hip propped against the door, sporting a smile that was a noble fight against the weariness that plagued a specialist with too many patients and not enough hours in the day. The man was a puzzle. Salt and pepper hair gave the impression of being older, but it was playfully mussed, his face practically unlined, his eyes of a penetrating blue that snapped. He crackled with vitality.

His typical, white doctor's coat couldn't hide his atypical jeans, T-shirt, and sneakers. He bowed her in his office, apologetically clearing papers off his sofa.

She hesitated, getting her back up. "Listen, it's Casey. I'm not his doctor now, I'm his girlfriend, and shouldn't you speak to Emmett first?"

Dr. Woods motioned for her to sit and situated himself beside her, turning her way. His face was completely open, inviting her to come in and stay a while. "Casey, no matter how well I do my job, he's going to have questions after I leave. You'll be able to answer them, and you'll serve him better as his eyes when you see the results."

He picked up a thick folder on his desk and started flipping through the pages, even though everything was clearly catalogued in that incredible mind of his, as the doctor would prove, rattling off observations, conclusions, and possible scenarios without looking through the file. "He's getting dressed right now. My assistant will show him to my office in a few minutes. I have to thank you for all of your excellent groundwork. You made my life easier, showed me exactly where I had to go." Dr. Woods settled on a starting point, an image of his patient's brain, and set it on her lap.

Casey glanced down, closed her eyes, and swallowed hard. "Tell me one thing, Doctor. Is his life in danger?" It had been that fear that kept her awake nights and made her push Emmett to come here. If anything were to happen to him—

Jason Woods took her hand and shook his head.

Her breath let out slowly, like a balloon losing air. She met his eye and asked the million-dollar question of the day. "Can you help him?"

Casey was crying in his arms when Emmett arrived.

෧෨෬

"Tell me again. In terms that can be understood by horse farmers and normal human beings. Break it down into small pieces."

Dr. Woods was on his way to surgery. He'd told Casey and Emmett to take as long as they liked, sitting in his office, going over the thick folder in her lap. He'd been right on the money. As soon as the man walked out, Em was firing off questions, pacing, knocking into things, as tense as a tiger trapped in a cage.

"Em, please. Come sit down. You're making me nervous." He obliged, propping an elbow on one knee, kneading his neck. She laid her fingers on his, and they stilled, but the crease between his eyes grew deeper in concentration.

"Okay. When you were injured, you actually had tiny fragments of bone that have been pressing on your optic nerve. You also have new fluid building up. That accounts for your recent problems. I figured on the fluid, but not the bone. The original testing you went through missed it. Even the testing I put you through missed it. Dr. Woods has the equipment and the experience to catch something so important."

Emmett was out of his seat once more, pulling away from her, trying to process. "Bone chips? You're trying to tell me this is all from bone chips pressing on my nerve? What can he do about it? It's too late, isn't it?" He stopped and leaned against the wall, his palms pressed flat.

Casey was up in a flash, standing in front of him, resting her hands on his hips. "There's a lot of ifs." Her voice broke, and she had to take a deep breath before forging ahead. "If Dr. Woods can remove the bone splinters, if he can drain the fluid, there's a chance you'll see again."

His face crumpled. Emmett shook his head and fumbled his way out of the hospital, stumbling outside into the rain, lifting his face to the sky, letting it come down on him. Casey rushed after him and took hold of his hand, "Em, what is it? What's wrong?"

He turned her way, and the storm brewing in his eyes

reflected insides in as much turmoil as the outside. His feelings poured out in a voice gone hoarse. "I'm—I'm scared, Case. I didn't think this could be changed. Now that there's a chance, I want it so bad, I can taste it. More than anything, I want to see you. What if it doesn't work? I don't know if I can take it."

Casey pressed her palms to his cheeks and found steel in her words *and* her backbone. "I *know* something good will come from this. See me or not, you're going to be all right. No more dizzy spells. No more headaches. Nothing worse—Don't get this taken care of and there could be much worse. That's all I care about, Emmett." She leaned forward and covered him with kisses.

Emmett leaned his forehead against hers, brushing noses. "Tell the truth. You just want to see me in a hospital gown one more time." His arms came up around her as she buried her face in his chest, their laughter and the rain covering their tears.

☙ℰ☙

He was sporting that hospital gown the next day. Emmett was a priority. If his optic nerves hadn't been irreparably damaged or severed yet, it was imperative that the fluid be drained to relieve pressure. If Dr. Woods could remove the splinters to eliminate any more risk, that would be ideal. If his vision could be restored, better yet. The procedure was incredibly delicate and fraught with risks. Any slight shifting of the bits and pieces in the process and their hopes could be dashed—permanently.

Prepped, disinfected, hooked to an IV for hydration and anesthesia, Emmett sat on the gurney, waiting to be rolled in. He was joking with the staff, smiling and laughing, but Casey couldn't miss that line between his eyes or around his mouth. Putting up a brave front for everyone else, that was his way.

Good thing he couldn't see the way the nurses were drooling over him, otherwise she'd be absolutely green. "You sure do look sexy in your hospital gown. It's making it really hard to resist temptation. I'll have to be on guard. One of these nurses might try and take advantage of you."

The smile slipped from his face as he reached for her. One hand hooked around her waist, drawing her closer. The other disappeared under his pillow and emerged with a velvet box. If Emmett hadn't been holding her, Casey was sure she'd be on the floor.

He cleared his throat as his voice dropped down low. "I want to ask you something, want to ask you now. If this doesn't work, you might say yes because you feel sorry for me and if it works, how will I know if you would've gone for rich or for poor, better or worse and all that, right? If I ask now, I'll know your mind, not that I want to put you on the spot—"

Her finger touched his lips, effectively stopping the steady stream of words. "Will you shut up? Yes, a thousand times yes. I'd say yes no matter when you asked or where or how. I will marry you, Emmett Henry."

Powerful emotion flashed across his face as he pulled her into the shelter of his arms. A few deep breaths, a gathering of composure, and he broke away, the sheen of tears making his eyes even brighter when he opened the box. A smile bloomed at her gasp and kept on growing.

Emmett fumbled until he'd found the ring, caught her left hand, and counted his way across to slide it in place.

"Oh, Em. It's simply gorgeous." It was a simple band with tiny diamonds and emeralds alternating all the way around to create an unbroken circle.

"That's what Sammie said. I figured I needed a woman's opinion the day we went ring shopping. She kept coming back to this one. I think she wanted it."

Casey leaned forward, stopping the flow of words by sealing his mouth with hers. Sliding over, he made room for her, and they stretched out on the gurney, playing the waiting game.

Emmett gazed up at the ceiling with an empty stare, a hush falling in the room, despite the noisy hallway, as well as the expected hustle and bustle of a hospital. His hand found her hair, started to toy with it, his voice husky when he spoke again. "I want to tell you something, now, while I can. No matter what happens with this procedure, I wouldn't change a thing, hindsight or no, because it brought you into my life. If I could have seen you that night we met, I might have said or done something stupid, or you wouldn't have felt sorry for me."

She started to protest, but his finger on her mouth quieted her. "Yes, you felt sorry for me, at least that first night. Not since. If I could have seen you, everything would've been resolved wham-bam thank you, ma'am, and you would have been on your way, out of my life. Wyatt and I probably would've delivered that baby—Lord only knows. All I know is I would do it all again, everything in the same way, to have you."

"I don't know what to say to that, except I feel the same way." Casey rolled on her side and nestled her head against his shoulder while his hand continued to rhythmically stroke her hair. Her heart swelled, and she couldn't speak, could only rest her hand on his cheek to reassure herself he was solid and real, that this was not a dream.

Emmett turned her way and pressed his forehead to hers. "You don't have to say anything." He kissed her and laid his hand on her chest to feel the steady thrumming within. "Your heart says it all."

cంంంం

The chapel was quiet, cast in a soft blue glow from a stained-glass picture of Mary, her hands open in welcome, offering a mother's comfort to all. Casey bowed her head and closed her eyes tightly, searching for a peace that would not come. The surgery was running long, five hours and counting.

When a nurse checked in with her for the fourth time and couldn't give any answers, it was time to do *something*. Casey told them where she would be, had been there for nearly another hour. The clock ticked on the wall and the blood rushed into her ears. Gulping down a sob, she leaned forward and pressed her hands to her face.

Footsteps sounded, and someone dropped into the seat beside her, an arm coming around her shoulders. It was someone with a strong back, one that reminded her of Emmett. "He's in recovery. Everything went well. There was more going on in there than I thought, some other areas that had to be addressed. I'm sorry to keep you waiting so long."

She opened her eyes to find Dr. Woods covered in perspiration, exhaustion clouding his gaze and lining his face, but his smile spoke more than his words. For the second time, Casey grabbed hold of the man and cried her eyes out.

cంంంం

"Em, stop! Wait until the doctor comes."
It looked like there'd been a war with the bed, and it

was questionable about the winner. Somehow, he'd managed to raise the mattress, pillows were on the floor, the covers in a tangle. The bullheaded man was sitting up, tugging at the bandaging that wrapped his head, giving him the appearance of a rush-job mummy that was left undone. Casey hurried to his side, careful of the tubes running to his arm, and sat down on the edge of the bed, laying her hand on his.

He stilled, but only for a moment. The part of his face that was visible was whiter than paper, his jaw clenched. "What does it matter, Case?" he asked tightly, his words clipped. "Either it worked, or it didn't, nothing in between. No sense waiting for a drumroll or public presentation. I just want to get this over with."

Swallowing hard, forgetting herself again, Casey nodded. Her hands were trembling as she helped him, carefully pulling at the outer wrapping, giving him a shoulder when he started to sway.

"I'm all right. Keep going."

"Okay, okay. Try to be patient, okay, Em. I don't want to tug at your incision or cause any bleeding. They've got you on some pretty serious stuff. When it wears off, you're going to feel it."

A little more finagling and the last of the gauze was off, leaving two, thick pads of white that covered his eyes. Her heart began to thud painfully, echoing in her ears. If she was anxious, imagine how he must feel after a year in the dark.

Cautiously, Emmett peeled each bandage away. His eyes cracked open, and he winced. "Too bright! The light. God, it's too bright!" He made a shield with his arm.

Casey hurried to draw the blinds and turn off the lights, leaving only the light in the bathroom, the door slightly ajar to cast a soft glow in the room. Her hand found the way to his shoulder and held on tight.

Emmett moved his arm away from his face and breathed deep. In. Out. In again. "Okay, all right then. Here goes. One…two…three." His eyes opened slowly, and his pupils responded to the light, shrinking in size.

He turned to Casey, and his hand trembled as he reached for her face. "My God! I knew—I *always* knew you were beautiful, but more so than I could have imagined. The color of your eyes, the gloss of your hair. I have tried to build a picture of you in my mind, but it would always crumble."

His face caved in at that moment, a sob breaking his dam of self-control. He bit it off, but his shoulders began to shake. Casey held on and began to rock, her heart fit to burst with joy.

"Wyatt! Come quick!"

Sammie sounded fragile, as if she was about to fall to pieces. His wife never sounded that way. Wyatt dropped the harness he was working on in the barn and rushed out, heart hammering, head beginning to pound. *The baby? Dear God, don't let anything be wrong with the baby!*

Sammie was on the porch, taking clothes off the line, and Jackson's little arms and legs were waving from his carriage. All clear on the home front. His wife was gesturing toward the driveway with a towel before she buried her face in it, the tears flowing down her cheeks.

A truck. His brother's truck was rumbling down the long lane and rolling to a stop. The doc was on the passenger side. Incomputable. The driver's side opened with a creak. Scuffed boots dropped to the ground, followed by jean-clad legs that stretched to a flannel shirt and broad shoulders on a body that stood straight and tall.

Emmett glanced his way and tossed him a smile, an over the top, out of this world, sun-coming-out-after-a-bad-storm smile, and then his long legs were eating the distance between them. Wyatt's knees gave out, and he fell to the ground, burying his face in his hands, afraid that his eyes were deceiving him with a mean mirage of something prayed for on a daily basis for the past year.

A few heartbeats later, a hand clamped down on his shoulder. "Get up, Wyatt. I won't have you down on the ground today. This is a day for jumping up and down, time to celebrate."

A sturdy, calloused palm was offered and pulled Wyatt to his feet. The brothers slammed into each other with a hug, the tears coming from both and neither paying them any mind.

"But how?" Wyatt walked beside his brother to the house, a hand gripping him by the nape of the neck like a mother dog hanging on to her pup. He couldn't take his eyes off Emmett, afraid it was a dream. "Did I just wake up? Wait a minute."

He moved in front of Emmett and took hold of his shoulders, staring him up and down, lifting his bangs with a tentative touch to reveal the bandage peeking out below his hairline. "I *knew* it! I knew you lied to me about that trip with Doc. I'll forgive you this once, Em, but never again, got it? Henrys tell each other everything—good, bad, and the ugly."

Emmett nodded and pulled his brother in for another bone cracker. "I promise. I didn't know how it was all going down. You've been through so much, Wyatt, I couldn't put you through more. I thought I might be in big trouble and, even if I wasn't, I was afraid to dangle hope and have it snatched away."

Wyatt stepped in and kissed his brother on the cheek, scraping his sleeve across his eyes. "I get it. My answer stands. Don't do it again." He hooked an arm around Emmett's neck and couldn't stop smiling.

They made it as far as the porch before the whirl-wind that was Samantha Henry plowed into her brother-in-law and knocked them both to the ground, laughing and crying. She kissed his forehead, his cheeks, his nose, and full on the mouth, pressing both hands to his face and staring intently into his gorgeous, golden eyes.

Casey stood with Wyatt on the steps, taking in the spectacle, arms wrapped around her middle while Wyatt held on to her shoulder. Sammie was on her feet first, lending Emmett a hand, covering him with a flurry of kisses and hugging him fiercely. "Oh, my God, Emmett! Except for the day Jackson was placed in my arms, you are the best thing I've seen in a lifetime."

"Hey, what about the face you wake up to every morning? I hear we do have a resemblance." Wyatt faked a hurt tone, but couldn't pull it off, not with the grin that couldn't be wiped off his face.

They all took the steps, flanking each other, every-one talking at once when Emmett broke away. He crossed the porch and caught Jackson in his hands, holding him aloft, laughing, choking up, burying his head in the little boy's hair. Emmett's shoulders began to shake, and he held the baby boy away from him again. "Will you look at that blondie and his baby blues? Beautiful, just like his mother, and his grandmama. But that face, whoa, baby, that's you through and through, Wyatt."

"Look in the mirror, Emmett. It's you, too. He's a Henry." Eyes filling up once more, Wyatt dashed a hand roughly across his face and cleared his throat. "Sammie, go get dolled up. We're going someplace nice to cele-brate."

Emmett turned with Jackson tucked in the crook of his arm, bouncing him, marveling at the sight of his nephew. For the first time in a year, he looked...happy. No lines marring his face. No lost look about him. All the walls that he'd been hiding behind had come down, leaving one thing out in the open...joy. "Wyatt, that sounds great, but there's something I want to do first."

$\infty\infty$

The sun couldn't hold a candle to Emmett, not with the light in his golden eyes, vibrant once more, and the brilliant flash of his teeth in a smile that couldn't possibly be any wider. Sitting on Bonnie's back, straight and tall, he looked like an extension of the great horse, completely at home in the saddle. He leaned forward, stroking her neck, and whispered something in her ear.

She set off like a shot, Clyde in her wake. Emmett let out a great whoop that carried over the field as Wyatt attempted to keep up. No chance.

"My God, look at him! Will you look at him?" Casey said in a hush—any louder, and she'd scatter to dust.

Sammie nodded, her eyes bright. "You know how it's wrong to cage a bird? I always thought it was worse to clip his wings, hang a taste of freedom in front of him, only to take it away. That was Emmett this past year, with his wings clipped. I thought he'd never be free again but look at him now. Look at him fly!"

The tears were streaming freely down her face, Jackson clutched to her chest.

Casey could only shake her head and cry with her. *If you can't beat them, join them.*

# CHAPTER 21

The cabin was perched high on a hill, on a dead-end road, the Adirondack mountains and a sea of wilderness acting as a backdrop. The truck coasted to a stop behind an old, Chevy truck in robin's egg blue and a beauty of a black GTO. Emmett let out a long, low whistle. "Sweet spot."

"Almost as sweet as yours—I mean ours."

His hand reached for Casey's thigh and held on. Now, more than ever before, he had to be in contact with her, couldn't get enough of her, didn't want her out of his sight. She turned toward him, and he caught her chin simply to stare at her and get lost in her eyes.

Emmett would never take the gift of vision for granted again.

Casey returned the gesture, her fingers soft and gentle, leaning in close to land a butterfly of a kiss on his lips. One more second...or was it a minute?...of staring into each other's eyes, and she nodded. "Well, shall we?"

He stepped out of the truck, holding Casey's hand as she slid across the seat and joined him. All was quiet, incredibly peaceful on a mild spring day, the air and sunlight like a kiss, everything popping with green. Emmett filled his lungs and mounted the stairs to the wrap-around porch made from logs to match the rustic home.

A hard rap on the door gained no response. Giving a shrug, he forged on, walking to one end of the porch, glancing to the side, making his way around to the back, Casey in tow.

Around one more corner and a soul-soothing view opened on a small patch of yard that was swallowed by a wall of forest. At the end of the porch, a couple sat in an Adirondack chair, taking in the day.

Both turned at the sound of footsteps. The man rose to his feet, bringing the woman with him and carefully setting her on her feet, his hand caressing her protruding, obviously pregnant belly for a moment before striding forward. He was tall, solid, and lean, with golden wheat in his hair and the sky in his eyes. The smile on his face, one that looked like habitual wear, could not stop growing as his steps quickened and he offered his hand.

"Emmett? Emmett Henry! Claire, can you believe this?" His wife, trailing behind him, wore a face-splitting grin of her own, her pixie cut of dark hair endearing, pale green eyes shimmering with tears. Emmett seemed to have that effect on people. *Like Lazarus rising from the dead.*

A handshake wasn't enough. Emmett pulled their host into a hug and received a good pounding on the back. "Joe, I had to come and say thank you, Casey and I both did. When we drove through town and saw that sign for Hope, we realized you couldn't live in a better place because that's what you gave me that day in the hospital. You were right. Dr. Woods is a miracle worker."

Claire stepped in next, offering a hug and congratulations, taking Casey's hand as well. They formed a circle, holding on tight, welcoming the spirit of celebration. Casey reached into her pocket and pulled out an envelope. "We've come for one more reason—to invite you to the wedding."

c/ɔc/ɔ

All was as it should be, the pasture used for its original purpose once more—to give his animals freedom, not as a boundary line to exercise himself like his livestock. The field was filled with horses again, one for every stall. Emmett stood at the fence, fingers digging into the wood, splinters drawing blood as he closed his eyes and pictured all those walks using the long, white stretch of railing as his guide. Keeping him sane. Until Casey walked into his life.

A puff of warm breath lifted his hair and a nose like velvet rubbed his cheek. His arms came up around the sturdy dark neck, and he stared into eyes as warm as melted chocolate. "It's good to see you, too, Bonnie Bell." Clyde was next, nudging Bonnie's shoulder, nuzzling *Emmett's* cheek, making his laughter bubble up. "All right, buddy, all right. I've got enough to go around. I'm happy to see you too." He patted the horse's cheek and grabbed hold to plant a kiss on his nose, then Bonnie's. "God, you are glorious animals."

A hand clapped him on the back, and Wyatt stepped up beside him, decked out in a matching tux. "Come on, Little Brother. Enough visiting out here. It's time. You don't want to keep Doc hanging." Side by side, as in so many things, they headed to the church…together.

c/ɔc/ɔ

Spring. It meant new beginnings, endless possibilities, the gift of hope. The perfect time to marry Casey Mitchell in the country church where his parents married, and his grandparents before them. Emmett stood by the altar where he and Wyatt were blessed with the holy wa-

ter in baptism. Now by the grace of God, he'd join Casey
in marriage.

His brother stood beside him, a best man in every
sense of the title. Sammie waited on the other side as Casey's matron of honor, Jackson in her arms, playing the
part of tiny ring bearer. Surrounded by the people he
knew and loved, those who'd seen him grow up, shared
in the good and the bad, everyone rose to their feet as the
music changed, announcing the bride.

Emmett lifted his head to see the most beautiful girl
in the world as it should be for every bride on her wedding day. Casey's dark hair was piled on top of her head
in an intricate arrangement of curls, baby's breath and
white roses entwined within the nest, a simple silver band
acting like a crown, her veil attached. That hair-do made
his hands itch to take it down, a pastime he enjoyed even
more with the gift of sight. All in good time. His heart
began to pound, the heat rushing to his face, and he
fought the urge to tug at his collar. She couldn't be by his
side, be his, become one with him soon enough.

In a break from tradition, Casey's mother did the
honors of giving the bride away. Unable to hide her emotion or control her tears, she lifted the veil and took her
daughter's face in her hands. Elsie kissed both of her
cheeks, did the same for her future son-in-law, and linked
their hands together. One more kiss for both, the congregation unable to resist chuckling, and she slipped into her
seat, burying her face in tissues shoved into her hand by a
kind guest.

From that moment on, Emmett knew nothing else but
Casey. He studied the way the light made her hair shine
and the weaving of flowers within the stands, watched the
bloom in her cheeks, and the way her mouth tipped up in
a smile as if guarding a good secret. He would never
grow tired of simply watching the wonder of that smile,

lighting her up like the fireworks on the Fourth of July. Her gaze locked on his, and he was swept away on a wave of green, rich and deep as the rolling fields surrounding his home. Looking at her would never grow old.

Besides, Emmett was making up for lost time.

His body did the motions, his mouth said the words, his heart kept beating, but his soul was hers. He was vaguely aware of the moment the pastor announced, "You may kiss the bride."

Emmett didn't know how his bride came to be in his arms, but he wasn't about to let go, dipping her until her hair brushed the floor, placing his mouth on hers, watching the splash of light dancing in her eyes.

❧❧❧

"Congratulations! Happy honeymooning," Sammie called after them from the reception hall as a crowd of well-wishers poured outside to watch the bride and groom depart. Bonnie and Clyde were hitched to a resplendent carriage of white, decked out with ribbons to mark the occasion, waiting to take the couple home.

Wyatt was the driver, tipping a top hat as he helped both aboard. A half hour later, he sprang from his seat at the Henry Homestead to offer a hand once more. Emmett accepted, turning back to take hold of Casey's waist to set her on the ground.

Wyatt hugged them both, stealing their breath away with his fierce grip. "I'll take care of the horses. For the weekend too. This is your honeymoon. Don't worry about a thing. Love you guys."

A wave of his hand and he set foot on the path that would lead him through the woods and back home, the same path Casey had taken on that fateful night when she first met the Henry brothers. Watching his brother walk away, Emmett could only smile. *What goes around, comes around.*

Casey squeezed his hand, reminding him, she was waiting. Lifting her in his arms with ease, he walked to the house, up the porch, and through the doorway. The voice in his head counted each step as he carried her, a habit from the last year, no longer necessary. A few steps more and they were in the bedroom, his feet crossing to the bed, his arms laying her down. He stretched out beside her, propped on one elbow, and began to stroke her hair. "You know, I would've taken you anywhere in the world for your honeymoon."

The tears welled up in her eyes, and her hands trailed up his arms, to his neck, finally cupping his face. "You are my world. Everything is here," Casey touched his chest and his head, "in you. The rest is geography."

Emmett proceeded to worship the treasure that was his wife. He began with her hair, releasing her curls, placing a rose in his teeth and another behind her ear. His fingers, once fumbling, were now adept at undoing the long, intricate row of buttons, slowly unwrapping his universe. No need to go anywhere with her in his arms. She carried him to the moon and the stars.

The next morning, in the early hours, even before the birds began to stir and chatter, Emmett rested a hand on his wife's cheek. *Wife. Can't get enough of that word.* "Case, wake up. I've something to show you." In a sleepy daze, she rose up out of the covers, leaning on him as he handed her a pair of pajamas. He led her out to the barn, settled her on Bonnie's broad, warm back, and mounted the saddle behind her.

"Emmett, I must look like an absolute fright." She patted at her hair, glancing down at her favorite worn flannels, at the ready to slip into after a wedding night when nothing more was necessary than the covers and shelter of his body.

Emmett's arm wrapped around her waist and pulled her close. The scent of her filled his lungs. Nothing could be better to wake up to the first thing in the morning. "Are you kidding? I could never get enough of looking at you, especially with your hair all mussed and sleep in our eyes. You look beautiful. Besides, there will be no one else watching where we are going."

They ambled out of the barn and out to pasture, the harness and stirrups ringing in the silence.

"What about Clyde? Won't he feel left out?" She need not have spoken. Hoofbeats behind her proved they had a shadow. Out to the field, at least a half hour, far from signs of anyone else, far off on Henry property, the sky began to lighten. It was soothing, the rocking of the sturdy horse beneath them and her warmth, her husband's strong arms, flannel, and denim rubbing against her. Emmett reined in and stopped, his chin propped on Casey's shoulder. Gradually, more light poured into a sky on fire with color.

"It's the most beautiful thing I've ever seen...well, except for you shedding your clothes piece by piece." They fell into a hush, watching the world awaken, listening to bird song, and Emmett's head pressed against hers. Casey could feel him shaking with silent sobs.

Somehow, she managed to turn around in the saddle, to rise on her knees and grab hold of the nape of his neck. "Em? What is it? What's wrong?" She began to tremble along with him, caught in a tide of emotion.

He shook his head, the tears raining down. He fought to brush them away, but they kept coming. "You—You gave this back to me. I never thought I'd see the sunrise or my land or go riding again. It's all because of you."

Casey kissed his tears, tasted their salt, and pressed her hands to his face. "No, not me. It was Doctor Woods. You have to give credit where credit is due. I made the appointment, that's all."

"No, it was you. You made me come in, you ran the tests, you knew the next direction to go. You never gave up on me. Because of you, I found my way back to who I was. How do I ever repay you?" Emmett's eyes were filled with wonder, reflecting the dawn, reflecting his love.

Casey turned his head toward the sky once more. She shifted her body, facing the breaking day, her back pressed against the solid, living wall that was her husband. "By watching sunrises, sunsets, and everything else in between with me for the rest of my life."

# About the Author

Heidi Sprouse lives in upstate NY in historic Johnstown. She attended college at St. Rose in Albany, knowing all along her two loves were teaching and English. It took four years before she landed the teaching job of her dreams, but over twenty years later she is still nurturing little ones in pre-K. She loves the privilege of watching brand-new little humans as they discover and begin to shape their own worlds.

Knowing what she wants and going after it in relentless pursuit is Sprouse's gift. Deciding to become an author can be downright unnerving, but Sprouse bit into the challenge, took off, and never looked back. Her perseverance proves success is not a matter of luck. It's a matter of finding what speaks to your heart and committing to do that thing until it makes a difference.

When she isn't busy teaching or with her husband Jim, her son Patrick, and her canine kids Chuck and Dale, she's cooking up her next novel. She dabbles in sweet romances, historical fiction, and suspense thrillers, depending on what pleases her reader's eye at any given moment. Sprouse is always in search of the extraordinary in the ordinary, writing about strong men with old-fashioned values and the women who pick them up when they fall. She'll tell anyone it's never too late to chase after your dreams, no dream is too small or insignificant, and any mountain can be moved with a proposal and a good plan.

Her past works include: *All the Little Things, Lightning Can Strike Twice, Aging Gracefully, Sunny Side Up, Against the Grain, Hope's Rise from Ashes, Adirondack Sundown, The Edge of Forgiveness on Blue Mountain, Sunrise Over Indian Lake, One Last Adirondack Summer, Whispers of Liberty,* and *Liberty's Promise. A Man of Few Words* is first in the saga of the Henrys of Charlton. Book three, *Making Mountains into Molehills,* is next in the series.

You can find Heidi at Heidi Sprouse Writer on Facebook, Heidi Sprouse Author @heidi_sprouse on Twitter, and http://heidisprouse.wixsite.com/heidi-sprouse.